Devotion

Devotion

by
Anna Denisch

To request permissions, contact Our Corner Publishing at info@ourcornerpublishing.com

First Edition

Design by Matcha Mochi | matchamochidesign@gmail.com

ISBN 979-8-9863336-0-1

www.ourcornerpublishing.com

www.annadenisch.com

Acknowledgments

It takes a village to raise a child but a whole army to finish and publish a book.

I would like to thank Maria Tureaud for her invaluable editorial services. Her expertise truly helped this book shine.

Many thanks as well to my mom for her continued belief, initial feedback and editing help, and to my dad for his support and encouragement.

A big shout out to all of my friends who read this when it was in its infancy. You all loved these fools when their names were different, and their story not as developed. Your continued support for this book has been a blessing.

Heaps of gratitude to my writer-in-crime Lydia Weltmann. Thank you for letting me borrow the muse long enough to finish this. Thank you for providing support through the ups and downs of the publishing process. Thank you for going through this journey with me (and sometimes dragging me along, kicking and screaming).

And last, but my no means least, thank *you*. Thank you for picking up this book and deciding to give it a shot. I hope you enjoy reading it as much as I enjoyed writing it (maybe even more).

Table of Contents

1

Enter Croften (stage left)

Croften had heard the rumors. The story differed depending on who you talked to, exactly, but Croften's favorite variation was that Graham had married a prostitute. He was fairly certain that one wasn't true, even if it was the most fun. The kid he had remembered meeting all those years ago certainly didn't seem the wild and crazy type. He figured, hey, people could change. So, when he received yet another invitation to one of Mara's parties, he agreed.

Usually, the kinds of parties Mara and Ursula threw were boring, but they lived in the same town as Graham and his hussy, so Croften was more than eager to go and see what he could see.

The town *was* just a short train ride away, after all. Graham and his boy-toy moving in had been the biggest news in not just that town, but all the ones near it. There were a few different reasons they had moved there, too, also depending on who you talk to. Everyone agreed that there had been a fight between Graham and his family. Apparently, this made it difficult for the two of them to remain in Graham's hometown, so they moved here. One particularly wild story told to Croften by a drunk stumbling home featured Graham murdering his brother in a fit of rage and the two of them having to move away to escape the police. That made absolutely no sense, but Croften was more inclined to believe it because he liked the bit about the murder.

Ursula met him at the train station.

"Well, well," she said, arms crossed and smirking. "If it isn't Andrew K. Croften, darkening our little town once more."

Croften returned her smirk and hugged her. "Well, you know me, can't stay away from the gossip." He winked at her.

Ursula rolled her eyes and led him to the carriage waiting to take them up to her and Mara's house. "I knew it. I told Mara you were only coming to see Graham and Ainsley."

"Ainsley, huh?" Croften climbed in and stretched a bit. "Not a bad name for a

whore."

Ursula climbed in opposite of him and kicked his leg. "Ainsley is not a whore," she hissed at him. The carriage jolted and started to move away.

Croften grinned and shrugged. "That's not what I heard."

"Well then you heard wrong."

Croften shifted forward, elbows resting on his knees. "So. Tell me all about it."

Ursula shook her head. "I don't know much. They aren't inclined to talk about their past."

"So maybe he did murder his brother."

Ursula gave him a look. "You really mustn't believe everything you hear in the street."

"So, what *do* you know?"

Ursula sat back, her spine straight. "Well, Graham is quite protective of him, that's for sure. There's not much he can do when people just ignore him, but if anyone ever dares to insult him or anything...well, let me just warn you now. Don't insult him."

Croften smirked and leaned back, crossing his legs. "Murder is sounding more and more possible by the minute."

"Personally, I don't understand what everyone's problem is," Ursula said. "I think Ainsley is a darling."

"Well, he's probably used to being charming. Have to be in the escort business."

Ursula kicked him again, quite hard. Croften yelped and grabbed his shin, scowling at her.

"I'm serious, Croften! Do not treat him badly. And do not say things like that to anyone. The poor thing is having enough trouble adjusting as it is, and I won't have you making it worse for him."

"Ow, okay, okay." Croften rubbed his leg until it stopped hurting and then sighed. "Why do you always have to kick?"

Ursula smiled at him. "It's what you respond to."

Croften scoffed and smiled back.

There were two types of rich people, and you could tell them apart by the kinds of parties they threw. New money rich people threw great parties. Wild hooplas that

went long into the night and had all kinds of fun dancing and great food. Old money people threw boring parties. A lot like this one. Out in the garden, dull or pastel decorations, tea served at every table and little sandwiches being carried around on platters.

Croften faked his way through conversations with the rich and fabulous that were attending the party. He much preferred the company of the status-less, but every time he caught the eye of someone he'd like to talk to, he got dragged over by some lord this or lady that and forced into another dreary conversation about his work. It wasn't a total waste, as he did make a few commissions off it. Seems he was going to be spending a lot more time in this little town doing work in the future.

Croften sighed and pulled himself away from another conversation, grabbing Ursula's arm as she passed. "They are coming, aren't they?"

Ursula smiled at him, leading him over to where Mara was chatting with some old couple that Croften knew he knew but couldn't place the name of. "They're usually late."

"Fashionably late, huh?" Croften smirked. "Ain't that just like a-" Ursula's heel made sharp contact with his foot "-Ouch! A fine upstanding citizen!"

Ursula shook her head and Croften let her drag him over to the old couple. He smiled and acted polite as was necessary until they left. Ursula placed a kiss to Mara's cheek, rubbing her back a bit.

"Oh, don't look so upset," Mara said, catching Croften's glare. "People might think you didn't come to this party to be with your friends."

"I didn't," Croften told her. "I came here to get a look at…"

Croften's voice trailed off as he looked about. Two men were being led into the garden. One he recognized as Graham. The guy may have aged roughly twenty years or so, but he looked exactly the same: suit and tie expertly tailored with slicked down hair completely in its place. The man on his arm was another story completely, practically in stark contrast.

Ainsley was a bit shorter, his head resting at Graham's shoulder. His hair was a beautiful white blond, gently curled about on his head. He had bright blue eyes, that twitched about as he looked around the garden, his lips a quivering frown. His clothes were a lot less uppity than Graham's, too. His trousers had creases in them, and his coat was much too long for him. And he was awfully fidgety, his fingers picking at Graham's sleeve as they entered.

"Ah, here they are now," Mara said, heading towards them.

"Come on," Ursula said, dragging Croften and his open jaw after her. "I'll introduce you. And be nice!"

Croften couldn't think of being anything but nice to the man that he was being led to. *Very* nice.

"Graham, Ainsley, so glad you could make it," Mara said. The four exchanged greetings, little kisses on cheeks and small hugs. Croften noted how once Ainsley was no longer wrapped around Graham's arm, Graham's hand was on the small of his back.

"Graham, Ainsley, this is Andrew Croften," Ursula said, holding her hand out to him. "He's a portraitist, has done a lot of amazing work."

Graham shook his hand and Ainsley fidgeted, seemingly surprised when Croften held his hand out to him. Ainsley gulped and shook his hand, a twitch of a smile on his lips.

"You know that portrait of ours over the fireplace?" Mara said. She smiled proudly over at Croften. "All him."

Graham's eyebrows rose. "Excellent work," he said.

"Thanks," Croften said, not wanting to drag his eyes away from Ainsley but finding he had to.

He opened his mouth to say something else but someone else came up, eager to drag Graham away. Croften was perfectly fine with this as that meant he would get to talk to Ainsley a bit more. But the hand on Ainsley's back pulled him away with Graham, the two of them moving out of view. Croften scowled.

"You stop that thought right now," Ursula told him, smacking him lightly on the head.

"Ow." Croften rubbed the point of impact. "What was that for?"

"He is married, Croften," Ursula hissed. She pointed a finger at him. "Leave him alone."

"I have no idea what you're talking about. I'm a saint."

"Oh, please," Mara said, rolling her eyes. "We know you, Croften. But I'm telling you, this isn't some bored house spouse you can just get off with, okay? Graham will kill you if you even think about touching Ainsley."

"So, not above murder, eh?" Croften smirked.

Ursula rolled her eyes. "Honestly. Why do we ever invite him to anything?"

"What are *they* doing here?" Croften's voice oozed with the contempt he felt for Léon and Henri. Well, the contempt was mostly of Henri, but Léon was contemptible by association for marrying him.

Mara and Ursula exchanged glances.

"What?" Croften asked in their silence.

"You tell him," Mara said.

"He's your friend, you tell him," Ursula countered.

"Are you saying we're not friends?" Croften asked.

Mara and Ursula ignored him, staring each other down until, eventually, Mara sighed. "The mayor's commissioning a town mural," she said. "Henri's here applying for the job."

"What? Why didn't you tell me earlier? I would be perfect for that job!" Croften crossed his arms and gave Mara his best disappointed look. It didn't come anywhere as close as hers, but it got the job done.

"We didn't want to tell you because we knew Henri would be here," she said.

"So, you don't think I could beat him, is what you're saying. You think he's better than me?"

Ursula stepped up to help. "We think that he has a long-standing history of getting jobs over you, and we didn't want to bring up any…past trauma."

"Wow." Croften let his mouth hang open as he looked at his so-called 'friends'. "Nice to know you have so little faith in me. Thanks."

He turned and walked away, ignoring their further comments. He didn't need to stand around and be insulted like that. Sure, yes, Henri *has* always beaten him whenever they were both vying for the same job, but that doesn't mean this won't be the chance Croften needs to finally get back at him. He didn't even really care about the town mural or the money, he just wanted to beat that snooty Henri into the ground where he belongs.

But there was nothing he could do about it right now. He couldn't just leave the party without getting nagged at later. Plus, he had come here for a very specific reason…

So, Croften spent the rest of the party practically stalking Graham and Ainsley. Graham never seemed to stop touching Ainsley in one way or the other, Ainsley either draped about his arm or Graham's hand somewhere on Ainsley's back. Possessive little fuck, Croften thought, growling as he watched them. The worst part was how miserable Ainsley looked. No one spoke to him. No one. He stood there next to Graham and fidgeted as he listened to the conversations happening around him.

Croften simply couldn't stand it. He strode over as Graham spoke with that one older couple.

"Hey, Ainsley," he said.

Ainsley startled, blinking wildly as he looked at Croften. "Oh. A-Andrew, was it?"

"I go by Croften, actually," he said, smiling to try and ease the other man's anxieties.

Graham glanced over at him, eyes squinted and face stoic. Croften felt a pang of fear shiver down his spine, but he ignored it.

"Oh. Croften. Hello." Ainsley's face did that little twitch smile again. "Uh," he looked up at Graham, who had turned his attention back to the old couple but whose hand had moved lower, more possessive. "You're an artist, were you?"

Croften nodded and leaned himself against the nearest table. Not very proper of him, but who cares? He wasn't rich, he didn't need to try. "Yep! Lot of rich people portraits, you know."

Ainsley nodded. "Do you enjoy it? What you do?"

"Well, it's money," Croften said, shrugging.

"Oh?" Ainsley turned to face him. Graham gave him a look that Ainsley didn't catch, but Croften did. Graham's hand fell away from Ainsley and Croften could see his teeth clench tight as he listened to the old couple. "What would you rather be doing? I mean if money wasn't an issue."

"Money will always be an issue," Croften said, chuckling. "I do like painting though. I just prefer animals and plants to humans."

"Oh! Oh, I just love paintings of plants!" Ainsley's face brightened up and he jumped a bit.

Croften couldn't help but smile, a little surprised at his outburst. "Is that so?"

Ainsley nodded. "Oh yes. They're simply wonderful! Oh! Oh, could I see them? Your other paintings? Would that be alright?"

Croften chuckled a little, despite himself. "Yeah, of course. I'd love to. I could bring them by."

"Tomorrow?" Ainsley had his hands folded together and was biting his lip ever so slightly.

"Uh, yeah, sure. Tomorrow."

"Excellent! I-"

"Ainsley." Graham was holding his arm out and Croften noted how the old couple had moved away.

"O-oh! Sorry!" Ainsley smiled at Croften. "I'll see you tomorrow." Then he grabbed Graham's arm and let himself be led away.

Graham shot Croften a warning glance over his shoulder and Croften felt that shiver of fear run down his spine again. Oh well, he figured. Graham could give him all the threatening glares he wanted. Croften was going to see Ainsley again tomorrow, away from the party and his 'husband'. It was going to be great.

Ainsley could feel Graham's gaze on him as he undressed, carefully undoing the buttons on his shirt. He bit his lip, waiting for whatever he was going to say.

"You know," Graham finally spoke, breaking the tension in the room. "You don't have to go to these things."

"It would be rude to turn down an invitation," Ainsley said, slipping his shirt off and untucking his undershirt.

Graham sighed. "You know the invitations are only for me," he said. Ainsley looked up, watching Graham on the other side of the room through the mirror. His back muscles were tight.

"Yes, dear, but I am your husband. What would it look like if I didn't go?"

Graham turned around and Ainsley looked down, avoiding his face. "It would look like they're all a bunch of stuck-up pricks who aren't worthy of your time."

Ainsley smiled, closing his eyes softly. "Well, think of what they would say."

"Who cares?" Graham said. "They say things anyway. This way you don't have to go through hours of boredom."

"Yes, but the things they say now are about me. If I was to stop going places with you, well, they might start saying things about you, too."

"Good," Graham said. "Let them."

"No!" Ainsley spun around, grabbing the vanity to steady himself. "Graham, don't say such things!"

Graham frowned. "It's better they talk about me than you."

"No!" Ainsley stormed over, his face growing hot, tears stinging at his eyes. "You have been so good to me, Graham, and I simply won't have anyone saying anything about you!" Graham opened his mouth to speak but Ainsley placed a finger to his lips. "You already had to leave your family and home because of me, and I will not stand for it happening again. I'm fine. I can handle this life. I choose it. But I will not let you live miserably for me!"

Ainsley kept his finger on Graham's lips, mainly because he was afraid of his response. Eventually Graham reached up, gentle fingers wrapping around Ainsley's wrist and pulling his hand away.

"Ainsley," Graham whispered. He sighed and looked away. "Very well."

"Good." Ainsley placed his hands on Graham's chest. "Besides, today wasn't all that bad. I did get to talk to that Croften fellow. He was quite nice."

"Oh yes," Graham said, looking down. "Him."

"I don't know if you heard any of what we were talking about-"

"I heard every word."

"Oh, good. So, you don't mind if I put some of his paintings up. Our walls here are terribly bare."

Graham placed his hands on Ainsley's waist. "You know I don't care what you do with this place."

"I really wish you'd care a little, dear. It is your house after all."

Graham growled. "It's our house."

"Yes, and that makes it part yours and you should have things you like in it."

Graham leaned his head down, pressing their foreheads together. "What I like is already here."

Ainsley huffed out a chuckle. "You sweet talker, you." He tilted their heads back and kissed him.

"Just...be careful with him, okay?" Graham said, nuzzling his nose against Ainsley's cheek.

"Hm?"

"That Croften. I asked about him. He has a bit of a reputation."

Ainsley kissed his cheek and then pulled away, wandering back over to his vanity to finish getting ready for bed. "A reputation for being a good painter?"

"For being a homewrecker."

Ainsley's body froze. He swallowed hard, tears stinging his eyes. A few escaped. He turned around slowly. Graham was standing exactly where he had left him, frowning deeply and looking away.

"Graham," Ainsley croaked, hating the way his own voice sounded. "Y-you know I... I wouldn't." He bit his lip, but more tears fell anyway. He could feel snot forming in his nose and he sniffed it away, trying not to go into full teary hysterics. Graham still hadn't moved so he crossed the room, grabbing his hand tight. "Please, you must believe me. I wouldn't dream!"

Graham looked at him, all that hurt and pain from the past clear on his face. Ainsley's jaw started to quiver. He pressed forward, wrapping his arms around Graham, his face pressed tight to his chest, tears wetting his skin.

"Please, Graham. Please, you have to know! Never! I would never!"

Graham's arms wrapped around him, and Ainsley found he could breathe easier.

"Of course, I know," Graham whispered. Ainsley felt his whole body relax. "I didn't mean anything by it. I'm sorry."

Ainsley sniffed away the last of his tears, sinking into Graham's embrace, suddenly quite tired. "I'll tell him not to come," he said.

"No," Graham said, smoothing down Ainsley's hair. "It's alright. Just...keep an eye on him. I don't want him to hurt you. And... just, tell me if he tries anything."

"Of course." Ainsley nodded against Graham's chest. "But you'll probably be able to tell by him walking away with a painting broken over his head if he does."

Graham pressed a kiss to the top of Ainsley's head. "I love you, Ainsley."

Ainsley smiled softly. "I love being with you." It wasn't what Graham wanted to hear, what he deserved to hear. But they both knew that if Ainsley had returned the sentiment, it would be a lie. And they had agreed a long time ago that lies didn't belong in their relationship.

2

Two Slaps for the Price of One

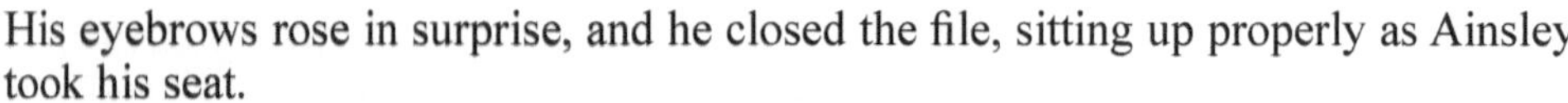

Graham was already half-way through his breakfast when Ainsley joined him. Their butler rushed out of the room to go grab Ainsley his food, but Graham didn't seem to notice. He was reading something out of a file, which was odd, because of the few times Ainsley managed to get up early enough to see him off he was usually reading the newspaper.

Ainsley pulled out the chair next to him, feet dragging against the ground, and Graham glanced up.

His eyebrows rose in surprise, and he closed the file, sitting up properly as Ainsley took his seat.

"Ainsley," Graham greeted. "You're up early."

Ainsley gave him a smile, face lighting up as his breakfast was placed before him. "I figured I'd try and get some writing done this morning. I'm not sure how long the visit with Croften is going to be after all."

Graham nodded. "That seems like a wise choice. I'm sure he won't take up too much of your time, however."

"Oh, I wouldn't say that. He seems like a sociable fellow. I thought he might stick around to chat."

Graham's face twitched a bit, but he didn't say anything. The conversation from last night was still fresh in both their minds, and as much as Graham was still deeply worried about Croften and his reputation, he also knew that Ainsley didn't have anyone to talk to. He had no friends. And if there was someone around that wasn't going to snub him, Graham couldn't in good conscious stand in the way of that.

"Well, as long as he isn't too sociable," he said.

"Of course."

Graham's eyes glanced at the clock in the corner of the room, and he sighed. "I should get going."

Ainsley eyed his plate up. "You've hardly touched your breakfast."

"I'm not that hungry," Graham said, standing up and fixing his jacket.

"But dinner's so far away," Ainsley said, glancing at him with worried eyes. "That's hardly enough to get you through the day and don't tell me you'll be fine because I know you don't eat lunch!"

Graham smiled and crossed over to him. He cupped the side of Ainsley's face with one hand and leaned down, placing a soft kiss to his forehead. "Have a good day," he said, thumb rubbing over cheek before pulling away.

Ainsley pouted. "You, too," he said.

Graham left and their butler came over to clean up his plate.

"What are we going to do with him, Benson?" Ainsley asked, sighing heavily.

"Well, I could always tie him to his chair and force the food down his throat."

Ainsley chuckled softly. "I don't think that would work. No, just, please make sure that dinner is something hearty. Maybe a stew? He likes stew."

Benson nodded. "Of course, sir." He picked up the plate and carried it away.

"Thank you!"

Croften had an extra pep in his step as he bounded up the street to Ainsley's house. They lived not too far from Mara and Ursula, and he had been able to hitch a ride from the station with Ursula's chef, returning from a much-needed vacation.

"Don't even think about trying anything," Ursula had said, spotting his goofy smile as he headed off.

Croften grinned, adjusting the paintings under his arm. He was going to try so many things. He rang the doorbell and bounced on his heels, waiting. The door swung open, revealing the butler, and a wafting scent of vanilla.

"Uh, hi!" Croften said, one of the paintings almost falling out of his grasp. "Andrew K. Croften, here to see Ainsley."

The butler stepped to the side, holding the door open for him. "Please come in, he has been waiting for you."

Croften walked into the warmth of the house a bit nervous. Was he late? They hadn't exactly agreed on a time. It was late morning, maybe he should have come earlier. But that would have been a little hard considering he slept in so late. (Not his fault, thinking about spending the day with Ainsley had made him really excited and anxious, and falling asleep hadn't exactly been easy).

The butler led him into the drawing room. It was light and airy, the windows open, a gentle breeze blowing past silk coverings. It was well decorated too; a fancy rug beneath two plump couches and a wall in the back covered in bookshelves, each with no room to spare. Ainsley was sitting at a desk in the corner, writing in a journal.

Croften smiled inwardly as the butler announced him and then shut the doors to the room, closing the two of them off from the rest of the house.

"Croften, I'm so glad you could make it." Ainsley got up, closing the journal and slipping it in a drawer before walking up to him.

"Wouldn't miss this for anything," Croften said. "Sorry if I'm late."

"Oh! Not at all! We hadn't agreed on a time anyway." He chuckled softly and then his eyes landed on the bundles under Croften's arms. "Are these them?"

"Yeah."

"May I?"

"Sure, sure, just be careful."

"Of course."

Croften placed the bundles down on the table and Ainsley sat down, pulling one open. He gasped. "Oh, they're simply beautiful."

Croften stalked around to the side, leaning in to see which one he had picked up. It was the scattering of roses on a dark cloth. Perhaps a bed, if one wanted it to be. Croften licked his lips and looked at Ainsley, wondering what he saw in the image.

Ainsley looked through the rest of the pictures, murmuring praises at each one, as Croften circled around the room, hands behind his back, taking in the sights of both decor and man. Ainsley's face looked so pure and adorable as he studied the paintings. And every word of praise sounded like a heavenly song. Croften had no idea how anyone could think anything other than the world of him.

Ainsley sighed, content, leaning back against the couch as he put the last painting away. "You are incredibly talented," he said.

Croften smirked. "Talent's only half of it."

"Oh of course! I'm sure you've worked very hard to get this far. And I am very much interested in hiring you to paint such lovely things for me."

Croften smiled. His first, immediate response was 'you're a lovely thing, how about I paint you' but he wasn't entirely confident in the vibes of the room so he just said, "I would be more than happy to be under your employment."

Ainsley's eyes lit up as he smiled. He looked so different from the fidgety, shy mess he had been at the party. Croften wondered why Ainsley didn't just walk away from it all, and the husband who dragged him around to everything.

"There's this garden," Ainsley said, "over by Bell Street?"

Croften nodded. "I know the one."

"Well, I've always thought it was the most beautiful place ever and I would be absolutely tickled if I could have some paintings of it in my house."

Tickled...Croften's eyes wandered over Ainsley's body, wondering what it would be like to run his fingers over it, making Ainsley laugh, making him smile that bright smile of his. "Well, then, allow me to tickle your fancy."

Ainsley giggled and the way he looked up at Croften, through his eyelashes, hint of a blush on his cheek...Oh yeah. Next time Croften would turn the flirt on.

"You got a lot of books," he said, steering the conversation away from business.

Ainsley wiggled in his seat, hands in his lap, looking positively pleased. "I love books. I spend so much of my time reading. Do you read?"

"Eh, not much." Croften shook his head, eyes scanning over the titles of the books.

"No? Nothing?"

"Well," Croften shrugged, slipping his hands into his pockets. Not very posh of him but he had a feeling that Ainsley wouldn't mind. "I do like those Dangerous Dan books. You heard of them? Raleigh something or another?"

Ainsley's eyes grew wide, and he gulped. "Raleigh Mayans," he whispered.

"Yeah! That's the one. Great books. Lots of fun." Croften caught the pale expression on Ainsley's face. "You alright?"

"Oh, yes, I'm fine. I just, uh…"

Croften chuckled. "Hey, it's alright. You can admit to me you like them."

"What?"

"I know they're not exactly high-brow, but I won't tell anyone." He wandered back over the couch, leaning over the back. "Everyone needs a little adventure in their lives."

Ainsley's blush deepened and he scooted away a bit. Adorable.

"Well, what's your favorite?" Ainsley asked. He picked up a cup of tea from the coffee table that Croften hadn't realized was there. He put the cup to his lips, soft and round, and took a tentative sip. Croften couldn't draw his gaze away from the motion.

"I like the one with the camel," he said.

"Oh? That's odd."

Croften furrowed his eyebrows, finally looking back into Ainsley's bright blue eyes as he put the cup down. "Why is that odd?"

"It's just that most people prefer the one with the spyglass. Or the propeller.

That's a popular one. I don't think I've ever met someone who's favorite was the camel."

Croften resisted the urge to hop over the back of the couch, knowing that he had to have at least a bit of decency in such a house. He walked around and sat next to Ainsley; one leg curled up under him so he could face him better. "Talk to many people about these books?"

"Oh. Oh no. I just hear things is all." Ainsley looked away, biting his bottom lip a bit. He glanced at Croften, seemed a bit uncomfortable in his seat, but didn't move.

"Well, come on then." Croften scooted closer. "What's your favorite?"

Ainsley's hands started to fidget, picking at his fingernails. "I suppose the first one will always have a special place in my heart. See I... read it when...well during a very bad time in my life. It was quite helpful."

Croften smiled, forgetting his advances for a moment, watching every gesture of Ainsley's face as he seemed to think back on the past. Well, Croften's past wasn't exactly covered in roses either.

"Yeah," he said, scooting up another inch. Their legs almost touched. "I remember when I first read it. It was so different from anything else you could get, you know. So cool and unique. And I just love the mystery surrounding the author."

Ainsley smiled a bit, body calming briefly. "Yes, I know." He looked a little bit mischievous. "It's awfully exciting thinking about it."

One more inch. Touching now. Arm draped over the back of the sofa, hand a hair's breadth away from neck.

"I think he's some kind of like, eccentric old guy. The kind that's got a fuck ton of money and no fucks to give."

Ainsley looked up, lost in a bit of a daydream. "I like to think he really is Dangerous Dan. He leads this wildly extraordinary life, full of adventure, and exotic food and locations. It's partially biographical. And it doesn't matter what anyone thinks of him because he's got so much confidence."

"And the love of that one king's son certainly doesn't hurt."

Ainsley chuckled. "You're absolutely," he turned his head, face sobering a bit, "right."

He looked at Croften surprised, as if he hadn't noticed how close he had gotten. Croften could see his heart beating hard, pumping out gently against his neck. And his pupils were certainly very dilated, and they kept glancing down at Croften's lips. Ainsley didn't move when Croften's fingers brushed against his skin, a slight shiver if anything. That was all Croften needed. He leaned in, his own heart mirroring Ainsley's speed as the delicious lips crept closer by the second. Oh yeah, he thought, this was going to be great.

SMACK.

Croften shook his head, pulling back as Ainsley jumped off the couch, leaving a white handprint across Croften's cheek.

"How dare you!" Ainsley said, hand clenched to his chest as he walked a good distance away from Croften. Croften sat back, still trying to wrap his head around what exactly just happened. "I am married."

Croften scoffed, rubbing at the slap mark with more of a hurt ego than a hurt face. "Yeah. I'm sure that stiff bastard is totally worth it."

Ainsley was back by the couch in an instant, slapping Croften again, hard across the other cheek. "Don't you dare speak about him like that!"

"Wow, okay, sorry!" Croften rubbed at his other cheek. That one stung a little bit. He was actually missing Ursula's attacks.

Ainsley backed away again. He pointed to the door. His eyes were wet but held a great fury behind them. "Get out."

Croften scrambled off the couch. "Whoa, whoa, whoa, wait! Okay, I'm sorry."

"Take your paintings and get out of my house!"

"Look, I'm sorry, okay! I thought you were, ya know." He gestured to the couch. "I just misread the signals is all."

"You sure as hell did!"

"And I'm sorry for that." Croften held his hands out, licking his lips. "I didn't mean anything by it."

"Is that why you came over?" Ainsley sounded hurt, the sound reverberating off Croften's spine like prickly pines. "You just wanted to...to…" He wrapped his arms around his stomach, and the look he gave Croften made him absolutely sick.

"No! Of course not!"

"Then why?"

"Well, because you invited me. And I thought you were really interesting, and I wanted to get to know you."

Ainsley's arms moved to cross over his chest, glaring at Croften.

"Not like that!"

Ainsley shook his head. "I know about you, you know. And your reputation."

Croften rolled his eyes and put his hands on his hips. "My reputation, huh?"

"This is what you do. You pray on weak house spouses and use their loneliness to try and...and violate them!"

In all honesty, it was those 'weak' house spouses that often prayed on his loneliness. Croften cocked his head. "So, you admit you're lonely?"

Ainsley frowned, then huffed. "To think I thought this would be any different."

Croften shrugged. Ainsley already had his opinions about him, nothing he said was going to change that. "If you knew all this about me then why invite me over?"

"I didn't know when I invited you," Ainsley said. His jaw quivered and Croften's face softened. "I thought...I just thought you wanted to be my friend."

Croften felt something weird in his chest. Like a string being pulled tight and released, vibrating throughout his body. A tear slipped down Ainsley's cheek and the string broke.

"Clearly, I was wrong. Please just go."

Croften didn't move. "I did want to be your friend. I do! Look, I'm really sorry. I completely misread the situation and it's not going to happen again. Okay? Just, here." Croften picked up his notebook and sat down, opening it up to a blank page. "The garden on Bell, right? What do you want?"

Ainsley kept his arms crossed and stared at him. Croften gulped. If Ainsley didn't accept his apology he would have to leave. But the prospect of that made him sick. He really did find Ainsley interesting, and he did want to be friends. Having to leave? Having to never see him again? Croften couldn't stand for it.

Ainsley nodded slightly and sat on the couch opposite of Croften. "Why do you think I'm interesting?"

Croften blinked, pencil primed on the page, waiting. "Uh, well." He shrugged. "Nothing I heard about you seemed to match with what you looked like."

Ainsley uncrossed his arms, scowl lessening. "What did you hear?"

"Huh?"

"The things people told you about me. What were they?"

"Oh." Croften leaned back a bit. "There's a lot of different stories. Mostly that you're a prostitute. Or were one anyway."

Ainsley's face looked disgusted and offended. "They say I'm a prostitute?"

"Yeah. Or escort, whore, what have you."

Ainsley huffed, his face warping into something determined but sad. "What else have you heard?"

"Uh...there was a really great story about how your husband murdered his brother."

Ainsley looked horrified. "But that's simply not true!"

Croften shrugged. "I didn't say I believed it, just that I heard it."

Ainsley looked like he was going to cry again, and he swallowed hard. "What else?"

"Why do you want to know?"

"I need to know." Ainsley leaned forward, eyes pleading with him. "Please tell me everything."

"That's really all I know," Croften said. He had to look away from Ainsley's expression before he started crying himself. "Mara and Ursula probably know more. Just ask them."

Ainsley leaned back, shaking his head. "No. No, they won't tell me anything."

Probably because you look like a damn wounded animal, Croften thought. "So, uh, I mean, what-what did happen?" Clearly it must have been dramatic enough to sprout all these rumors.

Ainsley looked away. He licked his lips, and his face became stoic. Not happy, but at least not on the verge of crying. It was marginally better.

"So," Ainsley said with a little sigh. "I was thinking of a large painting, of the whole garden, to hang in the hallway. A landscape, you know?"

Croften nodded. He knew. But boy, did he ever want to know more.

3

Blue Flower in the Evening

Ainsley was waiting for Graham to fall asleep. His eyes were closed but his body was too tense, and his breath wasn't quite soft enough. It had been nearly an hour since they went to bed. Ainsley turned on his side, resting his head against his hand, propped up on his elbow. He reached over, gently running a hand through Graham's hair. Graham's eyes slowly opened.

"What's on your mind?" Ainsley asked.

Graham shook his head. "Nothing."

Ainsley frowned. He shuffled forward, snuggling up to Graham's side.

"You don't have to do that," Graham said.

"It helps you sleep," Ainsley stated, matter-of-factly. He placed one arm on Graham's stomach and rested his head on his chest, just over his heart.

Graham sighed, adjusting slightly, and brought one arm up to rest over Ainsley's.

"You're sleeping in tomorrow," Ainsley announced.

"I have work," Graham mumbled.

"You need your rest," Ainsley argued. He snuggled up closer.

He waited. A few minutes later Graham's heartbeat had slowed to an appropriate pace, his muscles relaxing under Ainsley's touch, his breath slow and steady. Ainsley waited a few minutes after, to make sure he was really asleep, before he slipped out of bed, tiptoeing across the room.

He winced as the door creaked behind him, but Graham didn't seem to move. With a sigh of relief Ainsley left the door open and crept his way downstairs. It was a lovely night, so he stepped out to their little garden in the back. It wasn't anywhere as large or lovely as Mara and Ursula's, but he loved it very much.

The moon was high in the sky and Ainsley decided to go for a walk. There wouldn't be anyone around on these streets at night, so he would be safe. He could visit his favorite place in the world without worry.

It was quiet at the garden on Bell Street. Ainsley found his way to the bench near the back that he loved to sit on. He took a deep breath in, the spring air light and cool, the smell of flowers abound. And then he sniffed, which could be confused as allergies, until the tears started to fall down his face.

Ainsley pulled his feet up, drawing his knees to his chest and hugging them close. He buried his face in his legs and cried. A prostitute. That's all that remained of his life now. His parents had really done a hell of a job erasing him if that was so easily believable. He shuddered. That wasn't the worst of it. He could handle that. He had brought that on himself.

But now there were rumors about Graham? People were out there saying he murdered someone? His own brother no less? Ainsley shook his head. He hated himself. He wished he could go back in time and stop himself from accepting Graham's proposal. Graham had been so nice and good to him and look where it got him? A suspected murderer married to a prostitute.

Ainsley was finding it hard to catch his breath. He knew he needed to stop but he couldn't. It had been a while since he cried like this and so it was a bit overwhelming. Back when they had first gotten married, back when they had that little place in their hometown. Ainsley had cried practically every night. That was when he had started writing, something to do to help distract him.

That was why they moved. Graham had caught him up in the middle of the night sobbing in bed or spending his lunch tearful at the desk as he wrote. The insults there had been personal. And they hadn't been hushed away and said behind his back. They had been shouted at his face. So, they were a lot harder to ignore. And Graham had gotten so upset that he moved them away. He left his home and his family (that still talked to him) to get Ainsley away from all of that.

And that was why Ainsley was determined to never let Graham see him cry again. He wouldn't have Graham uprooting his life anymore. Not for him.

"Ainsley?"

Ainsley's head popped up, wet and scared. But it wasn't Graham who had spoken, it was Croften. Croften, whose head was peaking over the row of bushes to Ainsley's right.

"Are you crying?"

Ainsley put his feet down, wiping his face off and hoping the light of the moon was dim enough to hide it. "No," he said, unable to keep the waiver from his voice. "Just feeling a little under the weather is all."

Croften grunted and the bushes started to shake as he climbed over them. He swung a leg over the top and then proceeded to catch his foot on the other side, falling to the floor with a thud. The case of papers he had been carrying bounced away, spilling a few pages over the lawn.

"Ow." Croften sat up and rubbed his head.

"Oh dear." Ainsley got up and rushed over to him. "Are you okay?"

"Yeah." Croften accepted Ainsley's hand and got up. "Sorry. That wasn't exactly cool."

"You could have just walked around," Ainsley said.

"This was faster." Croften shrugged and started picking up his papers.

"Why does that matter?"

"You were crying."

"I told you I wasn't crying." Ainsley crossed his arms over his chest. "I'm sick."

"Why were you crying?" Croften asked. He gathered the last of his papers, shoving them in the case and holding it under his arm. He looked at Ainsley pointedly.

"What are you even doing here?" Ainsley turned his back on him and strode back over to his bench. "I thought you lived out of town."

"Yeah, I do." Croften followed Ainsley over, sitting on the bench next to him, earning him a side glare he chose to ignore. "But I'm doing a lot of work in town so I'm shacking up at Mara and Ursula's."

"How kind of them to take you in," Ainsley said. "You must have met a lot of clients at their party."

"Oh, trust me, I pay for it in daily torture." Croften placed his case on his lap and rested his elbows on it, leaning over to Ainsley. "Didn't meet as many as I need. But I'm hoping some good word of mouth will help."

Ainsley turned slightly, intrigued by the working world of a painter. "Why do you need more clients, specifically?"

Croften bit his lip and looked around. "There's this commission the mayor is looking to get. Some town mural or something." He waved his hand about to indicate he really didn't care about it that much.

"Oh yes," Ainsley said. "I've heard about that. It should be a very prolific piece. I'm sure it would be a boost to your career for sure."

"Yeah, yeah," Croften said with that same dismissive wave. "All I care about is making sure that *snot*, Henri, doesn't get it."

"That sounds like a story," Ainsley said. He was thankful that the conversation had steered away from his own sordid tale. He was much better at listening to others talk about their lives.

"He's just this prissy jerk I've known forever," Croften explained. "Thinks he's better than me and all that." He shrugged. "So, why were you crying again?"

Ainsley frowned at him. That little break wasn't very long-lived. He wiped his cheeks to be sure they were dry. "I wasn't crying."

"You are a terrible liar."

Ainsley folded his hands in his lap and looked away. He knew what Croften would think, and that nothing would change his mind. He would think that Graham was why he was crying. That he either hit him or yelled at him or any other number of things his brain was creating to justify his own ambitions.

"Ainsley, I don't understand it. Why don't you just leave? You're clearly not happy here."

"Don't make assumptions about me, Croften. I'll have you know I am very happy."

"Is that why you're crying? Why you look so miserable at the parties? Why you spend your days so alone you'd be willing to befriend a known homewrecker?"

Ainsley stood up and walked away. "You really must stop thinking that you know everything. Just because I wanted to be your friend doesn't mean I'm alone. And just because I was crying tonight doesn't mean I'm sad."

"Aha!" Croften jumped up, case falling to the floor. "You were crying!"

Ainsley opened his mouth then clenched it close. "You are infuriating!"

Croften smirked. "Thanks."

"What are you doing out so late, hm? Seducing another client?"

Croften chuckled and picked up his case. "Just doing some work on the garden paintings."

Ainsley wandered back over, looking around at the space around them. "But it's so dark. Surely you can't have been painting in the dark?"

Croften sat down, opening the case on his lap. He patted the seat next to him. Ainsley sighed. He checked the paths around them. Nothing and no one seemed to be with them, so he deemed it safe to sit.

Croften handed him a piece of paper. Ainsley squinted at it. It was a flower bush, painting in grays and silvers, plants diluted as they reflected the moonlight.

"Nighttime has some of the best views," Croften said. "As you can see," he gestured to the space around them.

Ainsley shook his head. "I…never really noticed before…how different it looks."

"Oh, you simply haven't seen the best parts! C'mon!" Croften jumped up again, placing his case on the bench. He held his hand out. "I'll show you around."

"I can't!"

"Why not?"

"We shouldn't be alone together in the middle of the night like this!"

Croften shrugged. "We already are alone." He laughed. "Ah, come on, where's your sense of adventure? Channel your inner Dangerous Dan, hm?"

Ainsley bit his lip. That was a damn good argument and he hated how well it worked. He knew that if Graham woke up and he wasn't there...well, he didn't even want to think about it. But Croften's eyes were shining at him, almost looking yellow with giddy joy. And Ainsley really always did wish he was adventurous.

"Fine." He took Croften's hand and let him pull him up. "But we have to be quick."

Croften smiled, watching Ainsley's face. It was lit up, and not just by the moonlight. He was gazing out at the garden, hands gripping each other tight. "It's simply marvelous," he said, his voice light and airy. "I've never been to this part of the garden at night before. It's true, the flowers really do light up wonderfully in the moon." He reached out and ran his fingers across a vibrant, lavender petal.

"Yeah. I told you." Croften shoved his hands in his pockets, mainly to stop from reaching out to touch Ainsley. "Beautiful."

"Thank you for showing me this," Ainsley said.

"Thanks for coming."

Ainsley smiled at him and Croften bit his lip. He could feel it. It was there. That spark of electricity between them. Ainsley wanted him. Was attracted to him. And Croften sure as hell felt the same way. He almost leaned in. In fact, he started to. But then he stopped himself, pulling back abruptly and turning his focus to the garden. Ainsley was too damn adorable for his own good.

"Thank you," Ainsley said.

"You already said that."

"For not trying to kiss me."

Croften glanced over at him. "Huh?"

Ainsley sighed, and turned to face him, fingers fidgeting. "I know that you want to. And I appreciate your restraint."

"Oh. Uh...you're welcome?" No one had ever thanked him for that before. Granted, he never had restraint before. "I mean," he shrugged, glad it was too dark to see the blush on his face properly. "It'd be pretty unfriendly of me if I did."

Ainsley nodded. "I should head back before it gets too late."

"One second." Croften disappeared into the garden, bushes rustling here and there as he moved. He appeared a few minutes later, holding a blue bell flower out to Ainsley. "Here."

Ainsley looked at it. "I really shouldn't accept any flowers from you," he said. "I wouldn't want to give you the wrong idea."

Croften rolled his eyes. "It's not anything like that, sheesh. I just," he shook the flower at him, "you know, if you ever get...if it ever happens again...it's good to have something to focus on. Something you can look at and think about a happy memory. At least, I hope this is a happy memory."

Ainsley smiled and took the flower. "A very happy memory," he said. "Thank you."

Croften smiled and they walked back home. Ainsley placed the flower in one of the bushes in his garden. Now, whenever he felt like he needed to cry, he could come outside and look at his flower, and think of a happy memory. And those were few and far between.

4

Spring Fling

Ainsley didn't usually eat breakfast at the table when he was alone. He preferred to eat at his desk, while he wrote. He had more than a few stains on his journals, but he didn't mind. Sitting at the table alone was insufferable. He didn't know how Graham did it every morning. But if he started to think about it too much, he would feel bad about how he didn't wake up with him, didn't sit and eat with him like he should.

"Good morning, Master Ainsley," Benson greeted as he wandered into the kitchen. "What shall I make for you today?"

"I'm not terribly hungry," Ainsley said. If anything, he was tired. And sick. There was a knot in his stomach that had formed the moment he thought Croften might try to kiss him last night. It pulled tight at his guts because for a moment, just before Croften pulled away, Ainsley would have let him.

Benson gave him a knowing look. "I'm sure Master Graham will be delighted to know he can get away with that excuse from now on."

Ainsley sighed and picked up a muffin from the counter. "I'll have one of these," he said, taking a small bite. It made his stomach churn.

"Very well, sir," Benson said.

Ainsley took his muffin and went to the drawing room. He stopped in the doorway. Graham was sitting on the couch, one leg crossed over the other, one arm resting on the back of the couch while the other held a book open before him.

"Graham?" Ainsley said, mouth going a bit dry. "What are you doing here?"

Graham raised an eyebrow at him. "I'm pretty sure I live here."

Ainsley chuckled, a bit nervous. "I meant why aren't you at work?"

"Oh, well, you said I needed some rest." Graham shrugged. "So, I took the day off."

Ainsley smiled and entered the room. "But you've never taken a day off!"

"That's alright with you, isn't it?" Graham asked.

"Oh, but of course!" Ainsley knelt on the couch next to him. "You really do deserve some rest." He craned his neck to see the cover of the book. "What are you rea-"

Ainsley snatched the book out of Graham's hands, holding it close to his chest, heart pounding against it so hard he was sure it would break something. He felt hot, like sparks of energy were traveling all over his body.

Graham blinked at where the book had once been. He placed his hand on his knee and looked over at Ainsley with a slightly bemused expression.

"Sorry," Ainsley said, blushing at his rushed actions. "I just…why are you reading this?"

"Because you wrote it."

"But you've never read anything I've written before."

Graham shrugged. "I never had the time. But I do today."

"It's just…this is personal, okay?" He bit his lip, wondering if Graham had gotten to the bit with the prince yet. Worrying over what he would think about it.

"Thousands of people read these books, Ainsley. If they were so personal, then why did you publish them?"

Ainsley shied away. He looked down, picking at the edges of the book. "Well, yes. But those people don't know I wrote them. It's different."

Graham sighed and leaned back on the couch. "If you don't want me to read them, then I won't."

"Thank you." Ainsley got up and put the book back on the shelf. He was relieved. Graham wouldn't read them and find out all his secrets and desires. But he was also guilty. Graham had tried to show support of his work and he had denied him that. He sighed and turned around. "So. What would you like to do today?"

Graham shook his head. "What would you like to do?"

Ainsley waved a finger at him. "I asked you first." He sat down on the couch, hands in his lap. He eyed the way Graham's arm hung against the back of the couch, opening his side up. Ainsley would fit quite nicely up against that side.

Graham took a deep breath. "To be honest I'm not sure. As you said, I haven't had a day off in a while. I'm afraid I'm not sure what to do with myself."

"Oh. Well, we could go for a walk," Ainsley suggested. "It's really quite nice outside. And the fresh air does wonders for you."

Graham shook his head. "I don't think that would be a good idea."

Right. Ainsley hung his head. No need to be out and about together, where people could see them and say things, if they didn't have to be. After all, what would people say if they saw Graham missing work to walk about town with Ainsley? There goes that murderer and his whore. Spending their money frivolously and doing nothing to earn it back.

He heard Graham gulp. "But if that's what you would like to do, we can go."

"No, no." Ainsley forced a smile on his face. "It's okay. There's plenty to do inside."

Graham nodded and waited for Ainsley to suggest something else. Ainsley's 'suggestion' was to scoot over, turning his body so he could lay against Graham's side.

"Ainsley, you don't have-"

"It's relaxing. Trust me." Ainsley reached up and grabbed Graham's arm, laying it over his shoulders. "Just close your eyes."

He closed his own, giving a soft sigh as he relaxed against Graham's body. He could feel Graham's pulse increasing. He shifted a bit, but away. Ainsley frowned and refused to move. They stayed there for a while, Graham stiff and warm, Ainsley quiet and still.

Ainsley only sat up when Benson entered, a small bundle of letters in his hand. "Mail's in, sir."

Ainsley reached out and took them. "Thank you."

Graham cleared his throat and settled back against the couch as Ainsley started to open the letters.

"The Crichton's are having a dinner next week," he announced.

Graham's eyes closed. "Great."

Ainsley smiled at him. "It's just dinner. At least there'll be good food. They have that new chef after all. The one from France? I bet he makes amazing meals."

Graham nodded. "At least there's that. Anything else interesting?"

Ainsley looked at the next envelope and handed it, unopened to Graham. "Something from your brother."

"Good." Graham took the letter, ripped it in half, and set it down on the coffee table.

Ainsley stared at it. "Don't-don't you want to at least see what he has to say?"

"No."

Ainsley sighed, eyeing up the torn paper as he opened the next envelope. He forgot the letter as soon as he read the contents of this one. "Oh, how wonderful!"

Graham sat up a bit. "What?"

"The town is throwing a little festival for the start of spring later this week. Are we going?" Ainsley looked at Graham excitedly, eyes wide and bright, smile hopeful.

"Would you like to go?" Graham asked.

Ainsley gave him a look. "I asked you first."

Graham smiled at him. "We can go."

"But do you want to?"

Graham leaned over, pressing a soft kiss to Ainsley's forehead. "We'll go."

Croften was finding it hard to focus. It had nothing to do with the young girl that was squirming in her seat as her mother pinched her shoulder to get her to stay still. His hand continued to draw. Luckily, he was so used to drawing people's faces he could sort of autopilot for a while. Lucky because he had caught sight of Ainsley.

He was draped around Graham's arm again, but he wasn't frowning. He was smiling, god bless his beautiful soul. And his beautiful face. He was looking around at all the stalls and decorations and the food. It didn't seem to matter how many people gave him looks or moved away from him. He looked determined to have a good time and damn if anyone ruined that for him.

Croften turned his attention back to his work, figuring he'd better finish up before the girl or her mom started to yell at the other. "There you are," Croften said, ripping the paper off his pad and handing it to the girl, who eagerly reached out for it.

She giggled. "Mommy, we look funny!"

Her mother smiled and agreed. She handed Croften a few bills and then the two left. Croften started cleaning up his area a bit. There had been quite a rush of people at the festival, and he hadn't really had time to keep organized.

"Croften!" A familiarly joyful voice said.

Croften smiled and looked up. Ainsley was standing before him, holding Graham's hand. "Hey there, Ainsley."

"What are you doing here?" Ainsley asked. Graham was looking around at the crowd as they talked, his grip pulsing on Ainsley's hand.

"Well, I was going to be here anyway. Figured I'd do some work, make a little money, eh?"

"You're doing portraits?"

"Caricatures."

"Oh, how fun!"

"You want one?"

Ainsley tugged on Graham's hand, getting his attention. "Would you do one with me, Graham?"

Graham gave Croften a quick glance but shrugged, nodding slightly.

Croften frowned as they sat in the seats. He had hoped to get Ainsley alone, monopolize his time while Graham went off and did who cares what. But no. Of course not. Graham was too possessive to have Ainsley be off in public alone.

"How are you enjoying the festivities so far?" Croften asked.

"Oh, it's so much fun! I love big events like this. Everyone's just having such a wonderful time."

Croften almost smiled as he started to draw. Graham looked miserable, sitting there with a frown, watching the crowd with uninteresting eyes as Ainsley chatted away. Serves him right, Croften thought. Dragging Ainsley to all those places. Now it was his turn to suffer.

"Yeah, things like this are great." Croften focused on Ainsley's face which was a bad idea. God, he was so cute. He accentuated his cheeks, reddening them to mimic the cute little blushes he had when they talked.

"Have you had time to try any of the food? The farmers around here grow some of the most delicious fruits."

"Not yet," Croften said. "But I'll take a break eventually."

"Don't your hands get tired?" Ainsley tilted his head, leaning forward slightly as if trying to x-ray Croften's wrists.

"Eh. They get over it eventually."

Ainsley pouted and sat back in his seat. Croften smirked and mimicked that pout in his drawing.

"You really should take better care of yourself. If you push yourself too far now, you'll be in terrible shape when you're older."

Croften shrugged. "I prefer to live in the present." He finally forced himself to glance at Graham. He cursed under his breath. Damn guy was too gorgeous to really find anything to make fun of. He could accentuate the sharp lines and angles of his face, but as he did that just made him look good. At least he had the frown to work with.

Ainsley's head shook. "I don't get it. Graham doesn't take care of himself either." At the mention of his name, Graham looked over. "He barely eats, you know." Graham looked back away, a small, fond smile on his face that ruined Croften's mood.

"Not eating is hardly a crime," Croften said.

Ainsley tightened his grip on Graham's hand. "I'm always dreadfully worried he's just going to work himself too hard and hurt himself." Ainsley's face softened a bit, less happy and more sincere. "I wouldn't want that to happen to you, either."

Croften gulped. Less at the things that Ainsley said and more at the way that Graham's eyes slid over to look at him, squinted.

Croften cleared his throat. "Well. All done!" He tore the paper off and rolled it up, tying a little ribbon around it. He handed it to Ainsley as they stood up.

"Thank you." Ainsley took the paper and dug into his pocket, pulling out some money.

"Oh, no, no," Croften said, waving his hand and standing up. "Please, it's on me."

Graham's body went stiff. Ainsley chuckled nervously.

"I insist." Ainsley held out money to him, a pleading look in his eyes. Croften frowned and took it. "Thank you very much. I do hope you get some time to enjoy the festival."

And with that Graham was dragging him away. Croften sighed and sat back down. Every time he saw Ainsley his desire to be with him grew. This was more than just a crush, more than just a hot employer he wanted to bang. He genuinely liked Ainsley and liked him more and more with each conversation.

"Croften, Croften, Croften."

The voice sent a terrible shiver down Croften's spine. He turned around, disgust on his face.

"Henri," he said. "What the fuck are you doing here?"

"Could ask you the same thing," Henri said. And what the heck was he wearing? It was some kind of suit but wrong. Like he was trying to be fashionable but had hired a two-bit tailor to copy a design.

Léon was there too, of course. The two were damn-near inseparable. They were holding hands. "Henri's been commissioned by the mayor," Léon said, proud smile on his face. "They just announced it."

Croften's mouth fell open.

"Don't act so surprised, Croften," Henri said. "What did you expect? You could just waste your time away doing caricatures and expect to get to my level?"

Croften closed his mouth, scowling instead. I do more than caricatures, Croften thought. But he didn't say it. It wouldn't mean anything. "What were you commissioned for? Oh, oh, wait! Let me guess. He wants you to paint the trash? That is all you paint, after all."

Léon took a step forward, glaring at Croften. "You can insult him all you want, Croften. But he's better than you and you know it! Besides." Léon smiled, a real sickening sight. "He's not a trollop."

"*Trollop*?" Croften said. "Really? That's the best you've got?"

"Henri is faithful." Léon stepped back, rubbing Henri's arm. "Something you would never understand."

Croften scoffed. "Faithful cause he hasn't gotten caught."

Léon's face fell.

"Come on," Henri said. "No need to waste our time on this filth!" Henri spat at him, *literally* spat at him, and walked away.

Croften stared at the mucus spot on the ground by his feet. Great. He was stuck in this town doing all this work, and Henri had already scored the commission. He considered just canceling everything and going home. And he would have. Except he was working for Ainsley. And he could never cancel on him.

5

Dinner Disaster

Ursula's heels tapped sharp against the floor as she entered the room. She sighed. "Croften, get your feet off of my couch."

Croften didn't move. He lay sideways, head thrown over the arm of the sofa, his feet resting on the other. "I can't," he mumbled. "I'm in mourning."

Ursula groaned and clicked her way over. She shoved his feet to the floor and Croften let the momentum carry him, rolling off the couch and landing on his face. He didn't even wince. He did moan though, low and guttural.

"Get over it, Croften." Ursula sat on the couch and placed her feet on his butt. She shook him a bit. "Laying around moping isn't going to make anything better."

Croften's response was a groan.

"Ursula," Mara said, entering the room, looking around. "Did you bring another cat home?"

Ursula laughed and lightly pushed at Croften. "Not a cat, but a stray for sure."

Mara stood before Croften and looked down, arms crossed. "Croften, get up."

Croften groaned. "Can't you just let me be miserable?" He flopped onto his back, arm and leg pressed against the coffee table. He frowned up at Mara.

Mara's head tilted and she tapped her foot. "You're being ridiculous. So what if Henri's been commissioned to paint the town mural? You're probably making more money than him with all your portrait work."

Croften grimaced at the mention of that name and crawled under the table, rolling himself into a ball.

"Really, Croften, this is no way to behave." Mara sighed and sat down on the couch next to Ursula. "If you don't pull yourself together, I'm going to kick you out."

"Good," Croften mumbled. "Let me lie in the gutter where I belong."

Ursula rolled her eyes. She looked over at her wife. "We have to find a way to

cheer him up. He's ruining the ambiance of the room."

Mara kicked a leg out, nudging Croften with her foot. "Hey, lump."

Croften groaned. "Whaaaaat?"

"The Crichton's are having dinner tonight, and you're going with us."

Croften huffed.

"They've invited Graham," Mara added.

Croften moaned and shivered.

"Which means," Ursula said, "that Ainsley will be there."

Croften didn't make any noise. He stilled, and then looked over his shoulder at them, still pouting a bit. "Do I have to wear anything fancy?"

Graham had tried to trick him. It wasn't the first time it happened. And it still hadn't worked. Because even though Graham was smart, and knew Ainsley like the back of his hand, Ainsley had a secret defensive weapon. Benson.

Ainsley knew that Graham was up to something whenever he bought him a book. Unless it was his birthday or Christmas. Ainsley usually bought his own books. So, when Graham came home from work and handed him a new one with a kiss on the cheek, Ainsley knew it was a diversion. And of course, it would work because Ainsley was many things, and a lover of literature was one of them.

He would sit down and start to read, of course. Partially because he didn't want to ignore a gift from his husband, and partially because Graham was really good at picking out books he liked. And, as always happened when he was reading, he'd get so engrossed that he'd lose track of time.

"Ahem," Benson said, a clear fake cough.

Ainsley startled and looked up at him.

"I am to remind you that you have dinner at the Crichton's tonight."

"Oh yes! Oh, thank you so much, Benson."

Benson nodded and walked away. Ainsley closed his book, shaking his head as he went to get ready. He had a whole shelf of Graham's failed attempts at distraction. He kept them on a little bookshelf in Graham's home office.

"A nice try, my dear," Ainsley said, entering their dressing room. He crossed to his closet to find what outfit would be best for the evening. "But doomed to fail."

Graham sighed and shook his head, buttoning up his shirt. "Why does he always listen to you over me?"

Ainsley laid his outfit on the chair and started to undress. "It probably has something to do with the fact that I pay him." Graham hadn't wanted a butler. Ainsley was the one who insisted, citing that Graham was so used to one it would be a terrible adjustment if he suddenly was without. The truth was that Ainsley knew he would be terrible at taking care of a house and cooking and all that and he didn't want Graham to suffer for it.

"Would it really be so bad?" Graham asked. He smoothed out his sleeves and buttoned the cuffs together. "If we didn't go to any of these things? Would it be that horrible?"

Ainsley stepped into his trousers. "It would be rude. If you started turning down invitations, you'd be ostracized."

"I don't care."

Ainsley gave him a look, shrugging his shirt on. "I thought we agreed on no lies," said the biggest hypocrite on Earth. He knew Graham about as well as Graham knew him. If Graham was guilty of any sin, it would be pride. He was proud, and Ainsley thought he had every right to be. He was proud of his job. Proud of his house. He had once been proud of his family. And one day, Ainsley hoped, he would be proud of his husband. He had an in with the upper circles of the world and he liked it. Ainsley had let Graham give up a lot of things for him in the past, but this would not be one of them.

Graham sighed, grabbing his tie and wrapping it over his neck. "Why don't we just find someone who looks like you and hire them to go to all this stuff?"

Ainsley smiled at him. He crossed the room and took the tie from Graham's hands, knotting it for him. Not because he had to, but because he wanted to. "I think it's cute how you think that anyone out there could pull me off."

Graham smiled back at him. Soft and sweet. He placed a warm hand on Ainsley's cheek. As always, it was Ainsley who had to lean in, to press the kiss of their lips together. Graham? Initiating an actual kiss on the lips? Unheard of.

"Come on then," Ainsley said, patting Graham's chest and very unwillingly moving away from the touch of his hand. "We don't want to be late."

Croften had stopped paying attention to the conversation a long time ago. He nodded his head, sipped at his drink, laughed when those around him laughed. He kept his eyes trained on the door until his salvation arrived. He knew Graham was coming, which meant Ainsley would be here. Mara and Ursula had been right about that. But they had conveniently left out the fact that Henri and Léon would be there, too. Watching them smile and flit about the room, never more than half an inch away from each other made him sick. And a little lonely.

Mrs. Crichton led Graham and Ainsley into the drawing-room. She said something, gave a truly disgusting glance at Ainsley, and then flitted away. Graham's body went stiff, and he shook his head. He whispered something to Ainsley, who shook his head back at him and patted his arm. With what Croften knew was a contained groan, Graham led Ainsley further into the room, hands held tight.

Croften pulled away from the conversation as Ainsley and Graham met with Mara and Ursula. He didn't bother to say anything or even indicate that he was leaving. These snobs had snubbed Ainsley so many times he didn't even care if he did the same. Serves them right.

"Ainsley, hi," he greeted, smiling that deviously charming smile of his.

"Croften? I didn't know you were coming."

Croften shrugged and grabbed Ainsley's elbow. "Let's go chat." He started to pull him away, but Ainsley didn't budge. He gave him a look and shook his head. "Oh, I'm sorry. I didn't realize you were completely engrossed in the conversation not involving you."

He gave the other three a hard look. He hadn't meant to mean anything terribly malicious by it. Mara and Ursula had given him a whole spiel about how everyone thought it was rather 'charming' that he was making an acquaintance with Ainsley, but that if they were to do so outside the privacy of their own homes, they would face a similar fate as him. Croften thought that was absolutely ridiculous and had refused to talk to them for all of two hours before getting over it. He understood high society. He hated it, but he got it.

It was an awkward moment. Graham glared at Croften intensely, his eyes on fire. Mara and Ursula were looking away, almost as if ashamed. And Ainsley, poor, precious Ainsley, was trying to stutter out an excuse for them.

"That's what I thought," Croften said. He pulled again and Ainsley stepped with him, stopped only by Graham's hand.

Croften rolled his eyes. Ainsley gave Graham a small smile and then opened his hand. Glare never leaving Croften, Graham released Ainsley's hand, letting him be dragged off to the corner of the room.

Croften stood with his back to the rest of the room, wanting to focus his attention on Ainsley only (and ignore Henri's presence). "He's still glaring at me, isn't he?" He could feel the heat on the back of his head.

"Yes," Ainsley said. Croften sighed and shook his head. "He just wants to make sure I'm okay."

"What does he think I'm going to do? Rip your clothes off and ravish you right here on the floor?"

Ainsley chuckled softly. "Well, that would be a show." He licked his lips and quickly looked Croften up and down. He noticed it.

"What?" Croften stepped back a bit, holding his arms out and looking down at himself. He had borrowed a suit from Mara, finding that it actually fit quite well, if not a little sung down south. He had even gone so far as to slick his hair back. "Something wrong with my outfit?"

"Oh, no," Ainsley said. And there was that blush. "I've just, I've never seen you so...put together before. You look...nice."

Croften stepped back up, closer than he had been before. "And if Graham wasn't standing ten feet away, you'd say…"

Ainsley gave him a look but went along with it. "I'd say you look rather handsome."

Croften smiled. "You don't look half bad yourself."

Ainsley's blush deepened and he looked down. "Thank you."

Croften could actually feel the rage in the room that was radiating off of Graham. He sure did love to mess with the guy, but he also liked not losing his head to a 'misplaced' knife over dinner. He reluctantly took a step back.

"So, what was with the whole, look thing when you got here?"

"Hm?" Ainsley looked up at him, relief in his eyes.

"When you guys got here. The old crone said something, and Graham did that whole, statuesque frown thing."

"Oh yes, that! You know, I think you captured that face quite well in your drawing! How do you do it?"

Croften smirked. He was impressed. For someone who didn't seem to talk to people much, Ainsley was quite skilled at deflecting topics of conversation. "Don't change the subject," Croften said. "What did she say?"

Ainsley frowned. "It's really not important."

Croften waited.

"She was just thrown off is all. She had sent the invitation to Graham, alone. And hadn't expected him to bring a guest. So, she had to adjust things and really, it was all last minute so it's understandable."

"Huh." Croften let his mouth hang open. "That's strange. Cause, you see, I hadn't been invited either. Mara and Ursula decided to bring me along last minute. She said she was pleased as punch to have another guest and that it was no trouble at all."

"Don't play dumb, Croften," Ainsley snapped with a fury that surprised him. "You know exactly why she said that."

Croften gulped, feeling very warm and ashamed. He hadn't meant to make Ainsley upset. He just wanted to let him know he was on his side. He wanted Ainsley to know that if he was his husband, he'd never let anyone get away with saying something like that. He would yell at them, say something snarky back, maybe even punch them, and then leave, taking Ainsley with him. He would never put Ainsley in the kinds of situations that Graham did.

Before any apologies could be made a bell was rung, announcing dinner was ready. Ainsley pushed his way around Croften and joined back up with Graham. Croften sighed and downed the rest of his drink.

Dinner had been both good and bad.

Good: the food. Bad: the wine.

Bad: Couples usually sat across from each other at events such as this. If they could help it, no host had ever sat Ainsley and Graham across from each other. Good: Ainsley got to sit across from Croften.

Good: Mr. Crichton had decided that dinner was the perfect time to recount his trip to Venice, which was long, boring, and that he demanded everyone paid attention to. This turned the lack of talking to Ainsley from a conscious choice to ignore him to the rapt attention of someone else. Meaning Croften wouldn't make any more rude comments about it. Bad: Ainsley and Croften didn't get to talk. (And he had been meaning to apologize about snapping at him). Somewhere between good and bad: Croften's foot kept touching his.

Good: Graham went to work early and had managed to successfully talk their way out of staying for post-dinner drinks. Bad, very, very bad: Upon saying goodbye, Croften had, in front of everyone, taken Ainsley's hand and, because he clearly had no self-preservation, pressed a kiss to the back of his knuckles.

Ainsley pulled his hand away as soon as the lips touched it. He shook. He tried to give Croften a pompous look that said, 'how dare thee kiss me, serpent' but could only muster fear and panic that said, 'how could you be so stupid'. It was the one time Ainsley was glad that people ignored him as everyone shuffled off to the drawing-room.

But Graham hadn't been ignoring it.

His grip tightened on Ainsley's other hand. (He had been holding Graham's hand, Croften, you absolute idiot!). It hurt a bit. Ainsley wanted to tell Croften off, to yell and scream at him, maybe slap him again if he could stop shaking. But he was in so much shock that all he could do was let Graham pull him away.

He said nothing as they got in their carriage and headed home. Ainsley sat on the other side of him, still shaking. If he closed his eyes, he could see it, Croften's lips, puckered and placed against his skin. Good: it had at least felt nice. Bad: Ainsley kept thinking about those lips on other places. His cheek. His lips. His neck.

"Please say something," Ainsley blurted out. He couldn't be left alone with his thoughts.

Graham had been looking out the window. He didn't move. "How did you like dinner?"

"The food was good," Ainsley said. Breathing was hard. "Wine was horrid, though."

Graham nodded and Ainsley's jaw started to shake with the rest of him, his teeth chattering. He felt so abuzz inside that he was sure he was just filled with flies.

Eventually, Graham's head slowly turned to fix a hard stare on Ainsley. Not scary. Not angry. Not threatening. Hurt.

"Do you like him?"

"No! I mean...he's my friend. Was! Was my friend. I liked him as a friend but nothing more!"

"He likes you." Graham's attention went back to the window.

One more bump from the carriage and Ainsley was certain he would throw up. His stomach flipped and turned inside him, his back ached, his muscles grew tired. Breathing. Had he even ever been able to breathe?

"I'm never seeing him again! I'm serious! You know I would never let anything happen! And so does he! He's just...he's like that! He likes to upset people. And I'm never going to forgive him for that! Never!"

Graham didn't say anything. Ainsley leaned forward, hands on Graham's knees.

"Graham?"

He didn't say another word all night long.

6

That One Window Apology Scene

Croften moved slowly throughout the house. He had successfully avoided Mara and Ursula all morning. That was one of the good things about being in a big house, lots of places to hide. Unfortunately, Croften was getting rather hungry. He had walked back to the house last night after the incident, not wanting to spend the carriage ride back being berated. He had changed, grabbed some blankets, and found a nice little wardrobe in an unused room he could curl up and die in. If only he had had the sense of mind to grab some food.

Well. Being smart wasn't exactly on his resume.

The floor creaked under his toe, Croften wincing as the rest of his foot followed the step. He tensed, waiting. He heard heels clicking their way towards him. His eyes glanced to the nearest door, and he rushed inside. To the library. To where Ursula was standing at a shelf. Holding a book in her hand.

Shit.

"*You!*"

Croften turned to race out of the room, but Mara was approaching, blocking his exit. He grimaced and ran further into the room. His only option. Ursula chased after him, brandishing the book like a weapon. She managed to catch up, hitting him with the book as he tried to get away.

"You idiot!" Smack. "You big dumb idiot!" Smack. Smack. "What is your problem?" Smack.

Croften had let himself get cornered, falling backward onto the couch his only saving hope for getting away. He didn't. Ursula fell on top of him, straddling him so he couldn't get up, continuing to hit him with the book. Thankfully, it wasn't a terribly large one.

"You are so stupid!" Smack. "I can't believe it!" Smack. "Do you have brain damage?"

Croften brought his arms up to protect himself from the onslaught. "I might if you keep hitting me!"

Ursula stopped, breathing hard above him. She lowered her weapon. "What is wrong with you?"

He didn't know. He hazarded a, probably correct, guess. "I wasn't held enough as a child?"

Ursula's face scrunched up and she started hitting him again. Thankfully she only managed to get a few swats in before Mara grabbed her around the waist, pulling her away.

"What were you thinking, Croften?" Mara asked, continuing to hold her wife, who struggled slightly with her constant need to be hitting him.

Croften shrugged, letting himself sit up. "I wasn't."

"You had to be thinking something. I mean, why would you do that? What did you hope to accomplish?"

Croften frowned. "I just wanted…" I wanted to know what it was like. I wanted to let Ainsley know that I liked him. That I loved him. I wanted to show him how it could be, with me. How better his life would be. How good we could be together. He sighed, deflating against the couch. "I just wanted to mess with Graham was all."

Mara shook her head and released Ursula, who was on him in a minute.

"Stupid, stupid, stupid," she said, hitting him three more times for good measure. Then she seemed to tire of it, putting the book down and walking away.

"Look, I know it was dumb. But I'll fix it."

"No!" Ursula spun back around holding her hands out like she was going to choke him. "You do not fix this, Croften. You let it go!"

"But I like him." Croften pouted. They couldn't say no to his pout.

"He's married, idiot!" Ursula rolled her eyes and huffed. "God, you are so dumb!"

"So what if he's married." Croften crossed his arms, pout turning to a scowl. "That doesn't mean anything."

"You don't get it, Croften." Mara had taken over for Ursula in the ongoing lecture of his life. "Ainsley is not going to leave Graham for you." His scowl deepened and he looked away. "He just won't."

"He likes me," Croften said. "I know he does, I can feel it!"

Mara shook her head. "It's not going to happen."

"Right. Well. I'm going over to apologize."

"No!" Mara and Ursula both shouted, arms extended to stop him from getting off the couch.

"What?"

"If Graham sees you, he will kill you," Ursula said.

"Oh, please," Croften rolled his eyes. "He's not gonna hurt me. He's too posh for that."

"You don't understand." Mara crouched down, eye level with him. "He was here this morning. Looking for you. I have never seen that look in his eyes before, Croften. It was...Do not go over there."

Croften gulped. Mara has never been scared for as long as he's known her. Nervous? Sure. She was an absolute wreck on her wedding day. But scared? Never. The fact that she was scared enough to be speechless? It certainly held some weight.

But not enough weight.

"I don't care." Croften pushed himself off the couch. "I'm going over and I'm not leaving until Ainsley accepts my apology."

"It doesn't matter if he does," Ursula said.

Croften gave the two of them a smirk. "That's where you're wrong. *All* that matters is if Ainsley forgives me."

He turned and raced out of the room, already picturing Ursula picking up the book to chase after him.

"Croften, wait!" Mara called out.

Croften had the door opened but he stopped. He rolled his eyes and turned around. "What?"

Mara glanced down at his feet. "You aren't wearing any shoes."

Croften looked down. "Oh. Right. That would hurt." He raced upstairs to grab some, not a moment to lose.

And he was very thankful he had done that as he ran down the street to Ainsley's house. And Graham's, he had to remind himself. He pounded his fist against the door, not caring if Graham opened it, not caring if he attacked him or tried to kill him or whatever. All he cared about was seeing Ainsley again. At being able to at least apologize, even if he was bleeding out on the carpet from Graham stabbing him.

But thankfully it was Benson who opened the door. "Can I help you?"

"Hi, yeah, I need to see Ainsley."

"I'm afraid he's not seeing anyone today. He's rather ill."

Croften bit his lip. It's okay, he told himself. It was just a lie, is all. A lie Ainsley was giving to make him go away because he was still mad. Graham hadn't hurt him. Croften hadn't caused that.

The door started to close. "No, no, no, wait!" Croften stuck a hand out, pushing the door back open. "Please. It's important. I need to see him."

Benson stared at him and Croften didn't even have to pout. He knew he looked pathetic and wrecked. But hey, at least it worked.

"I'm afraid he really is quite ill. Taken to bed, you see. On the East side." He gave Croften a look. Croften shook his head. Benson sighed. "Second floor? Third window?"

Croften's mouth opened in understanding, and he nodded.

"Good day, sir. I'll be sure to let him know you stopped by."

The door closed and Croften let it. He jogged around to the side of the house and smiled. He had always been a fan of trees.

What was even the point of trying anymore? Ainsley sniffed and hugged the pillow closer to his chest. He buried his face against it, pretending it was Graham. But it wasn't. And it hadn't been last night either.

As soon as they got home Graham had gone into his office and closed the door. And he hadn't come out until morning.

Ainsley wasn't even sure if he had slept at all. He just remembered crying. Thinking his terrible thoughts about how he was the worst husband and Graham deserved so much better. Next thing he knew Benson was knocking on the door asking if he wanted a tray brought up for breakfast. He had sent him away. He didn't deserve food and even if he did, he couldn't possibly eat with how sick he felt.

There was a soft tapping against his window. Ainsley rolled over, taking the pillow with him, curling deeper under the covers. It was probably just some bird. He hoped it wouldn't start singing. That would really kill the depressed mood he had going on.

Tapping again. Louder, faster. It was probably just the wind knocking a branch against the window. That's all.

Harder. A palm being slapped against glass; so loud Ainsley was sure even Benson could hear it. He groaned and rolled out of bed, shuffling over to the window. He pulled the shades back, saw Croften's face, and immediately closed them again.

"I'm not leaving this tree until you talk to me!" Croften called out as Ainsley shuffled back to his bed.

"I'm sure you'll have a lovely winter." Ainsley cursed himself. He hadn't meant to engage in conversation with him. Now he really wouldn't leave.

"Please! I'm sorry, okay?"

Ainsley crawled into the bed, pulling the covers over his head and screwing his eyes shut. "Go away!" He cursed himself again. Stop talking to him!

"Look, I get it, okay? You're mad. And that's fair. But just...look, just come back to the window, and hear me out. You don't even have to talk, just look at me and listen. And after I'm done, if you still feel like this, you can push me out of the tree. That's totally within your rights."

Ainsley scowled. If Croften was serious, and he sometimes could be, he really would be in that tree forever. Which meant he would be there when Graham got home. Which would make salvaging anything impossible. Plus. Ainsley rather liked the idea of pushing him out of the tree.

Ainsley got back up and pushed the blinds open. "What?"

Croften smiled. He climbed from the tree to the window ledge, sitting on the edge of it rather precariously. He tapped the glass. "Can you open the window?"

"No."

"Why not?"

"Because you'll crawl your way in here. You are not welcome in my house, Croften, and you are most certainly not welcome in my bedroom."

Croften held his hands up. "Yeah, yeah, that's fair. That was my plan, fair point." He leaned his head against the glass. "I'm sorry."

"I believe you said that already."

"I just...I wasn't really thinking straight."

"You rarely are."

"Ya see? That's my problem." He shifted on the ledge, turning a bit so he could see Ainsley better. "I really don't mean to do this stuff on purpose. I wasn't intentionally trying to cause trouble. I just...do dumb things. Can't you forgive me for that?"

"I could have," Ainsley said. "If we had been alone. If you had kissed me in the drawing-room, or the garden, where no one could see us. I would have understood. I would have told you not to do it again and we could have moved on. I know what it's like to love someone that you can't be with. Believe me, I understand. But you kissed me in front of people. Not just any people. But Graham."

Croften nodded, hanging his head. "Yeah. I know. It's not exactly my finest moment."

"I understand your motives, Croften. But I am very cross with you and I'm sorry, but I just can't be around you anymore."

"Wait, wait, wait, Ainsley, no!" Croften got to his knees, almost falling off, stopping Ainsley from closing the blinds. "I am more sorry for this than I've ever been for anything in my entire life. More sorry than I am for the fact that I exist! I can't even begin to forgive myself for what I did to you. I knew he was a jealous, overprotective prick but I kissed you anyway. And he hurt you and locked you away and it's my fault and I'm sorry. But look, you can open this window. Take your stuff and we can just go."

Ainsley huffed out a laugh, shaking his head. "That's just it, Croften. You don't even know why I'm mad at you."

Croften's eyebrows furrowed, and he sat down a bit, not too much, or else he'd fall. "If not that, why are you mad, then?"

Ainsley took a step closer to the glass. He wanted to make sure Croften heard him. "I care about Graham very deeply. And I honor the vows I made to him when we got married above all else in this world. You didn't hurt me, Croften. And neither did Graham. But you hurt him. And I cannot forgive that."

Croften's confusion deepened. "How did I hurt him?"

Ainsley sighed. "Have you ever been in a relationship before?" Croften looked half-ashamed as he shook his head. "Then I'm sure it's hard for you to understand. But try to use a bit of empathy. Imagine you're Graham. No. Imagine you're you. And we're married." Croften's face brightened up a bit. "Now imagine that someone else kisses me. Touches me. Flirts with me. How do you feel?"

Croften shrugged. "That wouldn't happen. You'd be happy with me."

"Croften! Imagine! It happens. How do you feel?"

Croften looked down. "Not great."

Ainsley placed a hand against the glass, to hold himself up. He hated saying it out loud. "Now, imagine that you have a history...of someone you're with...someone you're engaged to...leaving you for someone else. Quite suddenly. In the middle of the night." He could hear Croften's gulp. "The person you are with now is being kissed by someone else. How do you feel?"

"...Worse." Croften hung his head, forehead resting against the window. "Like it'll happen again." He sighed. "Fuck. I'm sorry. I... I didn't know."

"You shouldn't have to know."

It was quiet for a moment. Ainsley so desperately wanted to open the window and hug him. Mainly because Ainsley so desperately needed a hug.

"I know this isn't going to make much sense," Croften said, just as Ainsley thought about closing the blinds. "I know that we've only known each other a few weeks but...you're the third closest friend I have. The only two above you are Mara and Ursula, and that's 'cause I've known Mara since we were five." He still wasn't looking up, head still hung low. His forehead was actually smudging against the glass as he lost the fight against gravity. "It may come as a surprise to you but I'm not exactly great with relationships. Mainly 'cause I do dumb shit like this all the time. But…" he shook his head. "I really don't want to lose you, Ainsley. I like having you as a friend, and I will do anything, *anything*, to be able to keep that." Croften finally lifted his head. "Please. Please don't go away."

There were tears in his eyes. And then on his face. He didn't move, didn't say anything else, just sat there and waited. Ainsley sighed and cursed his bleeding heart as he unlatched the window and pulled it open. Croften still didn't move. He shook slightly but made no other mention of being alive as Ainsley reached out and wiped the tears off his cheeks.

"I'm going to need time," Ainsley said. Croften nodded slightly. "We can't even begin to think about this while Graham's in the space he is, okay?" Another nod. "I'm going to do everything I can but there's no promise." More shaking now, more tears falling.

Ainsley wiped the fresh tears away and then pulled his hands back. He hated to be so cruel, but he had to be strong. "And there's going to be some ground rules once we're friends again." He did not want to give Croften false hope with the use of the word once, but the poor guy needed something, or else Ainsley feared he would simply crumble and fall off the window.

"You will stop being mean to Graham," Ainsley said. Croften nodded enthusiastically. "And you won't say mean things about him when we're alone." More nodding. "And I know that it's in your nature, but absolutely no more flirting."

Croften shook his head. "None," he said. Well, sobbed.

"Just lay low for right now," Ainsley said. "Don't leave Mara and Ursula's unless you absolutely have to. And for the love of all that is holy in this world do not come near me, and certainly do not let Graham see you." Croften nodded, jaw shaking as he forced his tears to stop. "I will call for you...when he comes around."

Croften sniffed and rubbed his palms over his eyes, blushing a bit. Ainsley all too well understood that embarrassment after breaking down in front of someone. He knew, from the sincerity of Croften's confession, that he would follow his instructions. So, he saw no harm in reaching out and giving Croften's hand a squeeze before closing the window.

Croften took a moment to gather his strength, breathing deep breaths and calming his tears. Then he mouthed 'thank you' and turned around, climbing back into the tree. Ainsley stayed at the window and watched him climb down, making sure he reached the bottom safely. He wanted to crawl back in bed and have a crisis. But there was no time for that. He had a plan to make.

7

My Week was Worser than Yours

Day One:

Croften's legs cramped. He wanted to shift so badly, to just stretch out a little, get his arm moved so his shoulder wasn't pressed against the tip of a shoe. But there really was nowhere to go. The lid of the bench was already slightly ajar, pushing against his knee as Ursula sat on it, a slight ring of light filtering into the tight space.

He had been having a rather lovely evening. Ursula had stopped hitting him, and Ainsley was going to be his friend again. He was recounting all of this to Mara, who had left that afternoon for a bit of business, when there was a knock on the door.

Croften had followed her out to the hall, continuing to talk. She had opened the door, said, "Hello, Graham," and Croften had simply dove for the first cover he could find; a bench by the coat closet, filled with shoes.

Ursula had come out at the mention of Graham's name, had seen Croften not quite fitting in the bench, and had sat on it, making Croften bite his lip to suppress a groan of pain.

"Is Croften here?" Graham asked. He had been invited in, but he stayed by the door.

"I'm afraid not," Mara told him.

"He's off doing a portrait," Ursula said. "He's been gone a while. I'm sure he'll be back soon; if you'd like to wait."

Croften rolled his eyes and resisted the urge to push up, throwing Ursula off.

"No, thank you." Croften could hear Graham turn to walk away. He sighed in relief. Then Mara stopped him and Croften bit back a groan.

"I know it probably doesn't mean much," Mara said. "But I've known Croften practically my whole life. He really is just an idiot. I promise you he doesn't ever mean anything malicious by his actions. He's just...really, really dumb."

"You are my friend, Mara," Graham said. "Your opinion means a great deal."

53

And then he left.

Croften sighed and pushed up. Ursula didn't move. "Hey, let me out," Croften said, banging against the lid.

"Mara, did you hear something?" Ursula asked.

Mara hummed. "I don't think I did."

"Ha, ha, very funny. Let me out now." Croften pushed up with both arms and legs.

"Come to think of it," Mara sat down on the bench, digging the lid in deeper to Croften's knee, "I haven't seen Croften in a while."

"Do hope nothing bad happened to him," Ursula said.

"You're very funny," Croften growled. "Now move!"

When he pushed up again the two women laughed and stood up. Ursula reached in and helped him climb out. He stretched and rubbed at his joints, glaring at them.

"Maybe it's best if you aren't here when Graham leaves and comes back from work," Mara suggested.

Croften rubbed at his shoulder, feeling around the indent the shoe had made. "My thoughts exactly."

Ainsley cleared his throat and softly knocked on the door to Graham's office. He got no reply.

"Dinner's ready," Ainsley announced. Graham had come home, late, and once more had gone straight to his office. Ainsley knocked a little harder. "I know that you didn't eat breakfast. You simply have to eat something, or you'll waste away."

Still no response. Ainsley tapped his fingers against the door, trying to will it open. Of course, there actually wasn't a lock on the door, so Ainsley could walk in at any point. But if he did that, Graham might not come back home at all, choosing to stay safe in his work office where Ainsley wouldn't get in.

Ainsley sighed and went back downstairs.

"Any luck, sir?" Benson asked.

Ainsley shook his head and sat down. "I'm afraid not. Just me tonight."

Benson placed a plate of food before him. "Shall I bring Master Graham up a tray?"

Ainsley deflated in his seat. He wanted to be mean. He wanted to say no, let Graham starve unless he decided to come down and talk. But he really wasn't that vindictive. And besides, Graham did have a right to be mad. "Please do. And bring him extra, he's probably hungry."

Benson nodded and left. Ainsley sat at the table, finger tapping against the wood as he thought. First thing he had to do was get Graham to talk to him. No. First step was getting Graham to look at him. So, when Ainsley went to bed that night, he set his alarm for early.

Day Two:

Ainsley did not like waking up to an alarm. It ruined his sleep. But a ruined night's sleep was better than a ruined marriage, so he groaned, sat up, rubbed his face, and got dressed. It was a bit of a cold morning, so he wrapped his arms around himself as he shuffled down to the kitchen.

"Good morning, sir," Benson greeted. "Would you care for some breakfast this early?"

Ainsley shook his head. "No, thank you. I'm just waiting for Graham to get up."

"Oh. Master Graham has already left for the day."

"What?"

"Yes, he left a few minutes ago, in a bit of a hurry I would say."

Ainsley huffed. His guilt was slowly turning into anger the longer Graham avoided him. Graham must have heard Ainsley's alarm and raced out. No breakfast again, probably. Had he even changed his clothes?

"Thank you for telling me," Ainsley said.

He stomped his way over to the drawing-room, grabbed the chair from his desk, and dragged it out to the hall. He set it down directly in front of the door, sat in it, crossed his arms, and waited. No reading, no writing, he couldn't be distracted. He just waited.

Croften actually did have a portrait to do that day, so he got up early, which was torture enough, and spent his day at the Tilly's. They were a lovely family, sure. Their kids were well behaved and even the youngest one managed to sit still long enough for him to get a sketch out. The problem was, they had seven dogs and insisted they were all in the painting, too.

Dogs were a lot harder to get to sit still than kids. They kept wandering about, barking, licking things. Croften figured he would need seven baths, one for each dog that had slobbered all over him.

It may have been the portrait day from hell, but on the good side he was out of the house and Graham had no idea where he was. Plus, work kept him busy. And if he was busy with work, he wasn't spending all his time thinking about various revenge plots against Henri that usually involved maiming of some sort. According to Mara that 'wasn't healthy' for him.

The door opened and Ainsley sat up, keeping his arms crossed, putting on a face that said, 'I know you're mad at me, but you can't keep avoiding me like this. We are adults, and we have to talk, so please stop being so dumb'. At least, he hoped it said that.

Graham walked in, motions slowing as he saw Ainsley in the chair. He hadn't changed his clothes. They were wrinkled all over. And his eyes were sunken, his hair a mess. Ainsley couldn't believe it. Graham had gone out looking like that to avoid seeing him. It made his insides churn, and he lost his speaking face as he tried not to start crying.

They stared at each other for a while, the door still open. Not breaking eye contact, Graham shut the door with his foot. The space in the hallway felt very, very small, and Ainsley found breathing difficult again.

Eventually Graham looked away, placing his briefcase on the ground and shrugging off his coat. He hung it up on the rack next to the door. At least he hadn't tried to just go right to his office.

Ainsley cleared his throat. "How was work?"

Graham didn't look at him. "Fine."

Graham picked his briefcase up and stepped around the chair. Ainsley didn't stop him. It was okay. This was a good first step. He had gotten him to look at and speak to him. Granted, it was one word, but still, that was one word more than yesterday. He called that a win.

Day Three:

Ainsley's sleep was light to say the least. Fitful at best. He woke easily when he heard the clattering in the room next door. He sat up and scratched his head. The clock told him it was much too early for any human to be awake.

Groaning, Ainsley shuffled his way to the dressing room. Graham was there, squinting in the low light of early morning as he got dressed. Ainsley leaned against the door frame, muscles already tired of holding him up, and sighed.

"You don't have to get up so early to avoid me," he mumbled.

"I'm not avoiding you," Graham said, back facing him. Ainsley scoffed. "I was. But I'm not anymore." He paused. "I just...wasn't sleeping anyway."

Ainsley closed his eyes. "Me either."

He listened to Graham as he shuffled fabric around and made himself presentable. When he opened his eyes again, he couldn't help but smile. Graham's bed head was one of the reasons that Ainsley hated not waking up early. It was charming. Cute. But it was not something to take to work.

Ainsley picked up the soft brush from his vanity and crossed the room. "May I?"

Graham made eye contact with him in the mirror, low light masking the color of his irises. He didn't say anything, just looked back down at his cuffs as he buttoned them. Ainsley reached up, pulling the brush over Graham's hair, smoothing it down until it looked presentable.

"There," he said, stepping back and admiring his work.

"Thank you," Graham said. He shrugged his jacket on and glanced at Ainsley as he buttoned it up. "There's a meeting I have to go to after work. It'll probably run late. So, uh, no need to bring out the chair." He gave Ainsley a half smile.

Ainsley looked down, blushing a bit. "Don't work yourself too hard."

Graham nodded. "Get some more sleep, okay?"

Ainsley didn't.

Croften was a nervous wreck. It was only two and a half days since his talk with Ainsley. He knew, objectively, that it shouldn't be this early before he heard from him. But he still felt awful with every second that passed.

"Look, I want to help you, Croften." Ursula walked into his room, where he was laying on the bed, head hanging off the edge. "But," she closed the door behind her, "you have to promise: not a word of this to Mara."

Croften squinted at her, she looked a bit red with all the blood flowing to his brain. "I don't think Mara would believe you'd want to help me even if I told her."

Ursula rolled her eyes and sat on the bed, a box sitting on her lap. "I'm serious. She can't know."

Croften sat up, his curiosity overriding his despair. He looked down at the box. "Please tell me it's a box full of toys," he said, wiggling his eyebrows at her.

"You are so gross."

Ursula shoved the box at him. Croften adjusted, holding it on his knees as he peeked in. "Books?"

"Books I know you like."

Croften gasped and pulled one out. He turned a wide, devilish smile to Ursula. "You read the Dangerous Dan books?"

Ursula shushed him. "Keep your voice down. Mara can't know."

Croften laughed. "I didn't know you had it in you!"

"If you won't be quiet about it..." Ursula reached for the box, but Croften twisted to the side, keeping it out of reach.

"No, no, no, I wanna borrow 'em." He chuckled again. "So, uh, what's your favorite? One with the camel?"

"...Yeah. How'd you know?"

Croften shrugged. "Lucky guess." He flipped one of the books open, smiling over the words.

"I'm letting you borrow these to keep you busy. You read them in here and you do not let Mara know about them. Okay?"

"Yeah, yeah. Your secret's safe with me."

Ainsley knew someone had stepped into the room, but he was too busy trying to hold on to the remnants of sleep to pay attention.

"Why are you down here?" Graham asked.

Ainsley let the sleep go, turning over on the couch so he could look up at Graham. "I'm not letting you sleep in your office again. You have to work so you take the bed."

Graham sighed, rubbing at the bridge of his nose, eyes closed. "Just...get up."

Ainsley obeyed, tossing the blanket off and getting to his feet. Graham wordlessly walked upstairs, and Ainsley followed.

"Get in bed, I'll be there in a minute," Graham said, heading for the dressing room.

Ainsley climbed in bed, burrowing under the covers. He kept his focus awake, listening for Graham's movements. He didn't care about privacy; if he heard Graham go into his office he was going in after him.

The door squeaked as Graham closed it, and then the bed behind Ainsley dipped down. Ainsley curled himself up tight on his side. He wanted nothing more than to turn over and cuddle up to Graham, to know that everything was okay. But everything wasn't okay. It was getting better, however. And he let that thought lull him to sleep.

Day Four:

It was like reading his own life. Croften was the prince of course. Ainsley was Dan. Well, not really, in the sense that he didn't really do a lot of crazy dangerous things. But it made sense in the realm of their relationship. Or lack thereof.

The prince never was named. It was a funny thing that led to many mishaps and confusions, but it was also symbolic. See, the thing was, Dan and the prince were in love. It was clear to everyone, including them. The prince would do anything for Dan. Did do anything for Dan. But Dan was afraid. He worried that his life was too dangerous, that if he accepted and admitted his love, then the prince would get hurt. They couldn't be together because of his life, just as Croften and Ainsley couldn't be together because of his marriage.

The books kept him busy, but they did nothing to ease his pain.

Graham was eating breakfast back to normal, half his food untouched, newspaper spread wide before him.

"Good morning," Ainsley whispered, sitting down. Benson was nowhere to be seen, which was fine, as Ainsley wasn't hungry.

"Good morning," Graham replied.

"How did you sleep?"

"Fine."

Ainsley nodded. He watched Graham read the newspaper. He listened to the clock tick in the corner.

"Do you have any plans tomorrow?" he asked.

Graham put the newspaper down. "I could."

Ainsley shook his head. "I want to talk."

Graham looked down at the table. Ainsley reached out, placing his hand on Graham's arm, waiting to see if he would move away. He didn't.

"Please," Ainsley said. "I don't want to wait months for us to get back to normal." And he didn't want to wait months to see Croften again.

"Very well," Graham said. He pulled his arm away and continued reading the paper.

Day Five:

"Someone come stop me from doing something dumb!" Croften called out as he rounded the corner from the stairs and raced for the front door.

Ursula popped her head out from the library. "What are you doing?"

Croften threw the door open and glanced at her. "I'm going over to Ainsley's."

"Croften, no!"

Croften ran out the door, Ursula hot on his heels. He managed to get to the end of the walkway, just by the road, before Ursula tackled him, knocking them both to the ground. They rolled about for a bit, Croften struggling to get out from under her, Ursula trying to get a grab on his arms to hold him down. They settled with Ursula straddling his legs and pinning his wrists to the ground by his head.

"Let me go," Croften said. "I have to see him!"

"You're just going to make it worse!"

"I know but I have to!"

Ursula pushed him further into the ground. "You just have to be patient."

"Do you know me!?"

A dog barked. The two looked to the side, spying a little brown dog looking at them, tail wagging. Their eyes traveled up to the woman who was holding the dog's leash. She looked at them with a raised eyebrow.

"Uh, we…dropped something," Croften said, smiling at her.

The woman shook her head at them and walked her dog around them. Ursula took the moment to grab Croften's ear, tugging on it.

"Ow, ow, ow," Croften said, letting Ursula drag him to his feet and back into the house. She didn't let go until they were inside, and the door was locked.

"You're staying here," Ursula said. Croften rubbed at his ear. "I'm not having you murdered while you're our guest, understand?"

Croften rolled his eyes. "He's not gonna murder me, sheesh."

"Just a few more days, okay? If he's not here by the start of next week, then you can go be an idiot."

Croften frowned. "Fine." He pointed a finger at her. "But I'm holding you to

that.”

They sat on opposite couches. Ainsley rubbed his hands over his knees, swallowing hard. He kept licking his lips, feeling them go dry and chapped at every passing moment. He wasn't sure how much time had passed, just that it was a lot.

"Ainsley," Graham said, breaking the silence. "I figured that when you said you wanted to talk, you actually had a topic of conversation in mind."

Ainsley nodded. "Yes. Sorry. I'm just...have you ever had a conversation with someone, and you...you just knew that your entire future rested on it?"

Graham's face softened. "I think you're putting too much weight on this."

Ainsley chuckled. He thought he wasn't putting enough weight on it. "I just wanted to start by apologizing again for what happened at the dinner."

Graham's eyes closed, and he took a deep breath. "It's fine."

Ainsley's leg bounced, the only thing he could do to stop himself from exploding with how nervous he was. "I just...I need you to know, Graham, that I would never do that."

Graham looked at him, eyes hard to read, somewhere between hurt and angry. "I know he tried to kiss you that first day."

Ainsley felt like something had punched him in the gut. He literally couldn't breathe. "What?"

"Benson may listen to you more, but he still talks to me." Ainsley let out a sob. "Why didn't you tell me?"

"I...I... I didn't want you to do anything to him." Ainsley brought a hand up to this face, biting on the nails. A nervous habit he had ditched about five years ago.

"Because you like him."

"Because he was nice to me!"

They fell back into silence, Ainsley fidgeting and biting and shaking, Graham stiff and unmoving.

Time passed.

More time passed.

"Well, good talk." Graham got up.

Ainsley could feel his breakfast making a hurried comeback. "Wait." His voice was weak and broken. Graham remained standing, but he didn't move. "I don't get the opportunity to have many friends." He knew it was a low blow. He didn't want to use it as an argument, because his lack of friends had absolutely nothing to do with Graham. It wasn't fair. But it was all he had.

Graham sat back down.

"I know that Croften likes me." He hung his head, unable to meet Graham's gaze. "But he promised me that he wasn't going to be like that anymore. And I... I know I probably shouldn't, but I trust him."

"You've spoken to him."

"Yes."

"You said you wouldn't see him again."

"He's very persistent."

More silence. More time.

Ainsley sighed and risked looking up. Graham was staring at him. He looked... completely neutral. As if he had never felt an emotion in his entire life. It was wrong.

"I have lied to you more in the last month than I have the entire time we've been married," Ainsley admitted. "It's not right, and I'm sorry. I do like Croften." There was a twitch of emotion on Graham's face. He swallowed hard. "But I would never even think about leaving you. You have to know that, on some level."

Graham looked away. "If you wanted to-"

"No!" Ainsley couldn't take it anymore. He fell to his knees, shuffling over to Graham. With shaking hands, he grabbed Graham's wrist and placed a kiss to the back of his hand. "I will never leave you. And I'm not letting you leave me. Our marriage is the thing I care most about in this world. I value it above everything else. Everything."

Graham looked down at him. Confused. "You would give up running away and being happy with him to stay here and be miserable with me?"

"Oh, I could never be happy with him." Ainsley kept hold of Graham's hand and sat next to him. "How could I ever be happy knowing that I let you go?" Ainsley brought one hand up, running it through Graham's hair.

"But you don't love me."

The look in Graham's eyes killed him. He let go of Graham's hand and placed both palms on his cheeks. "But I like you."

Graham's lip quivered for a moment before his jaw went rigid, clenching his teeth together.

"You are my best friend, Graham," Ainsley said. "Why would I ever put that at risk?"

A single tear slipped out of Graham's left eye. Ainsley leaned in and kissed it away.

"Can we be good again?" Ainsley asked. Graham nodded, pressing their foreheads together. "Good."

Day Six:

Graham was still in bed when Ainsley woke up. He smiled and rolled over, reaching out to touch Graham's cheek. He blinked awake.

"What time is it?" Graham asked.

Ainsley chuckled. Graham was known for his strong internal clock. Even on days he didn't work he was up at six. "It's a little after nine."

Graham made a face and rolled onto his back. "Damn."

"You needed your rest." Ainsley shuffled closer, snuggling up to Graham's arm. "We both did." He placed a kiss to Graham's shoulder. "It's a good day to be lazy."

Graham smiled, lifted his arm up so Ainsley could crowd in. "You're going to have to teach me about this being lazy stuff. Already I'm thinking about all the work I should be doing."

Ainsley shrugged. "You'll get used to it. Just have to clear your mind. Deep breaths. Let your muscles relax."

Graham did take some deep breaths. But clearly, he didn't clear his mind. "Ainsley, how many friends do you have?"

"Well, there's you and Benson. And I suppose I would consider Mara and Ursula friends, but only in private, you know."

Graham groaned. "And this...Croften...he's a good friend?"

Ainsley blinked. He really hadn't expected Graham to bring it up. He thought he'd wait two or three more days before cracking open that subject. "When he's not being a major idiot, yes."

"Just...don't not see him because of me, okay?"

Ainsley furrowed his eyebrows and propped himself up on his elbow. He had to check to make sure that Graham hadn't been replaced by some kind of clone. "What?"

"If you don't want to see him again, that's fine. I just...I don't ever want to be the reason you don't have a friend."

Ainsley felt a buzzing energy in his chest. He felt light and happy. "Graham..." he bit back the words he couldn't say, could never admit. So instead, he leaned down and pressed a kiss to his lips. "You really don't mind? If we're friends? You aren't worried."

"I will never not be worried." Ainsley's joy faded a bit. "But...I want you to be happy. And if having him as a friend makes you happy...then I'll just have to make sure I stalk him better."

Ainsley laughed and settled back down. "I'll get his schedule for you."

Croften had gone to the garden. Because there wasn't a way to get there without passing Ainsley's house. Because if he happened to see Ainsley in his backyard it wasn't really like he was searching him out.

He hadn't seen him.

He sighed, letting out a deep breath as he steadied his hand and continued painting. Mid-morning light was weird, but he loved it. Gave a sort of energy to the flowers and their colors.

"Croften, Croften, Croften."

Croften hung his head, his hand hanging dead in the air above the painting. "Are you just physically incapable of saying my name once? Or do you just get joy out of being annoying."

Henri laughed. "Annoying you is one of the greater joys in life. Especially since it's so easy."

Croften rolled his eyes and turned his attention back to his painting. He pressed the brush to the canvas, only to have the painting jerked up, leaving a long red streak across half of it.

"Tell me someone isn't paying you for this," Henri said, looking it over.

"Your husband, actually," Croften said. "Yeah, he says your paintings are so shit he has to go to me to get anything half-way decent."

There was a terrible ripping sound that reverberated off Croften's spine as Henri tore the canvas in half. "Oops." He dropped the two halves on the ground and was sure to step on them, digging them into the soft soil, as he left.

Croften sat there, unable to move for many reasons. He understood the irony of it. There he had been, talking big talk about hurting anyone who hurt Ainsley. Yet he just sat there and did nothing as Henri ruined his work. He knew why. Ainsley didn't deserve to be unhappy. Croften did.

He packed up his stuff and went back to Mara and Ursula's. Guess it was just another day spent moping.

"There you are!" Ursula said, grabbing his arm as soon as he was through the door.

"Here I am," Croften said, letting her drag him into the drawing room.

She picked up a letter and handed it to him. He studied it. His name looked quite lovely in that handwriting. He turned the envelope over in his hand, no return name. He tried not to get his hopes up as he opened it.

"Yes!" He cried out, reading over the first half of the letter. "No!" as he got to the end.

"What?" Ursula asked. "What, what?"

"He wants to see me!" Extreme joy turned to intense frustration. "Tomorrow."

"Just focus on the positive," Ursula said. "He wants to see you."

Croften nodded. His body bounced on its own, legs begging him to walk. "You may have to sit on me."

"I'm okay with that."

8

Little Talks

Croften could not stop smiling. He hadn't slept all night. Might have had something to do with the whole being tied to the bed so he wouldn't try and slip out in the middle of the night. But there was also the unnerving buzz of getting to see Ainsley again. He was up with the sun, clawing his way out of the rope, out the door without even a thought of breakfast. Only Ainsley on his mind.

Graham opened the door.

Croften's face fell. His heart, once beating erratically with joy, seemed to stop dead in his chest. He stuttered. Normally when he stuttered, he just had too many things he wanted to say. This time, his mind was just completely blank.

"Croften," Graham said, looking him up and down. Fuck. He hadn't even gotten dressed, just ran over in his pajamas. Graham stepped to the side. "Do come in."

Croften didn't know a lot of things, but he knew he most definitely should not go in. Graham's stare gave him no room for argument. He gulped and entered the house.

A strong hand landed on Croften's shoulder, steering him into the drawing-room. The doors closed behind them.

"Make yourself comfortable," Graham said, gesturing to one of the couches. He sat down on the other, crossing his legs.

Croften bit his lip. He really should not be here. He knew that. Just because Ainsley wanted to talk to him did not mean that Graham wasn't still going to try and kill him. Why hadn't he just waited until the guy had gone to work? He sat down, still as could be. Any movement might be his last.

Graham didn't talk. Croften glanced around the room, not wanting to look at him. His palms grew sweaty, and he rubbed them on his pants. "So, uh, where's Ainsley."

"He's still asleep."

Croften nodded. He tried really, really hard not to think about Ainsley asleep. Cuddled up in bed. Soft face and soft breath. Peaceful and cozy. Maybe with Croften curled up around him. He was really bad at not thinking.

Graham took a deep breath and Croften risked a glance at him. His arms were resting on the back of the couch, spread wide, his chest pushing out. He looked completely at ease, but also in control of the room. Certainly intimidating.

"Look, if you're going to kill me could you just get it over with?"

"I'm not going to kill you, Croften."

"Punch me then. Stab me. Yell or whatever. Just get it over with so I can move on with my life. Please!"

Graham shifted, sinking further into the couch. "Ainsley tells me that you promised him there would be no more flirting."

"I, uh, guess you don't believe that, huh?"

"I don't trust you Croften."

"Okay, yeah, yeah, that's fair. I'm not a very trustworthy person." That certainly didn't help his efforts much. "But Ainsley has made it very clear that there is and never will be anything between us. And you trust him, don't you?"

"No."

Oh. Well. That explained...a lot. Croften furrowed his eyebrows. "You know, you really can't have a good relationship without trust." Graham glared at him. "Says the man who has no room to give you relationship advice."

"I trust that Ainsley is telling me the truth when he says he does not want to do anything. But I do not trust that he wouldn't."

"That...makes a little bit of sense. I suppose."

"And I know he would do something with you."

Croften could feel his hope slipping away. But he couldn't lose it. He wouldn't. And how dare Graham try to keep it from him. Keep Ainsley from him. He clenched his hands together. He wasn't going down without a fight.

"Just because you have weird trust issues does not mean you can keep Ainsley from having friends!" He stood up. "I don't care that some guy cheated on you, okay? Ainsley is his own person, and you can't just control his life!"

"He told you about that?"

Okay, not exactly the response Croften was expecting. "He...alluded to it, yeah." Croften sighed, his moment of anger edging away. "Look, I am sorry, okay? That's a shitty thing to go through. But Ainsley is Ainsley. And for some, strange reason, he's really devoted to you. So, you don't have to worry about it."

Graham looked to the side, ever soft smile on his face. His head shook softly. Croften felt a little awkward standing, especially in his pajamas, so he sat back down slowly, fighting the flush he could feel in his face. He cleared his throat, ticked his tongue to break the silence.

"I'm not stopping Ainsley from having you as a friend." Graham looked back at Croften, eyes a little bit glossy, but otherwise his face neutral. "I'm just not convinced that you're going to be a good friend. I care deeply about Ainsley. You will not hurt him."

"Exactly! See, you get it!"

"No. You misunderstand." Graham uncrossed his legs and leaned forward. "You will not hurt him." There was a threat behind the bite of his words.

Croften mirrored his lean, trying not to let the fear show. Because that was the look Mara must have seen. He did not like it.

"You're right. I won't."

They stared each other down. Croften didn't want to be the first one to move away, to break the contact and show weakness. But he was never very good at being still.

"Besides," he said, sitting back. "You should be glad Ainsley has a friend like me!"

"Should I?" Still leaning forward.

"Yeah! I mean, who else is gonna be friends with him in public, huh? With me here, he'll never have that bored, pained look at all that shit you guys go to. I can tag along with Mara and Ursula and keep him company." Graham squinted at him. "No kissing or flirting of course."

Graham finally leaned back. He studied Croften with an intense gaze. Croften wondered if he should keep going. He had a million reasons why he'd be a good friend to Ainsley.

"You'd take him out?" Graham asked.

"...Like, on a date?" Graham frowned. Croften put his hands up in defense. "Hey, hey that was a very open question!"

"Ainsley doesn't go anywhere. He...we both don't want him out on his own."

Croften scoffed. "People ignore him sure, but I doubt they'd do anything."

"They have in the past."

Croften's hands were in fists again. "I want names! You tell me exactly who the fuck I have to beat up!"

Graham smiled. "Good. I want you to take him out, okay? He likes to go on walks. Take him to that garden he loves. I'm never around enough to go with him, so just get him out of the house for me. Can you do that?"

Croften's anger dissipated. Graham was offering him literally everything he wanted. And he wanted to know if he could do that? Hell yeah, he could do that!

Croften nodded, too afraid he would squeak with joy if he spoke. The door slid open. Both of them looked towards it, where Ainsley was shuffling in, rubbing his eyes.

"Graham? Croften? What are you doing here?"

"I, you, well, the letter!" Croften said. He knew he was blushing. There was no stopping it. Not when Ainsley was looking like that. His hair was all messed up on the top of his head. His face was scrunched up, eyes squinting as he woke them up. His pajamas looked one size too big, hanging off his body so comfortably.

Ainsley shuffled over, feet never leaving the ground. He sat down next to Graham and Croften ached. He wanted to be the one sitting next to him, placing his hand on his thigh, pressing tight to his side.

"Is everything okay? I heard yelling."

"Croften just got a little over excited." Graham moved to place his arm around Ainsley's shoulders. Croften gulped. "But we've come to an agreement. Haven't we?"

Croften nodded. "Uh, uh, yeah. Yeah it's all...hunky dory."

Ainsley frowned at him. "Hunky dory?" He laughed and patted Graham's arm. "You're going to be late for work."

Graham nodded. The two of them stood up. Croften looked away as Graham placed a hand on the back of Ainsley's neck and pulled him in for a kiss. Ainsley was smiling at him when they pulled apart. It made Croften sick.

"Have a good day," Graham said.

"You, too."

Graham gave Croften a hard look before he left.

"I hope he wasn't too rough," Ainsley said, sitting back down. Croften fought the urge to jump over to him.

"He was just...ya know...him. But I don't wanna talk about that!" He jumped to his feet, too excited to sit still. "Wanna go for a walk?"

Ainsley chuckled. "Well, I don't know about you. But I need to get dressed first."

"Oh. Right. No yeah, yeah. Uh...meet you out back in a few minutes?"

They walked down to the garden. It was still pretty early, so not a lot of people were around. But any that were got a harsh glare from Croften, even if they hadn't looked at them. It did not escape Ainsley's notice. He stayed an appropriate distance from him, but he wondered what it would feel like to hold that hand. Maybe wrap around that arm. He shook the thoughts from his head.

"Oh, it's beautiful." Ainsley smiled and took in a deep breath, the fragrance of flowers filling his nose. "I've never seen it this early in the morning."

"Yeah. It's good to study things at different times in the day. The position of the sun can really change the view and color and stuff."

Ainsley grabbed his arm, one hand tight around his bicep. "You haven't shown me any of your work yet! How is it going? I want to see!"

Croften smiled at him. "Uh-uh. It's a surprise."

Ainsley gave him a look and stepped further into the garden. He looked around, rubbing his hands over leaves and flowers. He found the bush of blue bell flowers that Croften had picked his gift from. His face fell a bit. The flower had mostly wilted by now. It was a nice little gift while it lasted. He rubbed a petal between his fingers.

"They're so soft," he said. "And so bright."

"Like you."

Ainsley looked over, and Croften's face was scrunched up, nodding.

"Yeah, yep, I know. Sorry. Slipped out."

Ainsley sighed. He couldn't help but smile. He liked how Croften liked him. It wasn't that Graham didn't compliment him, but when he did it wasn't often. And it didn't come easy. Croften, however, would probably sing his praises all day long. It was vain of him, but he liked it.

"It's okay. It'll take a while to adjust, I know." He gave Croften an understanding nod.

Ainsley turned to move on, but his foot crunched on something. He scooped down and picked up half of a canvas. It was a painting of the garden, a red smudge running over it. He looked around and found the other half not too far away. "Are these yours?"

Croften had his hands in his pockets, shoulders hunched, face looking down. "It uh...yeah."

Ainsley studied it. He had a theory. Croften had somehow messed it up, had gotten that red streak across the canvas, and had ripped it up in frustration.

"I think it looks good," he said, putting the two pieces together.

Croften scoffed. "Don't be nice."

"Why did you tear it?"

Croften did a very good job of hiding it, but his face went through the motions of surprise, to panic, to quick thinking. "It was just shit I guess." He shrugged. "No need to keep it."

Ainsley stepped closer to him. "Croften, what happened?"

"Not important." Croften walked away. But Ainsley wasn't going to let him get away with that.

"We're friends now. You can tell me what happened." He wiped the dirt off the canvas, folded the pieces together, and stuffed them in his pocket.

"Nothing happened."

"*Croften.*"

"What do you want to know, Ainsley? You wanna hear about the asshole that tore it up and stepped on it? Wanna know how I just sat there and let it happen? Is that what you want to know?"

"Croften, wait." Ainsley grabbed his arm, pulling him to a halt.

Croften rolled his head back and looked at him. "What?"

Ainsley rubbed his arm gently. "You don't have to talk about it if you don't want to. But I want you to know that I'm here for you if you do. You can talk to me about anything."

Croften looked into his eyes and groaned. "It just...it happens, okay?" He shrugged. "Henri's just a bully, you know?"

"He can't get away with this."

Croften shrugged again looking away. "Can we just…forget it? I want you to see the roses before it gets too sunny."

Ainsley sighed and nodded, letting Croften lead him deeper into the garden. He had gotten a name out of him, at least. That was a good start. Croften may not do anything about it, but no one was going to get away with hurting his friend like that.

9

Chekhov's Mistake

Ainsley rubbed at his eyes, blinking to try and get them to focus. He had stayed up too late last night worrying. "Are you sure you don't want to stick around?" Ainsley asked, hoping that some conversation would help wake him up. "I don't want you to have to leave on your day off."

"It's fine," Graham said. He was actually eating for once, putting a smile on Ainsley's face. "I have some things I need to take care of in town, anyway.

Anything you need while I'm there?"

Ainsley sipped on his coffee. He didn't like coffee much, but he needed it. "I'm running out of room in my journal," he said. "If you wouldn't mind picking me up a new one?"

"Don't mind at all. Getting close to finishing the next book, then?"

Ainsley nodded and picked at his food. "Yes. I'm having a bit of a dilemma with how to end it, however."

"Oh?"

"Yes. There's this...relationship that I know everyone wants to become fully realized. It's just...well, I don't feel like the characters are quite ready yet."

Graham finished all of the food on his plate. "So, what do they need to do to get ready?"

Ainsley frowned, leaving his food uneaten. "That's the problem. I don't know."

"Perhaps if there's nothing that can get them ready, they aren't meant to be together."

Ainsley looked at him. If only he knew. If only he knew how much Ainsley wondered over that very fact every day. He shook his head. "No. They have to be together. They just need something."

Graham sat back in his seat; hands folded on his lap. "I'm sure I could help more. But someone won't let me read the books."

Ainsley smiled, blushing slightly. "You wouldn't like them anyway. They're not exactly your genre."

Graham shrugged. "I liked the bit I got through of the first one. I think you're an excellent writer, and I was enjoying it."

Ainsley's blush deepened. "You don't have to lie," he said. "They're not that good."

"Just accept the compliment."

Ainsley sighed. "Thank you."

Graham stood up. "I'm heading out. Don't forget to eat your breakfast, hm?" He kissed Ainsley on the top of his head.

"I'll try."

Ainsley stabbed at his eggs. He couldn't eat. He was too nervous. It was a good idea, he kept telling himself. Croften needed a partner. And he wasn't going to find one spending all his time hanging around Ainsley and doing family portraits. This was how he was going to get to find someone.

The door knocked. "I'll get it," Ainsley called into the kitchen. He got up and opened the door. "Croften? What are you doing here?"

Croften was smiling. "You invited me."

"Yes, my dear, but I invited you for this afternoon." Ainsley kept the door mostly closed.

"Yeah, but I saw Graham leave, so I figured I'd come hang out early."

"But I need some time to set up."

Croften's eyebrows furrowed. "Set up?" Then he smirked and leaned against the door frame. "Planning something fun, huh?"

The sooner he found someone the better. "Yes. It should be enjoyable. I just need you to wait."

Croften stepped closer, all but forcing his way inside. "Maybe I can help."

Ainsley took a controlling breath. "No. I don't think you can. I'm going to have to insist that you wait."

Croften's face fell. "Really?"

Ainsley nodded, looking away. If he looked at Croften's saddened face too long, he feared he would give in. "I promise it will be worth the wait."

Croften sighed. "Fine."

"And don't just sulk around in the front yard. You'll ruin the surprise. Go back to Mara and Ursula's."

"Seriously?"

"Seriously."

Croften groaned. Ainsley risked a look at him. He was pouting, clearly trying to get Ainsley to change his mind. Ainsley shook his head and gently pushed on Croften's chest, forcing him to back out of the doorway.

"Just trust me. You're going to like this."

"Fine, fine." Croften mumbled and walked away, hands in his pockets, shoulders slumped.

Ainsley rolled his eyes. Croften could be quite the drama queen. But he couldn't be there while Ainsley was setting up. And he really couldn't be there while the other guests were arriving.

With Benson's help it didn't take long for everything to get ready. It wasn't going to be anything big, just some tea and sandwiches out in the garden. Something small and comfortable, to hopefully help create a cozy atmosphere. Something Croften could enjoy himself with.

Of the people Ainsley knew, only about twenty or so would actually talk to him. Of those, seven just so happened to be single. (Technically there were eight, but the one not invited to the party was too old for Croften). They arrived mostly in a good mood. Ainsley was, after all, an excellent host. It wasn't his fault that practically no one would even think about going to a party of his. But a tea to meet a prospective date was another thing altogether. He had not planned to tell them, originally, but most of them had refused to come until he mentioned it.

Croften was scowling when he showed up again. "It better have been worth it," he mumbled, arms crossed.

Ainsley held the door open for him. "I told you it would be. Come with me to the garden." He grabbed Croften's arm and led him back.

"Uh, there's people here," Croften said as they stepped out. Said people were all looking at him. Ainsley smiled, they all certainly seemed interested. "Why are there people here?"

"It's a party," Ainsley said. "I wanted you to meet some of my friends."

"You have friends?" Croften asked. Ainsley gave him a look. "I-I mean, uh, you're the one who said you didn't!"

Ainsley rolled his eyes. "Come on."

Ainsley tightened his hold on Croften's arm and dragged him around, introducing him to everyone. Croften was cordial, he said hi, he answered when spoken too, but it was obvious that he wasn't making an effort. It must have been because Ainsley was there. That was it! Croften was just worried about flirting in front of him.

Ainsley got Croften talking with someone and then slipped away, rushing inside before Croften could realize he was missing.

"Everything alright, sir?" Benson asked. He was working on decorations for the little cakes that Ainsley had asked him to make.

"Oh my!" Ainsley's eyes widened as he wandered over. "Those look scrumptious! I say, Benson, you really are quite talented."

"Thank you, sir." Benson smiled. "Did you need something outside?"

"Oh, no, no. I'm just hiding out so Croften can mingle as he pleases."

"Well, he's not very pleased," Croften said.

Ainsley jumped and spun around. Croften was standing in the entry to the kitchen, arms crossed as he glared at Ainsley.

"Croften! What are you doing in here?"

"Could ask you the same thing."

"I was just...checking on the cakes is all," Ainsley said. Benson gave him a look but said nothing.

"I heard you talking, Ainsley. What is this whole party about, hm?"

Ainsley picked at his fingers. It wasn't like there was a point to lying anymore. "Well, I was just sort of hoping you might meet someone."

"Meet someone?"

"Yes. You know, someone to...occupy your time."

Croften closed his eyes and pinched the bridge of his nose. "Oh, I see. You weren't a prostitute; you were a pimp. You're pimping me out."

"I am not! I just wanted you to find someone you could date."

"I don't want to find anyone to date."

"I really think it would be good for you."

Croften opened his eyes and looked at him. He sighed. He bit his lip. He opened his mouth. Then he turned around and walked away.

"Where are you going?" Ainsley asked, chasing after him.

"I'm leaving."

Croften grabbed the handle, but Ainsley raced around him, slamming his back against the door to keep it closed.

"Please, Croften. You can't leave. They came to meet you."

"Yeah? Well, I don't want to meet them." Croften pulled against the handle, but Ainsley pushed back. "Move."

"I'm sorry. I really am. I didn't think you'd be so opposed to it. Just please stay. Just for a little longer?" Ainsley gave him his best pleading look.

Croften sighed, his body slumping as he let go of the handle and rolled his head back. "That's not fair," he whined.

"I'll make it up to you later, I promise."

Croften huffed, a bit of a growl to his breath. "You better."

"I will!" Ainsley grabbed his arm. Croften frowned and slumped about, but he followed him back out to the garden.

Croften grumbled and kicked a rock down the street. He wasn't exactly in the best of moods. Ainsley had totally blindsided him with that party. Which would be bad enough. And on top of that it was a party where everyone wanted to talk to him. It was exhausting.

He wasn't exactly looking forward to working. But he figured it was the best way to settle his nerves. He worried that if he stuck around Ursula too long, he'd get roped into accidentally talking about what happened at Ainsley's. And he had a feeling he'd somehow end up getting hit.

So, he just stopped by to grab his stuff and headed down to town, the walk calming him a bit.

Madam Lacy worked just on the edge of town. It was an older building, and it certainly looked exactly like what he expected a fortune teller's place to look like. Ivy crept up the sides of the house and broken shutters hung off the windows. Croften felt a shiver up his spine as he knocked on the door.

It swung open almost immediately. Madam Lacy stood before him, a long, intricate robe barely covering her body.

"Ah, sorry," Croften said, averting his gaze. "I didn't mean to interrupt anything."

"Oh, no interrupting at all," she said, smiling at him. "I knew you were coming."

"Oh, right the, uh, telling the future thing. So…" Croften risked looking at her. He couldn't seem to speak so he just gestured to the supplies under his arm.

"Oh, yes. Do come in."

Madam Lacy held the door open and gestured down the hall. Croften followed her lead to a small sitting room. It was decorated with dark colors, a lot of greens and blues. A couch rested against the back wall, with a chair facing it.

"You can set up here," she said, patting the back of the chair. Croften nodded and sat down, pulling out his paints. "I want something for my husband, you see."

Croften nodded. "A popular request. Minis make nice gifts." He pulled out the proper-sized canvas.

"I hope." Madam Lacy dropped the robe and laid down on the couch. "How's this?"

Croften cleared his throat. It was not the first time a customer had disrobed suddenly in front of him. He's become a pro at handling it, but it didn't make it any less awkward. "That's uh, good."

"Are you sure? I really want him to like it. Maybe I should adjust like this?"

Croften shook his head. "However you feel most comfortable."

"I think this is quite nice."

Croften took a deep breath and got to work. He wasn't unfamiliar with nudes, of course. But it was always harder when he wasn't prepared for it. Harder still as Madam Lacy couldn't seem to sit still.

Thankfully it was a mini painting, and Croften wouldn't have to put up with it for long.

"Are you married?" Madam Lacy asked. She kept not looking at him. Which was equally great and terrible.

"'Fraid not," Croften replied.

"Anyone special?"

"Ah...not, particularly."

Madam Lacy nodded. "Must be nice? Being free like that?"

"Uh, it's a thing." Madam Lacy stood up. "Oh, I'm not done...yet."

Madam Lacy walked around to the back of the chair, hands on Croften's shoulders. They massaged them gently. "I just wanted to take a peek," she said. Her hands slid forward, fingers brushing their way down Croften's chest.

Croften knew he should stop it. After all, what would Ainsley say?

Wait. What would Ainsley say? Had he really just thought that? What would Ainsley say? Who cared? He had made it very clear that he wasn't going to leave Graham, that he and Croften would never be together. Had made it so clear he had gone through that whole charade to try and set him up with someone.

Maybe a good night in was exactly what he needed to relax.

10

Brotherly...Something

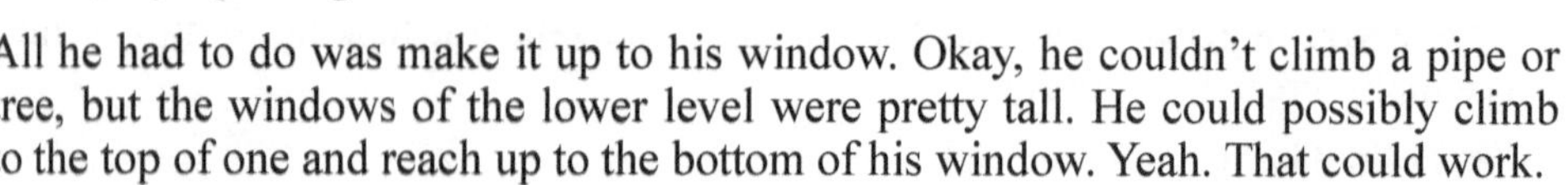

It was okay. He was going to do this. He's snuck into a house before. Just because this house was big and had a very aggressive doubter of his lifestyle inside did not make sneaking into it any harder. The fact that there wasn't a tree or drainpipe near his window, however, did.

The sun was still on its way up, the morning a light blue sky as Croften stalked around the side of the house, trying to figure out his best course of action.

All he had to do was make it up to his window. Okay, he couldn't climb a pipe or tree, but the windows of the lower level were pretty tall. He could possibly climb to the top of one and reach up to the bottom of his window. Yeah. That could work.

Croften grabbed the side of the window to the library and stepped up to the ledge. He reached for the top of the window but was stilled. The blinds had opened. Mara was there, arms crossed, staring at him from inside. Croften gave her a wide smile.

"Just cleaning the windows," he said, using the sleeve of his shirt to rub the glass.

Mara shook her head, face passive. She opened the window and Croften nearly fell in. "Where have you been?"

Croften carefully climbed inside, trying to smooth out the wrinkles of his clothes. "I was just having a few drinks, is all."

"Please tell me she wasn't married," Mara said, latching the window shut again.

"There was no she."

Mara's hand grabbed the collar of Croften's shirt. "So, when did you start wearing lipstick, hm?"

"Last week. Didn't you notice?" Croften pulled away and started heading for the stairs. Mara moved to block his path. "Look, I don't believe my nightlife is really any of your business. So, you can just go ahead and put that little judgmental face away, okay?" Mara did not put that judgmental face away.

"Either you tell me, or I'll wake up Ursula and you can tell her," Mara said.

Croften did not want to tell anyone. His life really was none of their business. But if Ursula knew he had come home so late, well, she would find ways to make him talk. He was pretty sure Ursula could make a good living as a torturer for the crown. She could get anyone to reveal all their secrets.

Croften took a deep breath and released it in a growl. "Fine. I'll tell you but you can't tell Ursula. She might actually kill me."

"My lips are sealed."

"Yes, I was with a woman. Yes, she was married. No, I don't know what's wrong with me. Can I go now?"

Mara shook her head. "Do you understand what the word no means? Do you... do you just need help learning how to say it?"

Clearly Croften was not going to be allowed to go. He walked back and flopped into a chair, scowling, legs draped over the arm. "Go on," he said. "I'm terrible, I'm disgusting, I'm gonna wind up dead at the hands of a jealous lover. Yada, yada, yada."

Mara said nothing of the sort. She walked over and sat on the edge of the coffee table. "What happened?"

Croften shrugged. "She came onto me. It happens. I'm hot, or didn't you know?"

Mara rolled her eyes. "Croften. I'm serious. I've known you since we were five. Did something happen with Ainsley?"

Croften crossed his arms and looked away, sinking further into the chair. "Nothing happened with Ainsley." And nothing ever would.

"You only do shit like this when you're hurt. What happened?"

"I do not only do shit like this when I'm hurt!" Croften looked back at her. She was not buying it. "I'm not hurt!"

Mara sighed. She stood up and stared at him with her hands on her hips. "I think you need to talk about it. If you don't want to talk about it to me, that's fine. But you gotta find someone. You can't keep doing this."

Croften was busy formulating a proper response when there was a knock at the door. Mara held a finger up to him and went to answer it, her feet soft against the floor. Croften huffed. He wasn't hurt. So what if Ainsley didn't want to be with him? So what if he tried to set him up? With an entire room full of people. That didn't matter. He didn't care. And he certainly wasn't hurt.

"Ah, Croften, good. You're up."

Croften scrambled to his feet, tugging his shirt down and trying to look half-way presentable. "Ainsley? What are you doing here?'

"Well, I was rather hoping you'd come over today?"

Mara hadn't followed Ainsley in, and Croften found himself wishing she had, so he had someone else to look at. "Uh...I mean. Sure?"

Ainsley had not explicitly asked Croften to come over since that first time, after the dinner incident. It was usually just expected that Croften would show up. For him to actually come over? And ask for him? In person? Something was up.

"Oh, good. We should hurry back before...uh…" Ainsley looked to the side, clearly trying to come up with a lie.

Croften looked down at his clothes, dirty and wrinkled. He usually didn't care what he looked like, but he really didn't want to hang out with Ainsley in the same clothes he had been wearing last night. Especially not if Graham caught him like that.

"Do I have time to change?" Croften asked. Ainsley looked at him. He was scared. He shook his head, quick but short. "Lead the way."

Ainsley was really hurrying down the street, Croften practically jogging to catch up to him. They stopped by the gate leading into the front yard. "Give me a few minutes and then knock on the door, okay?"

Croften barely got the, "What?" out before Ainsley was skittering away. Croften leaned over and watched as Ainsley started to climb the tree that led over to his room. What the actual hell was going on?

Croften waited to make sure Ainsley got into his window. Then he shook his head and walked up to the door, knocking as instructed.

It opened much too quickly, but it wasn't Benson who had opened it. It was a shorter man, balding, staring at him with a familiar gaze that Croften just couldn't place. "The charity house is on the other side of town," the man said.

"Uh." Croften looked down. No, yeah, that was a fair assumption.

"Croften!" Ainsley was at the top of the stairs, breathing hard. "What a surprise!"

The man's gaze changed and Croften realized where he recognized it from. It looked a hell of a lot like how Graham looked at him. "You know this...person?"

"But of course." Ainsley smiled, fake and wrong. He sped down the steps and stood behind the man, still blocking the door. "He's my friend. He comes by sometimes to chat and all that."

"Yep," Croften said, uncomfortable with how uncomfortable Ainsley looked. He elbowed his way inside, the man moving to let him in. "Andrew K. Croften, at your service." He slung an arm over Ainsley's shoulders, feeling his muscles relax beneath him.

"This is Alexander," Ainsley said. "He's Graham's brother."

Ah. There it was. Graham's brother, huh? Croften looked him up and down. How was Graham possibly related to...that?

"Anyway," Ainsley said, a slight nervous chuckle. "We'll just be out in the garden if you need anything." He grabbed Croften around the waist and pulled him down the hall to the back door.

"I guess good looks don't run in the family, huh?" Croften asked as they left the house.

Ainsley let out a big sigh and sort of leaned into their awkward hold a bit. "I'm sorry," he said. "I didn't mean to drag you into this. I just…"

"Scared?" Croften asked. His arm tightened around Ainsley's shoulder. "I won't let him hurt you."

"I just don't know why he's here. He showed up a few minutes ago saying he wanted to see Graham. And when I told him he was at work, he just came in and said he'd wait. I didn't want to be alone with him."

Croften turned to the side, pulling Ainsley into a proper hug. "Don't worry. I'm here now. It'll be okay."

Ainsley nodded and hugged him close. "Croften?" he asked. "Why is there lipstick on the collar of your shirt?"

"Uh...I'm sure there's a perfectly reasonable explanation for that."

Ainsley gasped and pulled back. "You met up with someone from yesterday, didn't you?"

Croften nodded. "Yeah! That makes sense."

"Oh! Oh, who was it? I knew it was a good idea! Please tell me!"

"No can do. She's, uh, shy." Ainsley's eyebrows furrowed. "Well, with this. She...doesn't want to tell anyone! Not until like, we know it's gonna work out. You know?"

Ainsley nodded. "Yes, of course. Do you think it'll work out?"

Croften's face tightened a bit. "It... could. But, uh, I wouldn't be surprised if it didn't, you know."

"I wouldn't be so sure. You're quite the catch. I'm sure the two of you will get along just fine."

Croften nodded. "Yeah. Sure." Got along pretty fine last night, at least.

Ainsley was normally happy to have Croften with him. He liked Croften. He was a good friend. But he had never been happier to spend the day with him than he was that day. He was not, as Croften had suggested, scared of Alexander. It was just uncomfortable.

Alexander and Graham may not look similar, but they were certainly related. They were both intimidating and imposing, but the difference was that Graham loved Ainsley. He was soft with him. Alexander...well, Ainsley hadn't seen him since before the incident. He remembered him being nice enough before. But that was before. And while Graham had not murdered him, the two did have quite a falling out once the marriage happened. Ainsley wasn't really sure what would happen, but having Croften there just made him feel better.

"He really is just going to stay there all day, isn't he?" Croften asked, coming back out to the garden with some fresh tea. They hadn't really needed it, but summer was quickly approaching, and they each took turns escaping inside for this or that to get a bit of relief from the sun.

"Yes, I'm afraid he is. Was he doing anything?" Ainsley accepted the cup from Croften with a smile.

"Just reading." Croften was smirking when he sat down.

Ainsley didn't want to know the answer. "Anything interesting?"

"Mr. High-and-Mighty in there was reading a Dangerous Dan book." Croften laughed.

Ainsley's eyes went wide. Oh no. What if he knew? Maybe Graham had told him. Or had told someone else who told him. Ainsley wrung his fingers together and prayed that he knew nothing.

"They're good books," Ainsley said. "I suppose he's allowed to enjoy them as we do."

"Oh! Speaking of. I just got to the part with the hippos. You read that?" Ainsley nodded. "Can we please talk about it? I mean...okay, look, I get it. He's scared. He has one fear and that's commitment. I understand that. I really do. But when a prince, not just anyone, but a prince comes to the fucking swamp to save your ass, you do not just say thanks and run off! You kiss him! You tell him you love him! Dan is an idiot!"

Ainsley smiled softly. "Yes, I suppose he is." When someone disowns their family and moves towns for you, you kiss them. You tell them you love them. Why couldn't Ainsley just do that?

"Hey." Croften nudged him with his elbow. "You okay?"

"Huh? Oh, yes. Sorry. I was just thinking."

"I've been told that's pretty dangerous."

"Is that why you never do it?"

Croften gave him a fake glare and Ainsley laughed. Croften really did always have a way of making him feel better. They talked and chatted and ignored Alexander as the sun started to dip low in the sky.

Croften stood up and stretched. "Suppose I should get going. I mean, I can stay here until Graham shows up and then just slip out the back, if you want."

"Actually," Ainsley stood up, "I was rather hoping you could stay."

"Stay? Like, with him here?"

Ainsley nodded. "I'm not sure what's going to happen between them. I just feel like maybe having you here could help defuse the situation, should one arise."

Croften sighed. He looked down at his clothes. "I mean, as long as Graham doesn't get any funny ideas seeing this."

Ainsley chuckled. "He won't. I haven't worn lipstick in years."

"You know, every time I come over it just solidifies the prostitute theory."

Ainsley shook his head and took Croften by the arm, leading him back into the house where Graham would arrive soon. Alexander apparently had the same idea, waiting out in the hallway.

"Coughten? Leaving so soon?" He asked.

"It's Croften," Croften said.

"And he's staying for dinner," Ainsley hurriedly added. Alexander's gaze wandered down to their linked arms and Ainsley dropped his hold. He already had to worry about Graham thinking things. Didn't need Alexander thinking as well.

A key turned in the lock and Graham stepped in. Ainsley held his breath as the two brothers looked at each other. He wished he was still holding Croften's arm, so he had something to grip other than his own hand.

"Graham," Alexander greeted. "How good to see you again."

Graham blinked. He stepped to the side and held the door open. "Get out."

"That's really no way to treat a guest. Mother raised you better than that."

"You are not a guest. No one invited you. Leave."

Alexander frowned. "No."

Graham's chest puffed out and he got that look in his eyes. Ainsley startled and rushed forward, hand on Graham's chest to avoid making a rumor a truth. "I invited him in," he said. Graham turned said look to him. "It's just that he came all this way, and, really, I think the two of you should talk. Over dinner, yes? Benson's really outdone himself with the menu tonight."

Graham's gaze didn't soften. Ainsley raised his eyebrows slightly. Please, he asked with his eyes. Please don't make this worse than it is.

"Fine." Graham moved around them and walked up to his office.

Ainsley let out the breath he didn't know he was holding. He looked back at Alexander who nodded his head.

"I should go check on how it's coming along," Ainsley said, mouth twitching into a smile as he raced to the kitchen, Croften hot on his heels.

"What was that?" Croften asked as Ainsley looked over the food Benson was preparing.

"What was what?"

"That! You told me you were uncomfortable with Alexander around. Why didn't you just let Graham throw him out."

Ainsley tapped a finger against the countertop. "Well...I'm sure it won't make much sense. But Graham and his brother used to be very close. They had quite the falling out when we got married. I'm certain if they just talked, they could work things out."

Croften shook his head. "You know, you really ought to try being mean one day. You might find it suits you."

Ainsley smiled. "Being nice to the people you care about is nothing to sneer at, dear."

"Yeah, yeah, whatever. I still think you should have let Graham punch him."

Thankfully, dinner was ready in a few minutes. There was no easy way to arrange how they sat. Ainsley insisted that Graham and Alexander sit across from each other to talk better. But opposite ends wouldn't work, as there would be too much space for proper conversation. But that meant Croften had to sit next to one of them. And for as much as Ainsley did not want to sit next to Alexander, he figured Croften would be more comfortable next to Graham. Not that he looked it.

No one had spoken a word in ten minutes. Neither Graham nor Alexander were eating. Croften was sipping at his wine, moving the food around on his plate and sometimes taking a bite. Ainsley cringed at every sound he made in the quiet.

"So," Croften eventually said, drawing everyone's attention. "Alexander, important question. Was Ainsley a prostitute?"

Ainsley kicked Croften under the table, doing his best to mimic Graham's murder-glare.

"What?" Croften asked, reaching down to rub his shin. "It's a fair question."

"About as good as," Alexander mumbled.

Graham stood up, chair scratching over the floor. "You will not come into my house and insult my husband. Now leave."

"I can't deny the truth, Graham. And neither should you. Marrying Ainsley was a mistake."

Ainsley bit his lip and looked down. It was true. Everyone knew it. There was a floral pattern on the rug beneath them. He found a blue patch and focused on it.

"Did you just come all the way over here to tell me that? You made your opinions very clear when we got married. But that's all they are, Alexander. Your opinions."

"Everyone's opinion, Graham. And if everyone thinks it, it must be true."

"Leave."

Alexander stood up. "I came to tell you that I've spoken with Father. He's forgiven you. You can come back."

"I'm not going back. But you are. Now."

"Don't do this, Graham. It's not too late to fix things."

"There's nothing to fix. If you don't leave this instant, I won't hesitate to force you."

(Croften had secretly hoped that Alexander would refuse, and Graham would punch him or something. Unfortunately, Alexander just nodded and left, much to Croften's despair).

Graham walked around the table. Ainsley felt a hand on his chin, gently pulling until he was looking up at Graham. Graham knelt down, head just lower than Ainsley's. His hand moved, rubbing the side of Ainsley's face.

"Marrying you," he said, "was not a mistake." Ainsley nodded. He could feel the sting of a tear in his right eye, and he blinked it away. "And I'm not going back. It's not what I want. And it wouldn't be good for me."

Ainsley could only nod, even though he wanted to shake his head. He knew that if he spoke all he would do is argue that it wasn't true. Graham had just been given his life back. A life of ease and comfort. Of not having to be miserable and worried about fighting everyone all the time. And, once again, he had thrown it all away for Ainsley. Who did not deserve that.

He held his breath, biting the inside of his cheek. He couldn't cry. He wouldn't. Not there, not in front of Graham and Croften. He would wait. He could wait. He had to wait. Croften would leave, and Graham would sleep, and then he could cry.

Graham moved his hand again, wiping a thumb over Ainsley's cheek as if he had already started crying. And then he did. Tears fell out of his eyes, breaking against Graham's thumb. He shook his head. He didn't want to be sad. He didn't want Graham to know he was sad.

"Alright. That's it!" Croften got up and stormed out of the room.

"Croften?" Ainsley called after him. He was leaving the house. Ainsley shared a quick worried look with Graham, and they were both on their feet, following him.

Alexander was a good bit down the street, but Croften caught up to him with the speed of a mad man. "Hey, asshole!"

Alexander turned around. His face only had a small moment of time to be confused before it was being punched. Ainsley gasped, and he and Graham raced up to them. Alexander stumbled back a bit, holding his nose. His eyebrows furrowed, and he pulled an arm back to return the punch. Then Graham was between them, catching the punch in his hand, holding Alexander back. Ainsley grabbed Croften around the waist and pulled him back.

"Walk away," Graham said, a warning growled out to his brother.

Alexander looked between the three of them, observing, calculating the risk of not following that order. He wrenched his hand free of Graham. "This isn't over, Coughten," he said, voice nasally.

"I sure hope not, *Sandy*," Croften said back.

Alexander started walking away, still holding his nose. Ainsley turned Croften around and hugged him. He was still crying but now he wasn't really sure why. He was still upset about what had happened at dinner. But he was also a bit happy. Happy that Croften had defended him. And, in turn, happy that Graham had defended Croften.

Croften hugged him back. "I can't believe you're related to such a tool," he said.

"Sometimes neither can I," Graham said.

At the sound of his voice, Ainsley was very aware of the embrace he had with Croften. Shaking a bit, he pulled back, wiping his face clean, using what energy he had left to hold the tears back again.

"You alright?" Croften asked.

Ainsley sniffed, trying not to wipe his nose on the back of his sleeve. "I'm okay, yes. Thank you. For all of today."

Croften glanced over to Graham and Ainsley followed his gaze. Graham had turned around, arms crossed, looking down at the road. As if giving them privacy.

"I should probably head home," Croften said. "It's really about time that I change."

Ainsley nodded, smiling at him. "Thank you again." Croften nodded back, patted him on the arm, and headed home.

As soon as he was gone Graham turned back around. He was clenching his one hand tight. But it didn't look like an angry sort of clench.

"Oh dear!" Ainsley grabbed it, looking it over gently. "That must have hurt," he said, referencing the punch he had caught.

"It's fine," Graham said. "Just need to shake it off."

"Come on, we'll put some ice on it." Ainsley continued to hold his hand as they walked back to their house. "That was really very nice of you, you know. Stopping that punch."

Graham shrugged. "I just didn't want things to escalate," he said.

"You know, I really do think the two of you would get along if you just spent a little bit of time together."

Graham was quiet for a moment. Then he said, "Yeah. Maybe." And Ainsley couldn't remember a time he was that happy.

11

Everybody Loves Somebody

"Ainsley! I need your help with something!" Croften grabbed Ainsley's arm and tried to pull him away. Ainsley's grip tightened on Graham's arm, and he pulled back, keeping Croften in place.

"There's no one else here," Ainsley said. "You don't need to steal me away."

Croften frowned, not releasing Ainsley's arm. They were at some fancy garden party for some event

or another Croften couldn't be bothered to remember.

"What do you need help with?" Graham asked.

Croften scowled at him. "I need *Ainsley's* help stalking someone."

"Oh? Who are we stalking?" Ainsley looked around the garden, hoping to spy the object of Croften's attention.

"Henri," Croften said. He wrapped an arm over Ainsley's shoulders and pointed him out. "He's here alone and I'm gonna catch him in the act!"

"Henri," Graham said, his voice musing. "Henri Shan?"

Croften squinted at him. "*Of course* you two know each other," he mumbled.

"We do," Graham confirmed. "He used to do my family's yearly portrait." Croften rolled his eyes. "I suspect he still does."

"Isn't he the one that tore your painting?" Ainsley asked. Croften didn't miss the look that Graham gave him.

Croften waved his hand. "Yeah, yeah, but forget that! This guy is never not with Léon! But he's alone now, and I'm gonna get him!"

"Get him how?" Ainsley asked, giving Croften a side-eye.

"He and his husband like to pretend they're so perfect." Croften growled. "But I know there's a flaw in their love and I'm gonna find it!"

"Exactly how many marriages are you trying to break up this summer?" Graham asked.

Croften glared at him. But before he could respond someone came over to occupy his time, which was fine, as Ainsley finally let go and allowed Croften to drag him away.

"So, explain to me exactly the situation with Henri and his husband?"

Croften pulled Ainsley behind a line of tall bushes, both just able to see over the top. "He and Léon like to pretend to be all in love and devoted. It's sickening."

Ainsley smiled and patted his arm. "Is it really that hard to believe that the two of them actually are in love and devoted?"

Croften scoffed. "You haven't met Henri, okay? The guys a dick. There's no way he's committed like that."

Ainsley's hand moved to his back, rubbing it gently. Croften looked over at him. There was a small smile on Ainsley's face and something like pity in his eyes.

"What is that face for?" Croften asked, trying to ignore the heat that radiated off Ainsley's hand on his back.

"What face?" Said face immediately dropped, turning into a fake innocence.

Croften shook his head. "How does Graham put up with you?"

Ainsley chuckled. "You know, I do wonder that myself."

"Shh, shh, he's coming this way!" Croften ducked down, attempting to pull Ainsley down with him.

"We're not going to hide from him, dear," Ainsley said, refusing to be dragged down.

"Is that you cowering behind that bush there, Croften?"

Henri walked around the line bushes, satisfied little smile on his face, arms crossed over his chest. Croften, still crouching on the ground, scowled up at him. "I'm not cowering?"

"Oh? Then what are you doing?"

"I'm, uh, just looking for...something."

Henri chuckled, shaking his head at him. "You really are pathetic, aren't you?"

Croften opened his mouth to say an equally jarring comeback when Ainsley cut him off.

"Excuse me," he said, crossing his own arms and giving Henri a hard stare. "But I am going to have to ask you to not speak to my friend like that."

"I'm sorry?" Henri said.

Croften hopped back up to his feet, hands on Ainsley's shoulders, trying to pull him away. "Let it go, Ainsley. It's fine."

"It most certainly is not!" Ainsley shook him off. "Now I really must insist that you apologize to Croften."

"Me?" Henri asked. "Apologize to him?" He laughed. "Oh, that's rich. Well, Croften, I must say, I think it's rather charming you've finally found someone who believes your charade. Tell me, are you naive or just an idiot?"

"Well, I-" Ainsley started.

"Love to stick around and chat," Henri continued. "But I have important work to do. I wouldn't expect you to understand." He winked at Croften and strolled away.

"The nerve of him," Ainsley said, huffing up, face tingling red.

"I'm sorry." Croften wrapped his arms around Ainsley's waist, head resting on his shoulder.

"Whatever for?" Ainsley's arms wrapped around him, hands rubbing over his back, more heat radiating all over his body now.

He didn't care how it looked. Croften hugged Ainsley tight. He had made all these big promises that he would protect Ainsley and never let anyone get away with hurting or insulting him. Yet there Henri went, calling him an idiot, and Croften had just stood there and let it happen.

"When it comes to Henri I just...can't..." Croften sighed and closed his eyes, just trying to make it up to Ainsley in any way he could.

"It's perfectly okay, dear," Ainsley said. "He really is quite the bully."

"Ainsley, we're leaving." It was Graham, grabbing Ainsley's arm, pulling him away.

"No, no, wait!" Croften said, standing up as panic boiled inside him. "I wasn't doing anything!"

"It's not that." Graham started to drag Ainsley away, with the strength of force Croften always expected of him.

"Graham, what's going on?" Ainsley asked. He loosely tried to wiggle his arm away, but otherwise didn't do much to stop him.

"You can't just take him!" Croften grabbed Ainsley's other arm, pulling back, unable to match Graham's strength. Please, please, please don't take him away.

"I told you it's not-"

"Graham?" The tug-of-war over Ainsley halted as a woman approached them. "I thought that was you I saw."

Graham released Ainsley's arm, and Croften took the opportunity to pull him closer, still afraid that at any second he was going to leave. He would not let that happen.

"Hello, Anabel," Graham said. "I didn't know you knew the Greens."

Anabel smiled, brushing a strand of hair behind her ear. "Ned went to college with Howard," she said.

"That makes sense," Graham said. He was acting strange. He wasn't looking at the woman, and he seemed to have no reaction to how close Croften was holding Ainsley. "How is...Ned?"

"He's good." A moment of silence. "How are you?"

"Fine."

Croften leaned down to whisper in Ainsley's ear. "This is awkward." Ainsley nodded and patted his arm.

"Well, it's good to know where you moved," Anabel continued. "Everyone's been wondering."

"I'm sure they have," Graham said. He finally looked at her, his jaw hard set but his eyes saddened. "I would appreciate it if you didn't tell them."

Anabel's mouth opened a bit, but she closed it and nodded.

"If we just start walking away slowly," Croften whispered, "maybe they won't notice."

There was a loud crash and everyone in the garden turned towards it. A young man with glasses had knocked into a table, sending it and the dishes on top falling over.

"Oh dear," Anabel said, "I'd better go help him." She reached out and placed a hand on Graham's arm. "It was nice to see you again, Graham. Take care of yourself, okay?"

Graham nodded and she left. Ainsley shook Croften off and walked up to him, placing a hand on his shoulder.

"Are you okay?" He asked.

Graham cleared his throat and looked at him. "I'm fine. Let's go."

"Wait, wait, wait!" Croften ran around to block them, arms splayed out before him. "It was just a hug! It wasn't anything!"

Graham rolled his eyes. It was Ainsley now who was holding onto him possessively. "I'm not in the mood for this, Croften. I just want to go home."

"It's okay," Ainsley said, walking Graham around Croften. "I'll see you tomorrow."

Croften wanted to protest more, after all, the party had only just started, and now he'd be stuck there the rest of the time without Ainsley. But it at least seemed like Graham wasn't mad at him, or not while he was dealing with whatever the heck that whole thing was about. Croften hummed, tapping his foot as he watched them leave. What was that thing about?

He looked over at the woman in question. She was drying off the young man's shirt with a napkin, shaking her head at him. Hmm. It could be possible that this Anabel person had been the one that Graham used to date. The one that cheated on him. Croften scoffed. With that guy? Not a chance.

Ainsley grabbed Graham's arm before he could scatter away upstairs. "Wait a moment," he said. "You haven't spoken a word since we left."

Graham shrugged. "I haven't had anything to say."

"I don't believe that's true." Ainsley grabbed Graham's other arm, rubbing them gently. "You have to feel...something. After seeing her again. So unexpectedly."

Graham's head shook. "I'm fine. Just tired is all."

"She was awfully pretty," Ainsley said. He stepped closer, moving his hands to Graham's chest, smoothing down the wrinkles.

"I suppose."

Ainsley slid his hands back, wrapping his arms around Graham in a hug. "Do you think you would have been happy?"

Graham didn't hug him back. "What?"

"With her. If things hadn't happened. Do you think the two of you would have been happy together?"

Graham sighed. "She was a good person. I'm sure she would have made a good wife."

Ainsley snuggled closer. "Too bad you got stuck with me, huh?"

Graham's arms finally came around him, hugging him back. "You know I have no regrets marrying you."

"Really? Not even one? Not even a tiny, teeny, little-"

"*Ainsley.*"

"Okay, okay. I believe you." Ainsley let them enjoy the moment for a while before bringing it up. "About Croften..."

Graham groaned. "I do not want to talk about him."

"It's just that the hug really was innocent."

Graham's arms dropped. "I suppose you're going to tell me he's just like that."

Ainsley didn't let him pull away from his hold. "I'm telling you that he had a run in with his bully, and he needed a friend. And we are friends, so it was a completely neutral interaction."

"Croften has a bully?" Ainsley nodded. Graham scoffed, Ainsley's head jolting at the motion. "Who could possibly bully him?"

"Henri. That horrible little creature of a man."

"Ah, yes. Fellow painter squabble I see. Isn't he doing some work for the mayor?"

Ainsley nodded. "He's also bullying Croften. And that's not the worst part."

"If I let you tell me the worst part, will you let go?"

Ainsley shook his head, tightening his embrace even more. "The worst part is he's obsessed with this idea that Henri's cheating on his husband because he can't stand the idea that this horrible man is better at him than something."

"Well, he must be. Croften is not the best at relationships."

"I know." Ainsley relented and dropped the hug, stepping back. "But I think he wants to be."

"With you."

"With anyone. In fact, that's why I threw that party earlier. To try and set him up."

Graham scoffed and shook his head. "Unless anyone you set him up with is you, I don't think he'll be interested." He walked upstairs.

Ainsley followed. "He has a mild infatuation with me," he said, chasing after Graham into his office.

"Mild infatuation?" Graham smiled at him, arms crossing. "Ainsley, he's completely obsessed with you."

"He is not!" Ainsley stomped his foot to help accentuate his point, but all it did was help deny it.

Graham shrugged. "Okay. He's not. He just comes over every single day because he's, what was it, mildly infatuated?"

Ainsley pouted. "Well-I-So what if he is? We just have to find him someone he's more obsessed with."

"Good luck." Graham sat down at his desk.

"I said we, Graham. If Croften has someone else to focus all of his, er, energy into, then he won't be around me as much. I'm sure you'll like that."

"Would you? I thought you liked having him around."

"I do." Ainsley wandered over, leaning against Graham's desk. "But I could use some time away. I haven't written a single word since we became friends."

Graham chuckled. "I suppose we could keep trying. Although I'm not sure who there is out there, he could like more than you. For all our differences we do share a similar taste. That being the best. That being you."

Ainsley blushed. "Stop it. There are plenty of people out there better than me."

"I disagree."

"Well, you don't have to agree." Ainsley stepped up to his chair. "You just have to help me find one for Croften."

"Can't find something that doesn't exist."

Ainsley leaned down and kissed the top of Graham's head. Graham could lie all he wanted, but there were people out there better than him. And Croften deserved to have someone of his own. Ainsley could tell he wanted that, more than just a fling, an actual relationship. He just had to find him someone.

12

Hate to Love (myself)

Croften's leg shook. Things had been back to normal for a while. Croften went over and hung out with Ainsley during the day, and he terrorized and was terrorized by Mara and Ursula during the evening. Thankfully Mara had kept good on her promise to not tell Ursula about the incident. It was good. It didn't matter that the garden paintings for Ainsley were all the work he really had left, he just didn't need to let anyone know that. Especially Henri.

Then Ainsley invited him over on Graham's day off. At first, he wasn't going to go. But, as Ursula had so kindly pointed out, Croften was whipped. Not exactly the phrase Croften would have used to describe his relationship with Ainsley, but not inaccurate. So Croften stood outside the door to Ainsley's house and shook.

He had been standing there for close to half an hour.

He was starting to get a bit sore.

Croften sighed and stretched. Okay. He could do this.

He could not do this.

Croften turned around, fully prepared to go back to Mara and Ursula's and just pretend to be sick or something. He stopped mid-turn. Graham was staring at him. He was sitting in the drawing room, looking out the window, an amused smile on his face. Fuck. How long had he been watching him?

Croften felt himself blush involuntarily. Well, at least that would help with the whole pretending to be sick bit. He prepared to zip away when Graham turned his head and said something into the room. Presently Ainsley's head popped into view. He smiled at Croften and waved before heading towards the door.

Croften groaned and worked up a good sick-voice to get him out of this. The door opened and Ainsley's smile was so big and genuine that Croften just couldn't bring himself to pretend to be sick anymore.

"I was beginning to worry you wouldn't show up," Ainsley said. Croften stepped in, and Ainsley gasped. "Oh. You've brought your supplies!" He pointed at the case under Croften's arm.

"Sketches, actually," Croften said, following him into the drawing room. "Some garden ones. Wanted to get your opinions on angles and stuff."

"Of course! We'd be delighted to see them!"

Graham didn't get up from the couch as they entered. Ainsley grabbed Croften's arm and pulled him over, sitting him down next to Graham, himself sitting down on the other side. Croften held the case on his lap and tried to make his body as small as possible. He could practically feel a knife or something reaching out from Graham's side, ending him.

But all he did feel was Ainsley's hand on his arm, rubbing softly. He gestured to the case.

Oh yeah. That was why he had him sitting between them. That made sense.

Croften cleared his throat, aware that any movement on his point would press him against Ainsley or Graham. He wasn't sure which would be the lesser of two evils.

"Sorry," he mumbled, struggling to get the case open. It was doubly hard as he tried not to push his elbows out towards either of them. "Clasp is broken."

"Perhaps you should get a new one," Graham suggested. He had leaned to the side a bit, graciously giving Croften a bit more room to work with.

The clasp popped open, startling Croften. When he jumped, the papers on the top of his stack slid off onto Ainsley's lap. Croften busied himself with gathering the papers on his own lap first, shuffling the drawings to a proper order.

"You can't go around as a respectable professional with a broken case," Graham said.

"I don't need a new one," Croften told him. He flipped through the sketches, pulling out the ones he was most fond of to show off. "This one works just fine."

"If you can't afford one, I'm sure we can-"

"I'm not poor!"

Ainsley gasped softly, then fell silent. Croften glanced over. Oh no. Oh no, no, shit, fuck, no.

Ainsley had gathered the papers in his hand, eyes scanning over them slowly. Croften snatched them out of his hands, shoving the papers back into the case. "Uh, those are just, uh…"

Ainsley's eyes were wide. He swallowed. "I suppose you're going to tell me you're Raleigh Mayans."

"Yes!" *No.* What the fuck? Why had he said that? He chuckled nervously.

Ainsley was giving him a look that said he didn't believe him. But there was no other way to explain it. He couldn't just go and admit that he wrote stories about Dan and the prince getting together as a way to deal with his own unresolved love for Ainsley. He chuckled nervously. "You got me."

Ainsley's mouth opened, but only a soft squeak came out.

Graham laughed. And it wasn't the kind of laugh that Croften had expected from him. It was like an actual laugh. Deep, meaningful, full of joy. Croften blinked at him. Then his shock wore away and his anger came out. Sure, the Dangerous Dan books weren't exactly acclaimed literature, but they were good. And fun. And how dare Graham laugh at them.

"Laugh all you want! But I'll have you know I make all kinds of money on those books!"

Ainsley's once pale face had started to blush. Graham's laughter calmed down a bit. "Not enough to buy a new case, apparently."

"I told you I don't need a new case." Croften closed it, fully ready to get up and leave if they were going to be that way about it. But the clasp didn't latch and when he stood up it opened, and all the papers fell to the floor.

His shoulders slumped, looking down at them. He should have just stayed home, damn it.

"Oh yes. That case works perfectly," Graham said, smirking at him.

Croften scowled and knelt to gather his things. Ainsley slid off the couch and helped, handing him pages. He stopped, standing up slowly as he studied one of them. Great. He probably had another one of the stories. Just what Croften needed.

"Who is this?"

Croften gathered the others and forced the case shut. He leaned over, glancing at the paper. It was a woman's reflection in a mirror. A self-portrait. She had a long face with sharp bones. Curly hair, red as anything, framed her face. "Ah. That's my mom," he said. "I think, anyway."

"You don't know?" Graham asked.

"Never really met her," Croften said. "I mean, obviously I met her. Like when I was born or whatever. But she died right after so like, ya know. Probably repressed that memory or whatever."

"Croften…"

"Ah, no, please. Look, it was ages ago. I'm over it. I don't need your pity."

Ainsley made a few noises, the starts of syllables, as if trying to come up with something to say. He settled for, "She looks an awful lot like you."

"Yeah." Croften was very aware of how quiet Graham had become. The last thing he needed was that guy feeling sorry for him.

Or was that exactly what he needed?

"Probably explains a lot of my early childhood, ya know." He sat down on the coffee table, fiddling with the clasp of his case. Ainsley sat down, still holding the picture. They both watched him with rapt attention.

Croften took a steadying breath. He hadn't really talked about it with anyone other than Mara. Even Ursula didn't know much about his early life. He was over it, though. So, it should be fine.

"My uh. My dad didn't exactly like me, you know? I think it's just the whole, 'hey you look like my dead wife' thing. He didn't look at me. Rarely spoke. Never even brought my mom up." Croften looked down at his case. He could feel a tear sting at his eye. He knew this was a bad idea. But now that he had started, he couldn't stop.

"We didn't even have any pictures of her in the house or anything. None of her stuff, either. I don't think he liked to be reminded about her. But when I was ten, I found this case. It was shoved in the back of a closet. Inside was all these art supplies and... that." He glanced up at the paper in Ainsley's hands. He shrugged. That one tear fell, but he wiped it away swiftly. "Anyway, yeah."

Ainsley's hand reached out and touched his knee. Croften stood up. Because he really didn't need their pity. He didn't want it. "Uh. I'll just leave the sketches here." He pried the case open again, turning around as he pulled them out. "You can just let me know which you like."

"Croften…" Ainsley stood up behind him.

Why were his eyes so tired? He blinked them hard, trying to get rid of the sting. "See ya later, yeah?"

"Don't you want-"

Croften didn't stick around to listen. He shouldn't have told them. He could maybe have told Ainsley. One day. In private. But in front of fucking Graham? What sort of demon had possessed him? He needed a nap.

Ainsley held the drawing of Croften's mother in his hand, felt the material of the paper between his fingers.

"You know," Graham said. "When I agreed to get to know Croften more I wasn't entirely expecting that."

Ainsley sat down. He couldn't take his eyes off the drawing. She really did look exactly like him. Even the eyes, a sort of golden brown. The drawing of her captured the light perfectly, that little bit of glow to them.

Graham reached forward and took the sketches from the coffee table. "He really is quite talented," he said, leafing through them.

Ainsley nodded. He couldn't focus on what Graham was saying. He was busy thinking about Croften. About how a lot of things made sense. About how Croften had grown up hated by his father for simply looking the way he looked. No wonder he was so...well...him.

"Ainsley."

Ainsley shook his head, forcing himself to look away from the picture. "I'm sorry. What were you saying?"

Graham gave him a small smile. "Would you like to go over and check on him?"

"No. No, I'm sure he's okay. He probably wants to be alone anyway." He did, of course, want to go comfort him. But Croften had looked so uncomfortable talking about it that Ainsley figured it was best to just pretend it had never happened.

"So. How long are you going to let him pretend he's you?"

"Oh! Oh, I had completely forgotten about that." He couldn't help but laugh a bit. "I can't believe he said that. Oh dear."

Graham's smile widened, turning mischievous. "We could always have some fun with it."

"I'm not sure that's a good idea, dear." He shuffled closer. "We really ought to be nice."

"Sure, sure. Nice." Graham wrapped an arm around Ainsley's shoulders. "Or…"

Ainsley nudged him softly with his elbow. "Well. Perhaps just a bit. It is rather funny."

"Anything interesting in the story?"

"No."

Yet another lie. This was a different lie. Graham would not want to know about what was in the few paragraphs he had read. Ainsley wished he could forget. They had been kissing. Dan and the prince. If only Croften knew who those characters were meant to portray. He probably wouldn't be so keen to have them be together.

But, oh well. He couldn't tell Croften how to think. And if writing those stories made him happy, then that was good.

13

The Art of Seduction

Croften made it his absolute goal to avoid Graham at all costs after that. He spent the weekdays with Ainsley, who kindly never brought up the story he had shared, and the weekends away. No need to spend time with Graham; he only cared about Ainsley. Plus, it was probably for the best, as he had found some new work to do. Mara had told him he couldn't just stay at their house to flirt with Ainsley unless he was going to pay rent.

The problem was that Ainsley didn't usually wake up until later. But Croften couldn't be bothered to wait around. Especially not inside somewhere. As soon as he was up and dressed, he was over to Ainsley's. He just hung around out front until he saw Ainsley in one of the downstairs windows.

Ainsley saw him, smiled, shook his head, and met him at the door.

"Mornin' Ainsley," Croften said, smiling. It was impossible to not smile around Ainsley.

"Come in," Ainsley said, opening the door for him. "Would you care to have breakfast with me out in the garden?"

"Love to!"

Benson brought them out some eggs and toast, with enough tea they could need. Croften chatted away; he could never seem to eat when he was with Ainsley. Every time he looked at him his inside just went all squishy and food wasn't very appetizing. So Croften rambled on about work or interesting anecdotes from his life while Ainsley ate.

Ainsley sipped at his tea and set it down, his plate empty. He looked at Croften's. "You didn't eat a bite."

"Eh. I'm not hungry."

"You're never hungry." Ainsley squinted at him. "You need to eat. If you don't, you'll never have enough energy to get through the day."

Croften smirked. "You give me all the energy I need."

Ainsley gave him a look.

"What? That wasn't flirting!"

Ainsley laughed and then his face sobered a bit, staring at Croften with a strange intensity in his eyes.

"What?"

"Could you...we're friends, right?"

"We better be."

"Could you teach me something?"

Croften leaned back in his chair, resting his arm over the back and smirking at Ainsley. "You want me to teach you how to paint, huh? Don't worry, I'll be more than happy to model for ya." Another look. "Okay, yeah, point for you that was flirting."

"I was rather hoping you could show me how you do...well, that."

"You want to know how to flirt?" Croften thought Ainsley did a mighty fine job of it. Maybe he really was just innocent and had no idea of the effect he had on others.

"Well, more than that." Ainsley picked up his cup, even though it was empty. He studied it, as if wondering where all the tea had gone. "You've been known to... seduce people."

"You want me to teach you the art of seduction?"

"Yes."

Croften smirked again, feeling it was better to be cool and collected. "Who you tryin' to seduce huh? Perhaps a devilishly handsome friend who lives down the street and has furiously fashionable red hair?"

Ainsley laughed at him. "You just keep wishing on that, dear."

"Oh, I will. But, seriously, who do you need to seduce? I thought you were terribly devoted to the st-to Graham?"

"I am. He's the one I need to seduce."

Okay. Croften had to have heard that wrong. He scratched his ear, checking for any wax. "I'm sorry. Come again?"

"I need your help seducing Graham." Which put a whole other image in his head that, surprisingly, didn't immediately disgust him.

"Uh...why? Can't you just be like, hey we're married let's go? Do you even...do you even want to have sex with him?"

"Of course I do!" Well, that ruined one of his plans of attack. Yeah, Croften may have agreed to play along for now but not for one second was he actually going to give up on trying to get Ainsley to be with him. "I just...have some trouble."

"He's bad at it? You're bad at it? Is it just bad overall? Cause you know I can show you some pointers on that-"

"I wouldn't know." Ainsley looked down at his empty cup. His face was almost as red as Croften's hair. "I... that is to say...we haven't exactly…" Croften gasped. "Yes. I know."

The light at the end of the tunnel. The silver lining! He scrambled out of his chair, pointing at Ainsley. "You're not really married!"

"Keep your voice down," Ainsley hissed. He had that fury in his eyes that Croften didn't like. "We are married. It's just that...well, it's just...We just haven't consummated it."

"Hey. I'm just going by the laws of the land. No sex, not really married." Croften got on his knee, right by Ainsley's chair, grabbing his hand. "Will you marry me?"

Ainsley pressed two fingers to Croften's temple and gently shoved him away. "Really, dear. You must get a hold of yourself."

Croften stood up and dusted himself off, giving Ainsley a disappointed look. "I can't believe you're really going to look me in the eyes and ask me to help you get in your husband's pants."

"I know." Ainsley sighed. "It's terribly mean of me. I'm sorry. I just know that you're an expert. After all, you did a very good number on me. So, I thought I'd ask."

Croften groaned. He did not want to help Ainsley have sex with Graham. That really defeated the entire purpose. Of his existence. But Ainsley looked so... saddened. Saddened that Croften wasn't helping him. Maybe even more saddened that he wasn't getting any. Which Croften thought was a very good reason to be sad. He growled and scratched the back of his neck. "Fine."

Ainsley hopped up in his seat, face brighter than the sun. "Oh really? Croften, thank you! Thank you! You have no idea how much this means to me!"

"I'm good not knowing, thanks."

"So," Ainsley settled back down on his seat, looking at Croften with rapt attention. He looked like he ought to have a notebook with him. "How does it work?"

"There are multiple ways to seduce, but I'll teach you my best method. Fool proof. Only one person has been able to resist it." He gave Ainsley a wink.

"Oh? I must be something special, then."

"Must be." Croften took a moment to just stare at Ainsley. So cute. So soft. So everything he ever wanted in life. And here he was, about to teach him how to get someone else in bed. He was either an idiot, or in love.

Alright. He was both.

"It's a two-step system." He turned away, walking around to the bushes in the garden. He ran fingers over leaves, seeming very interested in them. "First, I'm not interested in you. I'm exploring the surroundings. This flower is the most appealing thing in this room. Sure, I may look at you every now and then," at this he glanced back at Ainsley, who was nodding his head, "but you're really just a side thought."

"I see. So, ignore him without ignoring him?"

"Exactly. And another important aspect of part one. You don't do the talking. I'm doing it now because I'm teaching but in reality, you want them to be talking. Ask them questions about things they're interested in, get them chattering. Respond when prompted but keep it short and sweet. And always turn the conversation back to them."

"I see. Ignore him. Keep him talking. Got it. What's step two?"

Croften smiled and turned suddenly. He fell on the arm of the chair, sitting one leg up on it as he leaned in towards Ainsley, who gulped and leaned away.

"Now you're all I'm interested in. Rest of the world? It doesn't exist. Just you and me and the ever-closing space between us." He leaned in, closing said distance. "I'm hanging off your every word. I'm checking your face for the subtle signs of attraction; wide eyes, heavy breath, fast heart. I touch you, gently." He placed a finger to the side of Ainsley's neck, watching him shiver. "Last chance. If you pull away it's done. If you don't, well...nine times out of ten, I'm in. I lean closer still, we're going to kiss."

Croften leaned in, almost forgetting himself for a moment. Then he blinked back to his senses. If Ainsley had gone crazy over a kiss on the hand, what would he do to one on the lips. Croften really did briefly consider just going for it; it would be worth it. But he wasn't that dumb.

Croften pulled back, not missing the way Ainsley's lips were just slightly pouted out, a shake in his jaw as Croften stood up. He shrugged. "And that's how it's done."

Ainsley cleared his throat. "I... you do that very well." His cheeks were pink, the single most adorable color on him. "Thank you."

Croften sat down on his chair. Smirking again because he liked the confidence it gave him. "You wanna give it a go? Get some practice in?"

"Ah, n-no thank you. I'm sure I'll be alright."

Croften shrugged. "Up to you. I'm here if you change your mind." He settled back down as Benson came out to take their plates and refill Ainsley's cup. "Let me ask you something, if you don't mind."

Ainsley hummed and sniffed his tea. "Go ahead." He took a sip.

"Why, exactly, haven't you had sex yet?"

Ainsley thought about it for a moment, looking around the garden as he sipped at his tea. "I suppose, well, I think he's just afraid."

"Graham?" Ainsley nodded. "Afraid of what? I mean, clearly, it's not like you're going to leave him." Yet, he hoped. "Is he really that messed up from getting cheated on?"

"It's not that. I think...I think he's afraid of me."

Croften licked his lips. Oh, the thoughts he thought. "Real maniac in bed huh? A good ol' fashioned animal? Like it rough?"

Ainsley's face blushed deeper. "N-no! I-shut up!" Croften laughed. He really was adorable. "I just think he's afraid of my past, is all."

Croften squinted at him. "Were you actually a prostitute?"

"*No!*"

"I'm just asking! What else is there for him to be afraid of?"

Ainsley looked away. "It's probably best you don't know. I just...had an unfortunate incident in the past is all. Nothing to worry about. And I keep telling the same to Graham, but he won't believe me. I'm just hoping that this will help him to see that."

Croften nodded. "No, yeah, I get it. Well, if you ever did want me to know, I'm here. And I'm totally willing to kill someone for you."

Ainsley smiled. "I appreciate that, dear."

Ainsley took a deep breath. He could do this. He had to do this. After all, they were married. Going on five years. They really ought to be having sex by now. The door to Graham's home office was cracked open, so he slipped in.

Graham sat at his desk. He had his head in one hand, the other holding a file. He was rubbing gently at his temple, eyes squinted as he looked at his work. He glanced up briefly as Ainsley entered. "Dinner already?"

Ainsley shook his head. Oh yes, he wasn't supposed to be looking at him. He wandered over to the bookshelf, pursuing the titles. "Just thought I'd...look around."

"Okay..."

He could hear Graham flip the page of his file. He glanced at him, not long. "Interesting file?"

"Hm? Oh, no. Just some annoying legalities to work through."

Ainsley nodded. "Go on."

"That...that's it. Nothing to really worry yourself about."

Ainsley sighed. Croften really didn't tell him what to do if someone wasn't talking. He decided to find another topic of conversation. Oh wait, yes, glance at him. Just quickly like that. "Anything interesting in the newspaper today?"

"Not particularly."

Ainsley bit back a growl. Graham had never been one for much talk, but this was ridiculous. He couldn't work with him. He had to skip to stage two. After all, he didn't think stage one was all that important. The closeness was what had gotten him. That heat, that intense gaze, that touch.

Ainsley rounded the desk and stood next to Graham's chair. He stared at him, making sure to keep his eyes wide. Graham turned to look at him. He was squinting slightly, looking Ainsley up and down.

"Are you feeling alright?" Graham asked.

Ainsley leaned down, bringing his face level with Graham's. "I feel great. Better than, actually."

Just close in now. Graham was still squinting. His breath was normal. He didn't seem to be having any heart problems. Ainsley grabbed his arm. He didn't move away. There they were.

Ainsley closed the gap and kissed him. He could feel the muscles of Graham's face move as his eyebrows rose. Ainsley pulled back, satisfied with a job well done.

"Uh, thank you?" Graham said.

Ainsley sighed and deflated. "I'm sorry. I suppose I'm not very good at this."

"At what?"

Ainsley stood up and leaned back against the desk. "I was trying to...oh goodness, it sounds absolutely ridiculous."

Graham slid his chair closer, leaning forward to study him.

"I was trying to seduce you," Ainsley said, turning his head, unable to meet that intense gaze.

"Why?"

Ainsley was really tired of people asking him that question. Was it really ridiculous that he wanted to have sex with his husband? "Because, Graham. We're married. We should be having sex."

Graham leaned back in his seat. "Ainsley..."

"No! Listen. It's not fair! You have to deal with so much because you married me! And you don't let me do anything for you. The very least you should be doing is having sex with me! I don't see why you're so against this!"

Graham smiled, which was weird. It was soft, with a hint of pity, and Ainsley immediately felt guilty, but he wasn't sure why. "Ainsley, the reason you just gave as to why we should be having sex has nothing to do with being in love or you actually wanting to have sex with me."

Oh.

"If we ever did have sex, it's only going to be when you want to."

"But...I-I do...want...to…" Ainsley looked down. He thought he did, anyway.

"When you sound confident with that then maybe." Graham was still smiling. "But I appreciate the sentiment."

Ainsley rolled his eyes. "You really ought to try being mean one time. It might suit you."

Graham's smile widened, turning more sincere. "I'm sure as far as Croften's concerned, I'm the meanest guy he knows."

Ainsley stood up and kissed Graham's forehead. "He's coming around." Graham mumbled an argument. "Maybe you two ought to hang out a bit more."

"That will be the day."

14

Anniversary

The heat of summer slowly gave way to fall. It was almost time for Croften to go home. The only problem was that Croften had started to think of this town as home. He didn't even miss his old place, and he didn't have too many friends back there to miss either. He wondered if maybe he could just sneakily move in with Mara and Ursula. Surely they wouldn't notice.

One day Ainsley met him out on the street, already dressed and ready to go. "Good morning," he greeted. He linked his arm with Croften's and started walking them down towards the town.

"Uh, morning," Croften said. "Where we goin'?"

"I need your help with a bit of shopping," Ainsley explained.

"Oh? Need help trying on some new clothes?" Croften gave him a suggestive look.

Ainsley returned an unamused one. "No. I'm looking for something for Graham."

Croften groaned, rolling his eyes for added effect. "Really? Do I have to?"

"Yes. It's our anniversary tomorrow and I haven't gotten him anything yet. You're going to help."

Ainsley's arm tightened around Croften's, squashing any half-formed thoughts of escape he may have had. Croften grumbled and hunched his shoulders.

"Why do you even need my help? You know the guy more than I do."

"I know. But...you see, you're such a thoughtful person." Croften tried not to blush. "And so is he." That helped. Ainsley sighed. "But I'm afraid I'm terrible at gift giving. Graham always manages to find such perfect gifts. This year I'd really like to be able to get him something good, you know?"

"Yeah, yeah, I get it."

Maybe it wouldn't be that bad. After all, he got to spend the day with Ainsley, which was always a plus. A plan started to form in his mind. He smiled. Of course.

He could use this to his advantage. He'd help Ainsley pick out a gift alright.

"What's with that smile?" Ainsley asked, glancing at Croften as they entered the main streets. He seemed a lot more relaxed in the town. Less people there cared about his past, Croften figured.

"Oh, nothing. Just excited to help you pick out a gift is all." Croften's smile widened. Ainsley gave him a wary look but said nothing more.

They visited all the shops. Croften did a particularly good job at suggesting the worst gifts possible. Sequin suit? Graham would love that! A painting of a skeleton? Perfect! A book about dog training? That's exactly what he needs! They ended up spending way too long in the bookshop, Ainsley walking out with presents for himself.

Ainsley sighed. "It's no use. I'm never going to find anything good enough."

"It's not your fault," Croften said. He nudged him with his shoulder. "The guy barely has a personality. Hard to shop for people like that."

Ainsley frowned at him. "You haven't exactly been very helpful, you know. I know that you've been suggesting only the worst possible gifts."

"What do you mean? My gift ideas were great!"

Ainsley shook his head. "I thought you would at least try. Let's just go."

Croften growled and grabbed Ainsley's arm, pulling him. "Okay, fine. I'm sorry. I'll actually help." Ainsley crossed his arms and gave him a hard look. "If you want to find the perfect gift, you shouldn't think about what he wants."

"Fantastic gift advice. So glad I asked you to help."

"I wasn't finished. You need to find something that reminds you of him."

Ainsley's face softened. "Something that reminds me of him?"

Croften shrugged. Damn Ainsley and his stupid face. If he didn't look so thoroughly hurt, Croften wouldn't help. Whipped indeed. "What was your first date?"

"Huh?"

"Your first date. What did you do, where did you go?"

"W-why does that matter?"

God, pink really did look good on Ainsley's face. Croften smirked. "Terrible first date huh? It's understandable. He doesn't exactly scream romance."

"He was actually quite romantic."

"'Course he was."

"It was simple. We walked around in the gardens. He, uh, well, he gave me a flower."

Croften cursed his own bad luck. Of course, the first romantic thing he does for Ainsley is the same damn thing that Graham did. He'd have to come up with something big to make up for that.

"But I…" Ainsley sighed. "I threw it away." He looked away, picking at his fingers. "I feel awful about it."

Croften scoffed. Who would have figured that Ainsley, Mr. Lovey-Dovey Dedication would have thrown away a gift that Graham gave him? He hadn't thrown out Croften's flower, he noted with a smile.

"All right, come on. I have an idea."

"Where are we going?" Ainsley let Croften lead him further into town, out of the main shopping streets and towards the more run-down areas. He started to shake a bit, looking around them as if expecting someone to jump out and try to rob them.

Croften stifled a laugh at him and pulled Ainsley into a little shop in a fairly run-down building. He had found this place a few months back, when he was doing a little stalking about of the town.

The shop was dark, with lights focused on the wares. Glass sculptures of all colors lined the shelves on the walls. The floor dazzled with their shadows, creating a fun effect of light and color to walk on. Ainsley gasped, the floor creaking under his slow steps as he looked around.

The shop owner, Dalton, looked up from the book on the counter. "Oh. Croften. Come to break something else, are you?"

Croften chuckled. "Not this time." Maybe break his own heart helping Ainsley with this gift, but that was it. "My friend here's looking for a gift."

"I hope you have better reflexes than him," Dalton said, giving Croften a pointed stare.

"These are simply marvelous," Ainsley said, fingers ghosting over the shelves of animal sculptures. "You're really quite talented."

"I know." Dalton went back to looking at their book.

"C'mon." Croften took Ainsley's elbow and led him to the back wall of the shop. It was lined with flowers, each a little note card attached to them. "Which flower did he give you?"

"Oh!" Ainsley's eyes scanned over the display. "I do believe it was this one." He reached out and gingerly picked up the sculpture in question. He looked at the note. "Astilbe. What's this now?" He turned the note over. "Meaning patience and dedication to a loved one?" He looked to Croften for more information.

"Flowers mean things," he told him. "Giving certain flowers to people means certain things. But I'm sure Graham doesn't know anything about that. So just get him that and it can be like, symbolic or whatever."

Ainsley put the flower back and scanned over the flowers again. Croften gulped as Ainsley reached for the blue bell flower. He blushed as Ainsley read over the note. Desire, love, and the metaphysical striving for the infinite and unreachable.

Ainsley re-shelved that as well (thankfully not looking at Croften) and went around reading every note on the flowers. Croften sighed and wandered about the shop, waiting and looking. Dalton kept a close eye on him, and if Croften wasn't sure he would break something else, he'd pretend to.

"This one please," Ainsley said, smiling as he placed a red dahlia on the counter.

Croften didn't need to read the note. He was well versed in flower language. Commitment, strength, and support. Croften rolled his eyes, hands in his pockets as he waited.

They walked back to the house, Ainsley beaming. "Thank you very much for your suggestion, Croften. I think he's really going to like this."

"He better."

Ainsley stopped. Croften made it a few more steps before he even realized, turning around to face him. "You alright?"

Ainsley nodded. He looked down, shuffling his feet and biting his lips.

"I can guess what you're going to say," Croften said. "I didn't mean anything by the flower, okay?"

"But you knew what it meant." Ainsley looked back, gaze challenging Croften's.

Of course, Croften knew what it meant. He just never figured Ainsley would know what it meant. He scratched his head. "I didn't mean anything. Promise."

"You know, you do an awful lot of things you don't mean."

Croften shrugged. "Eh. I'm an artist. We're like that."

"And a writer," Ainsley reminded him, a smile twitching to his face.

"Huh? Oh yeah! That." Croften had just hoped that Ainsley had forgotten about that. After all, he hadn't mentioned it since.

Ainsley shook his head, smiling fondly at him. He walked up and took his arm again. "I suppose I just have to get used to having such a flaky friend, hm?"

"It makes things easier."

Ainsley was getting some writing done. He was running rather behind, and if he didn't hurry up, he'd be late with the newest Dangerous Dan book. His writing was interrupted by a colorful wrapped something being slid before him. He hadn't even realized that Graham had snuck up behind him.

"Happy anniversary," Graham said, placing a quick kiss to the top of Ainsley's head.

Ainsley leaned his head back, smiling up at Graham. "Happy anniversary." He reached into his desk drawer and pulled out his own gift. Also wrapped, but not nearly as well. He handed it up to Graham, who took it with a raised eyebrow.

Ainsley stood up and led the way over to the couch, sitting with his gift on his lap. Graham sat next to him. He gestured at the gift. "You first."

Ainsley studied the wrapping. He could tell it was a book. Which was strange because Graham rarely bought him books unless it was a distraction. He carefully removed the wrapping, excitement bubbling in his chest. It was a copy of *Wuthering Heights*. Ainsley tried not to look disappointed. On the plus side, his gift would be something spectacular compared to a copy of a book he already owned. Granted, a book he enjoyed.

Graham smiled and chuckled softly. "Open it."

Ainsley flipped the cover open, mouth falling open in tangent. It was signed. Not just that. It was signed *to Ainsley*.

"How, where, what!" Ainsley glanced between Graham and the book. Graham just smiled. "Don't just smile! How did you get this?"

Graham shrugged. "I have my ways."

Ainsley huffed, nowhere near satisfied with that answer. What ways did he have that got him in contact with Emily Bronte? And why hadn't he told him earlier?

But all thoughts of that fled his mind as Graham turned his attention to the box in his hand.

"No!" Ainsley reached out and stole it from him. "That's not your present!"

"You handed it to me."

"It was a mistake." Ainsley fiddled with the box, not looking at Graham. "I, uh…" he wasn't sure what he could do. He thought through everything in the house, wondering if there was something half as good to give him.

"Ainsley." Graham leaned over and took the box back. "You know I'll love whatever you got."

Ainsley blushed and settled back against the couch. "I know. It's just...well. You'll see."

Graham peeled back the wrapping and opened the box. He gingerly pulled out the flower sculpture, holding it up to the light. "Wow. Did you make this?"

"Goodness no! Although I'm flattered you think I have that kind of talent. I bought it."

Graham turned it around in his hand. The red of the glass reflected onto his skin. "What flower is it?"

"A dahlia. I just. I saw it and thought of you. Is all." Ainsley really, really hoped that Graham didn't know anything about the meanings of flowers. He couldn't stand it if he did.

"It's beautiful." Graham carefully placed it back in the box. Then he leaned back over, a soft kiss pressed to Ainsley's cheek. "Thank you."

"Thank *you*," Ainsley said. He hugged his book close to his chest. "Can you believe it? Six years?"

Graham's face was smooth and soft. "I can. No one else I could imagine spending so much time with."

Ainsley could feel the emotions inside of him lifting him up, making him feel light and airy. He kissed Graham properly. It hadn't been the easiest six years. But they hadn't been terrible. This last year, specifically, away from old families and enemies, had been good. Being away from all that old influence was peaceful. Sure, things weren't perfect, but they were better. They had both started to heal. And with that healing came an understanding that their life could be good. And, Ainsley figured, the next six years would only improve.

15

The Punch

Croften was not in a good mood. He had only agreed to go to this Gala thing because he heard Ainsley was going to be there. He did not want to be seen showing support for Henri and his stupid mural. But he figured that if Ainsley was there, he'd be fine. But Ainsley was not there.

"I can't help but notice a lack of charm on your arm," he said, approaching the solo Graham as he entered the room.

"He's staying home tonight," Graham informed him. He looked different. Relaxed. Meanwhile Croften was a nervous wreck.

"Great. Now I'm stuck here alone." He frowned.

"You're more than welcome to leave," Graham told him. "No one is stopping you."

Croften was going to argue but then he realized that Graham was right. There was no one stopping him from leaving. Sure, Mara and Ursula might give him a talking to about just slipping away from a party, but other than that he was free.

"You're right. Maybe I'll just stop by your place and keep Ainsley company." He smiled at the prospect. A night alone with Ainsley. His mood was improving already.

"You will not," Graham said, that familiar growl in his voice. "Ainsley is working, and you will not interrupt him."

"I didn't know Ainsley worked." He always just figured that Graham was rich enough. After all, Ainsley just spent his days lazing around with Croften.

"He does and you've been quite the distraction already. So, if you do leave, you are not going there."

Croften frowned again. If he left the party now, he'd just go back to Mara and Ursula's and sit around alone before getting bored and going over to check on Ainsley anyway. And if Ainsley was trying to work then he'd probably just get mad at him. He didn't like it when Ainsley was mad at him.

"What's he do, anyway?" Croften asked.

"Uh." Graham looked to the side. "He edits. Cookbooks."

"He edits...cookbooks?"

"Yes."

"Sure. So, he's just, at home, editing cookbooks?"

Graham nodded. "That's what I said."

Croften took a deep breath. "Wow, you are a terrible liar."

Graham frowned, and Croften laughed. It was kind of nice, actually. A flaw. Something Croften could utilize to get ahead in the game. The game that he technically wasn't playing but really, did Ainsley actually expect him to stop trying to woo him?

"Well, fancy seeing you here." Croften scowled and turned around, watching Léon approach him. "Didn't think you'd come around."

Graham stiffened beside him, face tight. He looked a bit like he looked whenever he was taking Ainsley around to these things. Croften didn't want to think about what that meant.

"Don't get any ideas," Croften said. "I'm here against my will."

"I'm sure." Léon's gaze flicked over to Graham briefly. "No boyfriend tagging along today?"

Croften balled his hands into fists, digging nails into the palm of his hand to stop from punching him, even though he was pretty sure no one would blame him. He didn't need any of that coming up, especially not when he was alone with Graham, no Ainsley there to interfere if he got angry.

He couldn't think of a proper response, so he turned around and walked away. After all, if you can't say anything mean, don't say anything at all. He didn't get very far before Henri was blocking his view. He groaned. Couldn't a guy get a break?

"I heard you were lurking about," Henri said, a gross smile on his face.

"Just leaving, actually," Croften said. "Wouldn't want to have to see your mural and get sick."

Henri laughed. Croften hated it when he did that. Not just because it was a bad laugh, but because it was a direct insult to whatever Croften had said.

Graham stepped up to them, standing behind Croften. Great. Just what he needed, an audience.

"I see you're still hanging around," Henri continued, as if Croften hadn't said anything at all. "Even though you have no work right now." His lips pursed. "Seems you should be heading back to that hovel you call a home."

"I have work," Croften said. He didn't need to know that Croften only had one job that he was purposefully putting off so he could stick around Ainsley.

"Oh yes," Henri said. "The garden paintings. Tell me, does it always take you half a year to do one set of paintings?" He scoffed. "I suppose that's why they chose me to do the mural. So it wouldn't take too long."

Croften scowled at him. "Well, they certainly didn't pick you for your talent."

Another laugh. Nothing Croften said ever seemed to actually upset him, and it ticked Croften off to no end. "It's charming how convinced you are."

Croften tapped his foot, trying to come up with something snarky to say back. Then something strange happened, and Croften had to take a moment to process exactly what that something was.

First: Henri said, "It's no wonder you can't find a relationship. How could anyone love someone worth so little?"

Second: Someone punched Henri. For a moment, Croften thought he had. After all, he wanted to. He had wanted to since the day he first met Henri and that weasel wormed his way to the job Croften was after. But it hadn't been him.

Third: While Henri stumbled back, holding his cheek, Graham stiffened, holding one hand tightly in the other and biting his lip.

The room around them grew quiet. Léon was, thankfully, nowhere to be seen. Those who were seen watched them. There was only a moment to react. After all, Graham had just punched the guy this whole Gala was for. They certainly couldn't stay there.

Croften grabbed Graham's arm and pulled him away, finding that he moved with him quite easily. Everyone was still too shocked to stop them as they fled the scene. Croften kept up the pace as they walked away from the building, looking over his shoulder to make sure no one was following him.

"Here," he said, slowing to a walk and grabbing Graham's wrist. "Let me see it."

Graham looked sick. His hand shook as he let Croften uncover it. Fuck. His thumb was purple and swollen.

"Yeah," Croften said. "That's broken."

He started leading them towards the doctor's office. Graham was unusually pale. He was still biting his lip, and he refused to look up. Croften figured it probably hurt. He had broken his toe once as a kid. It never did set properly, and it had hurt like hell. He had to give props to Graham. Croften had cried for a solid hour.

They had to wait for the doctor to see them, of course. They were given a small bag of ice and told to sit down and just wait. Graham didn't fight it as Croften continued to hold the injured hand, pressing the ice to it firmly. He winced once, but that was all. He still didn't look at him.

Croften was perfectly content to sit there in silence. For all of two minutes. "So, uh, you never learned to punch, huh?" Graham did not respond. On the plus side, Croften wasn't as afraid of being murdered by a guy who didn't know how to punch.

"What are you gonna tell Ainsley?" He didn't exactly want Ainsley to know the truth. Mainly because he was afraid Ainsley would go talk to Henri and things would just get more out of hand. Graham remained silent.

"Hurt that bad huh?" He figured Graham was just concentrating on not yelling out or crying. A noble goal. Still nothing.

Well, as long as he wasn't going to be talking…

"Thanks," Croften said. Graham didn't speak, but he did finally look up at him. Croften looked down at the hand he was holding. He didn't notice how smooth Graham's hands were before. And warm, despite the ice on the knuckles. "No one's… uh…no one's ever done something like that for me before."

He could feel himself blushing and it was stupid. Graham was the enemy. He was the block in the road that led to Ainsley. He shouldn't be thanking him. He shouldn't be drawn to the warmth his body radiated.

"You are worth more than you think," Graham said, his voice soft and quiet. Croften pretended not to hear him.

The doctor finally arrived, taking Graham back to an exam room. Croften waited. He could have left. But he didn't. Graham emerged with a much more normal face and a splint of sorts on his thumb and around his wrist.

It was quite late into the night when they walked home, Graham holding his injured hand and Croften with his hands shoved in his pocket, kicking a rock along the road.

"So, what's the lie?"

"Hm?"

"That you're going to tell Ainsley."

"I wasn't going to lie."

Croften scoffed. "That'll go well."

"I don't believe in lying in a relationship."

Croften looked over at him. His face was hard set. He seemed to be telling the truth, damn him.

"Well, ya know," Croften said, shrugging. "Some things need a lie. I mean, what do you think Ainsley is going to do when you tell him you punched someone?"

Graham didn't answer. Croften patted him on the back.

"Don't worry. I'll think of one for ya."

Ainsley worried. He had lost track of time until about an hour ago. He had gotten a fair deal of writing done, thankfully, but was still struggling to figure out how to end this book. When he had taken a break for tea, he realized how late it was. And how Graham wasn't home yet.

Ainsley had given Benson the night off and now he was regretting it. Usually, when Ainsley worried, Benson was there to listen and offer advice and calming thoughts. But now Ainsley was left to sit and wonder and worry alone.

What could have happened? Why was Graham late? Had he gotten hurt? Had he and Croften gotten into a fight, assuming Croften was there in the first place? Had Alexander shown back up and convinced him to return home? Ainsley was starting to get sick, sitting on the couch and hugging himself. He didn't want to think about it.

And then the door opened.

Ainsley jumped up and raced into the hall. Croften was there, standing next to Graham. They looked okay. And then Ainsley saw Graham's hand. He grabbed it, earning a bit of a grunt from Graham at his lack of gentleness. "What happened!?"

"He got it caught in a door," Croften said, nodding.

"I punched someone," Graham said.

Croften gave him an exasperated look and mumbled, "All that effort thinking up a lie..."

"What?" Ainsley asked. He knew that Graham had an intimidating aura, but he never really believed that Graham would hurt anyone. "Who? Why?"

"It's not important," Graham said.

Croften made a noise and his look of surprise turned murderous. "It was Henri," he said, squinting at Graham. Graham returned his glare.

What the hell had happened?

"Croften," Graham warned.

But Croften just crossed his arms, smirking at him. A challenge. "Yeah. He said some not nice things, and idiot over here punched him."

Ainsley had so many questions and thoughts he couldn't focus on just one. Henri had been bullying Croften. And Graham had punched him. He shook his head, trying to wrap his mind around the situation and their arguing over it.

"It's late," Graham said, still glaring at Croften.

Croften shrugged. "Yeah, should probably get back before Mara and Ursula start to miss me."

Croften left, and Ainsley still didn't know what to say. How on Earth was he supposed to react to this? He chose to focus on the immediate problem.

"Does it hurt?" he asked, running gentle fingers over the cast.

"It's fine."

"You're probably pretty tired."

"I could sleep."

Ainsley nodded and led Graham up to their dressing room. He wanted to know more about what happened. What did Henri say that made Graham punch him? It had to have been rather extreme. How did the other guests react to Graham punching him? How did Croften react?

He knew he would get no answers out of Graham, so he settled for waiting until he could get to Croften. He stopped, mid thought, as he heard Graham struggling. He looked over his shoulder and watched Graham fiddling with a button on his shirt, trying to undo it without his thumb.

"Here, let me help."

Graham let him. Ainsley stood before him, undoing the buttons, heating up at the closeness of him. He felt strange. Different. Like something was pulling him towards Graham. Like all he wanted to do was run his hands over the skin he had revealed.

"I think I can handle that myself," Graham said, voice strained as Ainsley started undoing his trousers.

"Nonsense. You're hurt, let me help."

Graham turned his head away and Ainsley helped him down to his underwear.

"I suppose you're going to say you want to help me into my pajamas now, too."

Ainsley shook his head. He placed his hands on Graham's hips and looked up at him. There had always been the promise of Graham protecting him. Of Graham doing something drastic if anyone tried to hurt him in any way. But there was also always a hint of doubt. What could Graham do, after all, if someone walked up to him and said something nasty? Now Ainsley knew exactly what. And even though he didn't approve of violence, he felt a warm, fuzzy feeling all the same.

Graham raised an eyebrow at him. "Are you going to take advantage of me in my weakened state?"

Ainsley nodded. "I want to."

16

The Truth Comes Out

Ainsley woke up with a deep breath and a smile on his face. He hadn't slept that good in ages. He sighed contentedly and snuggled up closer to Graham's side. Wait. He was snuggled up to Graham's side.

Ainsley blinked. There was certainly too much sun in the room for Graham to still be in bed. He tilted his head up. Graham was looking out the window, quite pensive, one arm wrapped around Ainsley and the other resting on the covers.

Ainsley reached over, grabbing Graham's free hand. "You're still here," he said.

Graham startled briefly, looking down at Ainsley as if he had forgotten he was there. Like that was possible, Ainsley thought, remembering the last night fondly. "Good morning," Graham said, leaning his head down to kiss Ainsley's forehead.

"Good morning," Ainsley said back, his voice a whisper. He was afraid that if he spoke too loudly, he might ruin the moment. "You didn't go to work today."

"No," Graham said. He hugged Ainsley closer, resting his chin on the top of his head. "Just didn't feel like it."

Ainsley closed his eyes, listening to the beat of Graham's heart. He wanted the reason to be him. He wanted Graham to choose to stay home to be with Ainsley the morning after they finally consummated their marriage. But he had a sneaky suspicion of the true reason.

"You can't just never go out in public again," Ainsley said. "Trust me. You'd never adjust."

"I'm not sure what you're talking about."

Ainsley shook his head. He pushed himself up, breaking free of Graham's hold and leaning over him. Graham's face looked so soft in the late morning light. Ainsley couldn't help but bend down and kiss him. Graham smiled at him.

"You'll have to face it eventually," Ainsley said. "The more you ignore it the harder it'll be."

Graham sighed. He wrapped his arms around Ainsley and pulled him back down.

119

"I know," he said.

"It's not like they won't understand," Ainsley mumbled. "Henri's a jerk."

Graham scoffed. "No kidding."

Ainsley figured he'd give it a shot. "So, what exactly did happen? I mean, what did Henri say?"

"It doesn't matter," Graham said. "It wasn't true."

Ainsley nodded. He could think of a few untrue things that Henri could say. But he was still itching to know which one of those had pulled such a strong reaction from Graham. "Well, it was awfully nice of Croften to wait with you at the doctors."

"Yeah."

Ainsley's fingers ran over Graham's skin. He had so much he wanted to say, and he could tell that there was more Graham wanted to talk about. And even though they had taken quite a step in their relationship, neither of them were quite comfortable enough to voice those thoughts.

"I suppose I should get up and go, huh?" Graham asked. He hugged Ainsley closer, as if hoping he would keep him there.

"You don't have to," Ainsley offered. "It's a special day. I'm sure you can afford to stay in. Unless you have something important to work on."

"Nothing more important than you," Graham whispered.

Ainsley smiled, a happiness swelling in his chest, and he nuzzled his head against Graham's shoulder. "Well, I'm not sure about that." He chuckled softly. "But if you do stay then I hope you know I am going to force you to eat a full breakfast."

Graham kissed the top of his head. "A small price to pay to get to spend the day with you."

They eventually untangled, got dressed and made their way downstairs.

"You know," Ainsley said, still holding Graham's hand as they sat down. "I'm surprised Croften hasn't stopped by yet." He looked out the window, trying to spot him on the horizon.

"Disappointed?" Graham asked. Benson had made them a lovely brunch spread, and Graham seemed to be enjoying it.

"No." Ainsley looked back at him. "Just curious. He's usually come around by now. But, hm, I suppose if he figured you were staying home, he might have decided to stay home himself."

"Is he really that opposed to being around me?" Graham had a small smile on his face, amused.

"He just has a preconceived notion of you, is all. I know that if he got the time to

hang out with you, you'd get along well. He just needs to come around."

"Do you think he will?"

"I sincerely hope. I look forward to the day where my husband and best friend aren't always at ends with each other."

Graham studied him with a face that Ainsley did not like. It made him nervous. Not afraid or uncomfortable, just worried. "I've been thinking about something," he said.

Ainsley chuckled, trying to ease the atmosphere that had settled between them. "Not too hard, I hope."

Graham did smile at that, which helped put Ainsley at ease. "I've just been thinking about this particular concept." That didn't really offer Ainsley any more information, so he raised his eyebrows. "Sharing."

The eyebrows fell, pulling together. "Sharing?" He looked down at his plate. He didn't have anything on it that Graham's didn't have. He looked then at his clothes. Did Graham want to share clothes? He didn't think they would fit well. "I'm not sure I know what you mean."

Graham's smile widened more, and he turned his gaze away from Ainsley. "It's nothing. Just a thought."

Ainsley frowned and picked at his food. He wanted to know what Graham was thinking, but he didn't want to push it if Graham wasn't ready to talk about it. And Ainsley certainly didn't want to ruin the mood of the morning.

Croften was torn. He didn't want to see Ainsley. But if he wasn't at Ainsley's, then he would have to be working. But he had done portraits for nearly everyone in the town that wanted one. Which left him with one option: finish the garden paintings.

Well. It wasn't that he didn't want to see Ainsley. He did. He really, really did. But it was...awkward. And he told himself it was because of what had happened at the party. And, technically, it was. But it wasn't because he was worried of what Ainsley would say or do, as he told himself it was. It was because ever since what had happened at the party happened, Croften felt odd.

If he didn't know any better, he'd say he felt guilty.

So, he avoided both Ainsley and his feelings and spent the next few days working on the paintings. He was a little saddened that Ainsley hadn't come by to check on him, at first. But two days after the party he had gotten a letter inquiring about his health. It wasn't exactly the rushing over in a panic worried he was hurt situation Croften had hoped for, but it was good nonetheless.

Eventually the work was done, and Croften couldn't put it off any longer. He gathered all the paintings, tied them together, and struggled down the street, carrying them in his arms. The door was opened for him before he could even try to knock with his foot.

"Croften! I was so worried about you!"

Croften could just see Ainsley around the pile of paintings. "Yeah, sorry, was just getting some work done." He jiggled his pile. "Special delivery."

"Oh, my yes, please come in!" Ainsley held the door open and grabbed Croften's arm, leading him to the drawing room. "Here, let me help." He took some of the paintings from Croften's arm and placed them on the table, Croften following suit.

"Thanks." He stretched his arms, a slight ache from carrying all the paintings over. He had gone ahead and framed some of them already, doubling their weight.

"I can hardly contain my excitement!" Ainsley said, glancing down at the covered art. Had to have some suspense. "But we'll get to that later." He turned, grabbing Croften's hands. "How are you?'

Croften flushed, and that strange feeling deep in his gut grew. Usually, a smiling or touchy Ainsley made him feel warm and happy. Now he just felt cold and sick. He hated it.

"I'm uh, busy," he said. He swallowed hard, trying to ignore the bile rising in his throat. "Maybe a little ill," he added. Surely he had to be sick. He had gotten something. That was the only explanation.

"Oh, dear." Ainsley released one of his arms and placed the back of his hand against Croften's forehead. "Hm, you do feel a little warm. We could perhaps do this some other time?"

Croften shook his head. "No, I'm okay, really. You wanna see 'em or not?"

Croften broke free of Ainsley's hold and uncovered the paintings. He handed them to Ainsley, one by one. Ainsley sat on the couch and gasped over each one, smiling brighter than ever.

"Oh, how marvelous," he said. "Simply stunning! Look at the colors!"

They had gone through all but one, and that Croften kept hidden behind his back as he watched Ainsley marvel at the artwork before him.

"You've simply outdone yourself," Ainsley said, looking up at him. "My house is going to look so lovely with these up here."

"Yeah." Croften rubbed at the back of his head. He really wanted this feeling to go away. But every time he looked at Ainsley it just got worse. "Glad you like them."

Ainsley placed the paintings back on the table and stood up. He opened the drawer in his desk, pulling out some money, counting out the agreed upon price. (Of which was more than Croften had quoted him, as Ainsley would not allow him to undersell himself). "You are taking all of this," Ainsley said, holding the money out to him.

Croften smiled. "I will. But you have to accept this as a gift." He held out the last painting.

It was smaller, easily fitting in one hand. Ainsley took it, smiling softly at it. It was a blue bell flower. Croften had painted it once the living one he had given Ainsley had died. But he could never seem to find the right moment to give it to him. Better late than never.

Ainsley held the painting to his chest, holding out the money. "Happily."

Croften smirked and took it. Compensation for his loss of love, he figured. He coughed and shuffled his feet. "I, uh...I'm...well…" he sighed and closed his eyes. "I'm gonna be heading home soon." Technically he was leaving tomorrow morning. But that was a part of soon.

"Oh?" Croften didn't open his eyes. He couldn't bear to see the look on Ainsley's face. Whether it was happy or sad, he couldn't take it. "So soon?"

Croften shrugged. "It's been half a year." He opened his eyes but kept them on the ground. "Figured it was time."

Ainsley was around him, hugging him, holding him close, squishing his face against his chest. "Promise you'll come back?" He said. "And not just to any parties. You're always welcome here, and you better visit often."

Croften gulped. He begged himself not to say it. "Come with me." He loathed himself.

Ainsley's grip loosened but he didn't pull away. "I'm sorry?"

Croften bit his lip to keep himself from going off anymore. He shook his head and hugged Ainsley back. Which was a bad idea, because that gave his mouth ideas, and before he could stop it, he was saying, "Come with me. Let's run away. We could go off together."

Ainsley's arms released him, but Croften just hugged tighter. "What do you mean, go off together?"

"Like. You and me. We just, we go off together. Away. Far away. Just you and me and we just...you know." Croften just could not shut up no matter how much he tried. It was a real problem, and he had to work on that.

"Croften…" Ainsley placed warm hands on Croften's shoulders and gently pushed him back. Croften let go, knowing already that his chances were shot. If he had maybe kept his mouth shut, he would have been fine. They could have been friends, and he could have visited. But he wasn't like that. And they wouldn't be like that. "I can't."

"But-" Croften snapped his mouth shut. He would let himself say a lot of idiotic things but not that. Never that. He couldn't allow it. "We belong together," he said instead, a sort of what he wanted to say.

"I can't just leave with you," Ainsley said, not denying the claim.

And that non denial was the littlest bit of hope that Croften needed to throw all caution to the wind.

He grabbed Ainsley's free hand, bringing it up to his chest, over his heart. "Come with me, Ainsley. Leave this shitty life behind and live with me. I know you'll be happier. You know you'll be happier. This is right, Ainsley. This is right, so let's just go!"

"I can't." Ainsley's head shook, but his eyes were locked onto their touched hands. "I can't...I won't do that to Graham."

Croften growled in frustration. Worse than that was the overwhelming feeling in his stomach growing about ten times worse. "Look. I get it, okay? But you can't plan your life around the fact that someone cheated on him. It sucks, and yeah, he probably didn't deserve it, but you don't deserve this! You deserve to be happy, Ainsley! And I can make you happy!"

Ainsley's eyes closed and Croften's grip tightened on his hand as a tear slipped down one cheek. "You don't understand," he whispered.

"So then help me! Help me understand, Ainsley. What is it about this guy that's got you all like this?"

Ainsley took a deep breath. "It was me." His eyes didn't open, and he shook a bit.

"What was you?"

"I was the one who cheated on him."

17

Flashbacks of Love

It had been a lovely service and that was that. Graham wasn't surprised. His family was never one to openly have emotion. He couldn't remember a time where he saw any of his family cry or laugh. They smiled, but only at parties, when they were talking to guests. He had learned to follow suit. But Sarah had been different.

Graham's younger sister was always expressive. He remembered times as children when she would laugh, and their mother would tell her to be quiet. Times when she would cry, and her father would tell her to go to her room. Despite being emotionally inept himself, Graham knew that Sarah couldn't be allowed to have her spirit broken, so he would always comfort her, allow her to laugh and smile and be joyful when they were alone.

He should have been a better brother. He should have spoken up more when she got sick. He should have told his parents to call the doctor when she got that cold. Because it wasn't a cold. And his sister shaking and throwing up wasn't an overreaction. It was the flu, and Graham held her through the night until she died.

It wouldn't have been proper to not have a funeral. So, they had one. And it was nice and lovely and proper. And then they went home and never spoke of it again. It was as if Sarah had never existed in the first place.

Graham wished he could forget her as easily as his parents and brother. But it seemed like everything reminded him of her. Especially the gardens. Sarah loved flowers and plants of all types. She wanted to study them. She wanted to be a botanist. Graham didn't have the patience or brain for science. But he could understand meaning. So he learned about the language of flowers as a secret rebellious memory of his sister. It helped ease his pain, but nothing would be able to take away the emptiness he felt with her gone.

And then he got some 'good news'.

"I'm sorry?" he asked, certain he had misheard what his mother had just said, not but a month after the funeral.

"We found someone for you to marry," she repeated. She had that fake little

125

smile on her face that always threw Graham off.

"I thought we were going to wait until I was a full partner at the company," Graham said. He worked with his father, of course, but was still learning. They had wanted to make sure he had a good standing, both financially and socially, before 'shopping around' as it were.

"We just feel like everyone could use a good celebration," his mother explained. "A lovely party to brighten things up."

Graham blinked at her. It was one thing to ignore the mourning period and push away their feelings. It was another to expect him to get married and be happy about it.

But there was no room for arguing, and his personal feelings on the matter were of little consequence, if of any consequence at all. "Who?"

"You remember the Angelos?" his mother asked. He nodded. They were a family from the town over. He had met them a few times at certain parties. "Well, they're having a bit of a trouble finding someone for their son. But they're a family of good standing, and we believe your union would be a fine idea indeed."

Graham was not aware that the Angelos had a son. They had never talked about a son. They had never brought a son to any of the events. And if this supposed son was having trouble finding someone, what did that mean for him? Graham had never been particularly interested in marriage as a whole. It was always something he had to do, certainly not an image of the concept of love. He wasn't particularly looking forward to marrying this guy, but he figured that didn't matter. He'd do it. And he'd live with it.

"We'll be visiting with them next week. I want you to get a new suit for it. We must be looking our best, yes?"

Graham nodded. He always looked his best.

The Angelo's home was nice. A little smaller than theirs, but certainly nothing to sneeze at. Mr. and Mrs. Angelo welcomed them into their home with the same fake smiles that Graham's parents greeted them with. Graham had his own fake smile, of course.

They were led into the drawing room where Graham got his first look at Ainsley. He was sitting on one of the couches, nose in a book. He wasn't unattractive. Cute, even, with little blond curls of hair and a round nose that moved slightly as he mouthed the words of the book to himself. He had bright blue eyes, as well, that moved across the page despite the five presences entering the room.

And he continued to read, even as the others filled in and started to talk. Graham didn't pay attention to what the two sets of parents were talking about. He was focused on Ainsley's focus on his book. It was kind of charming, the way he didn't even notice how other people had arrived.

And then Mr. Angelo grabbed the book, pulling it out of his hands. Ainsley jumped a bit, eyes wide as he looked up at the five of them. He looked sheepish as he stood to his feet, hands by his side, fidgeting with the hem of his jacket.

"This is Graham," Mr. Angelo said, a strong hand on Ainsley's back, shoving him forward.

Ainsley stumbled to a stop before Graham. "It's nice to meet you," he said, holding out a hand. He wasn't even trying to smile. Graham found it fascinating.

"You as well," he said, taking Ainsley's hand. It was a little sweaty. And cold.

Ainsley pulled away looking quite uncomfortable. His mother cleared her throat and Ainsley rolled his eyes. Graham's smile turned authentic. "A stroll?" Ainsley asked, teeth clenched together.

"Sounds lovely," Graham said.

Ainsley led him out of the room, four pairs of eyes on them as they left. It was the illusion of a choice. Graham and Ainsley were to be wed. But they would be given the chance to court, as if there was an end to that courtship other than marriage. But Graham wasn't as opposed to it as he had been before meeting his future husband.

They walked through the house and out to the garden, Ainsley setting a brisk pace, not speaking. For a while Graham kept up with him, but he slowed down as they entered the gardens, choosing to enjoy the scenery. Ainsley sighed and fell back into pace with him. He was frowning and looking at the ground.

"What were you reading?" Graham asked.

"Huh?"

"The book you were reading. What was it?"

Ainsley shrugged; frown turned scowl. "Why do you care?"

Graham could understand being moody around their parents, but they were alone now. And Graham was trying to be nice. "Just trying to make conversation."

"Well stop it. Just because we're getting married doesn't mean we have to talk."

Graham chuckled. He wasn't wrong. Graham's parents didn't talk to each other unless it had something to do with the house or their social life. And Graham had once been content to have such a marriage himself. But something about meeting Ainsley had changed that.

"Just because we're getting married doesn't mean we can't talk."

Ainsley finally looked up at him, expression half confused and half curious.

"We may not have chosen each other, but we can choose to accept the truth of our lives and live them happily."

Ainsley stopped walking and Graham slowed before him.

"How can you be happy in a relationship you do not want?"

Graham thought about it for a moment. It was difficult to answer that, as he decidedly did want a relationship with Ainsley. But he had once not wanted to. And he had figured he could be happy with it. Luckily his sister had also been quite fond of poetry and gave him the perfect answer.

"Who ever loved that loved not at first sight," he said.

Ainsley's eyebrows furrowed together. He looked up, thinking. "Shakespeare?"

"Marlowe. 'It lies not in our power to love, or hate, For will in us is over-ruled by fate. When two are stript long ere the course begin, We wish that one should lose, the other win. And one especially do we affect, Of two gold Ingots like in each respect, The reason no man knows, let it suffice, What we behold is censured by our eyes. Where both deliberate, the love is slight, Who ever loved, that loved not at first sight?'"

Ainsley's frown deepened. His eyes squinted. Graham chuckled.

"I suppose Hero and Leander isn't on your reading list." He turned and kept walking. A brief moment passed and then Ainsley caught up to him.

"Look, I'm marrying you because I have to. Don't go expecting me to ever be happy about it."

"You don't even know me," Graham said. "How can you be so sure you won't be happy?"

Ainsley crossed his arms, his scowl almost adorable. "I'm being forced to marry someone I don't love. I'm being forced to marry in general! You could be the greatest guy in the whole world but you're still the one I'm being forced to be with."

Graham nodded. Seemed like the guy was just letting the anger and frustration of his life poison his outlook on things. Nothing Graham could do about that except hope that time would cure him of his negative thoughts. "You are free to feel how you feel."

Ainsley practically growled. "Stop being so nice!" He stomped his foot a bit. "You can't be happy about this, either."

"What if I am? What if I want to marry you?"

"You can't."

"Can't I?"

Ainsley huffed and looked away. They had nearly completed their circuit of the garden. Graham's eyes caught attention of a particular flower. He smiled and picked a sprig of the Astilbe. He held it out to Ainsley.

Ainsley stared at it. "What?"

"I want you to have this," Graham said.

"You want me to have a flower that I already own?"

"Well if you don't want it."

Ainsley rolled his eyes and grabbed the flower out of his hand. "You better not make a habit of giving me things," he warned.

Graham looked into his eyes and knew he couldn't make such promises. For all he wanted to do was give Ainsley the world.

The wedding date was set for a year from that day. They had an engagement party the next week, of course. The celebration that his parents had been looking for. But Ainsley and Graham spent little time together, as they were both pulled away for congratulations and questions from friends and family.

Graham did get the time to speak with some of those on Ainsley's side. Apparently, everyone was very relieved he was getting married. No one would give any specifics, but Ainsley had been 'like that' for years.

But that was what Graham liked about him, he supposed. Ainsley reminded him a lot of his sister. Not because they acted the same, but because they both refused to give in to the constructs of their lives. He supposed Ainsley was giving in by marrying him, but he certainly wasn't going quietly. He refused to smile when talking about it or show any signs of being happy about his upcoming nuptials. Not even when his mother pinched him about it. He was his own person, and he was letting everyone know that. And Graham, who was so much a miniature version of his father, both envied and respected that.

They didn't even see each other much during their engagement. Ainsley still did not accompany his parents to any of the events they attended, but about once every other month their parents planned some event or another for them to be together, be it tea or dinner. Never alone, as they had been in the garden.

The only alone time they got was the month before they were to be wed. Graham had gotten the day off work because there was a case much too complicated for him to understand. He figured it might be nice to go see Ainsley, get to know him a little bit before the big event. He hadn't been home, but one of the maids had given Graham the directions to the lake he usually visited.

Ainsley was sitting on the bank of the lake, skipping rocks against the surface of the water. He didn't react as Graham approached. He thought maybe Ainsley hadn't noticed he was there.

"What do you want?" Ainsley asked, squashing that theory.

Graham sat down next to him, and Ainsley shuffled away a bit. "Just thought we could chat."

"I have nothing to say to you."

"Well, it'll be a pretty quick chat then, huh?"

Ainsley said nothing. He stopped throwing rocks, drawing his knees to his chest and wrapping his arms around them. They watched the water ripple.

"Look, Ainsley. I'd like to marry you. I think you're fascinating, and I believe we could be happy together. But if you are really so opposed to the idea, then we simply don't get married."

Ainsley scoffed. "Yeah. You go tell our parents that and let me know how that goes."

"We can come up with something."

Ainsley shook his head. "Will in us is over-ruled by fate," he mumbled.

"There is no fate but what we make," Graham told him. Ainsley simply shrugged.

Graham stood up and dusted off his clothes, stretching a bit. He wondered if their marriage would be like this. If Ainsley would always spend his time ignoring and avoiding Graham. If they would have short, meaningless conversations in passing.

Graham decided he wouldn't let that happen. He would devote his time to making Ainsley happy, and one day, he hoped, Ainsley would be. They would be happy together, as Graham knew they could, and everything would turn out okay. He had a feeling about it.

"I look forward to marrying you, Ainsley," Graham said. "But let me know if you change your mind. I'd rather you be happy."

Ainsley hugged himself closer and looked away. Graham waited a moment, and then finally left when Ainsley made it clear he was done talking.

The last month passed slowly. Graham was a mix of excited and anxious. Excited to be married to the enigma that was Ainsley. Anxious that it was more of a challenge than he was ready for. But he wouldn't get the chance to find out.

It was the night before the wedding, and the house was filled with muffled yelling.

Graham could not find his parents, who he assumed was the source of the yelling, so he found his brother instead.

"What's going on?" he asked.

"Bad news," Alexander said. "Seems your betrothed has skipped town."

"What?"

"I didn't get the full story. But apparently Ainsley was a frequent visitor of a... Gentlemen's club." He wiggled his eyebrows a bit to imply exactly what Graham figured. "Ainsley and one of the 'gentlemen' seem to have run away together."

Graham should be relieved. He didn't have to get married. He didn't have to spend his time worrying about how Ainsley felt, or what he thought of him. It was a good thing, he figured. But he felt a great sadness, nonetheless.

He told himself it was just worry. After all, who was he going to marry now? His parents were probably already on the hunt for someone new for him to marry, especially since he had become a partner a few weeks ago. That was all. He was just nervous.

And heartbroken. But he wasn't going to say that.

His parents found someone for him pretty quick. They didn't want to wait another year. Graham had hoped for it, to give him more time to get over the pain he most certainly did not feel from losing Ainsley. A spring wedding turned into a summer one in an instant.

Graham only had two months to get to know his new betrothed. A young woman named Anabel. She seemed nice enough. He couldn't picture quite the happy life with her as he had with Ainsley. But he figured he could marry her and be happy or marry her and be sad. He didn't know why anyone would choose the latter, so he committed himself to being okay with it.

But life was not done tripping him up.

He was having breakfast with his family. Everything was normal. Then he got a letter. Which was strange because he rarely got letters. But, as usually happened when he got mail, his father opened it for him. Graham watched his father read it, before folding it up and placing it in his pocket.

Graham didn't have the energy for that kind of a fight, so he let it go. It was probably just something to do with the wedding. Alexander, as per usual, was not as satisfied with not knowing. He didn't make a scene at breakfast, of course, but later that day he wandered into Graham's room, holding the letter in his hand.

"You are never going to guess what it says," he said, smiling a bit.

"Is everyone going to read my mail in this house?" Graham reached for the letter, but Alexander pulled it back.

"I don't think you're ready for this," Alexander said. "It's much too scandalous."

Graham rolled his eyes and leaned over, grabbing the letter from him. He really wasn't ready for it.

The letter was from one of the maids at the Angelo's house. She was writing to inform Graham that Ainsley had come home the other day. She didn't know what happened, but he was hurt. And his parents had turned him away. She wasn't sure where he was, but she figured he'd like to know all the same.

Graham didn't know what he was feeling. But it was hot and uncomfortable. There were a lot of things troubling about that letter but more so than all of them was that Ainsley had been hurt. He wasn't sure how much. Not enough to not walk, of course. But there could still be a lot wrong. And if his parents had thrown him out, he could be on the street, hurt and alone.

Except Graham knew exactly where he was.

"Where are you going?" Alexander asked, following Graham as he raced out of the room.

"I'm going to go get him," Graham said.

"Are you crazy?" Alexander raced ahead, blocking the front door of the house. "Why would you do that?"

No reasoning Graham could think of seemed good enough. He just knew that this was what he had to do. That if he didn't, he would never be able to live with himself. "Because I am." He pushed Alexander out of the way and stormed down the path.

"Ainsley isn't worth anything," Alexander said, jogging after him. "Mother and Father will never approve of it!"

They didn't approve of getting Sarah a doctor either, Graham thought, all the past resentment and hate bubbling up to the surface. He had stood by and been submissive to his parents while someone he loved died once. He wouldn't do it again.

"I don't need their approval," he said.

"But they'll disown you."

"So let them."

The club wasn't as run down or dirty as Graham had expected. It was actually quite put together. He gave a fake name and paid for entry. It was clear what happened in this place, but it was still much more sophisticated than anticipated. Graham got a few inquiring looks as he searched around, but none of them were from Ainsley, so he didn't care.

"Not seen you before," someone said, an arm blocking him in a hallway. The man attached to the arm was attractive enough. But also not Ainsley.

"I'm just looking for someone."

"Aren't we all." The man smiled and pulled his arm block, crossing them over his chest. "Who ya after?"

"Ainsley Angelo."

The man squinted at him, looking him over. "Why?"

Graham shrugged. "I heard what happened. I'm worried about him."

The man hummed softly as he studied Graham. Then he gestured down the hall and led Graham to a room.

Ainsley was sitting on a couch, hugging his knees to his chest and crying. Another man was sitting next to him, leaning against his shoulder while a third one was pouring out some tea.

"Angel, ya got a guest."

Ainsley looked up, face covered in bruises. He shook slightly. "Graham? What are you doing here?"

Graham almost cried himself. Ainsley, who had been so strong and resistant and fiery, looked so weak and scared. It wasn't right. And it was a sight that Graham never wanted to see again.

"I came to take you home," he said.

More tears spilled out of Ainsley's eyes, the man next to him rubbing a hand over his arm. "I can't go home. They don't want me."

"Not there." Graham shook his head. "Home with me."

"With you?"

"We are engaged."

Ainsley's mouth opened slightly. "I-I-I-"

The man from the hallway stepped further into the room. "Why don't we give them some privacy, lads." He shooed the other two men out of the room.

"We aren't engaged," Ainsley finally managed to say. "I left you."

"I said I would marry you," Graham continued. "I intend to keep my word."

Ainsley's body shook and his blue eyes were stained red with tears. "I don't understand."

Graham had to get Ainsley to stop crying. He couldn't stand to see him so upset. Ainsley deserved to be happy. He knelt before him and reached out, wiping the tears off his cheek, even as more fell down.

"I still want to marry you, Ainsley. If you'll have me."

"If *I'll* have you?" Ainsley asked, his voice a sob, his breath heavy and hard. "I left you," he repeated. "I ran away with someone else the night before our wedding."

"I know." And it still hurt. "But you were only chasing happiness. Which I told you to do."

Ainsley buried his face in his knees. "Some happiness," he mumbled.

Graham got up and sat down on the couch. He'd get the name of whoever Ainsley had been with, and he'd deal with him later. Right now, he had to cheer Ainsley up. He placed a hand on Ainsley's back. "You can't stay here forever." Eventually he would need money. And there's only one way to make money is a place like this. "So, let me take care of you. Choose me, Ainsley."

Ainsley's head turned, looking over at Graham. "But I don't love you," he said.

Oh, but how Graham loved him. He smiled. "Who ever loved that loved not at first sight?" Him apparently.

Ainsley looked away, his body stilling a bit. He uncurled slightly, rubbing his eyes on the back of his sleeve. "What would your family say?"

"It doesn't matter."

Ainsley sniffed and sat up straight, rubbing his eyes dry. "I can't let you do that. I left you and I have to live with that."

"Don't be difficult, Ainsley. I don't need you to pretend to be selfless. Just let me make you happy."

Ainsley looked at him, fresh tears forming in his eyes. He blinked them back. "You really still want to marry me?"

"I really still want to marry you."

Ainsley hesitated for a moment, then he leaned to the side, head resting against Graham's body. It was a choice. And it was a start. And even though Graham knew that their marriage would be harder now than before, he also knew this was still what he wanted. He wanted to spend his life making Ainsley happy. And he swore that one day he would, even if it was the last thing he ever did.

Croften couldn't believe it. It had to be a lie. No guy would do something like that.

"So, you see?" Ainsley said, after he finished speaking about his past. "Graham chose to help me, even though I had been so terribly mean to him. And I can't hurt him. It doesn't matter how badly I do want to be with you. I won't treat his act of kindness with such disrespect."

Ainsley was waiting for a response. But Croften didn't know what kind of a response to give him. He saw it, of course. He sure as hell understood. Ainsley may have enough of a bastard energy in him to be worth liking, but if he did something like run away with Croften, he would step into true bastard territory.

But where did that leave Croften? He loved Ainsley. But it was clear that Graham did too. And even though Ainsley loved Croften, he would not, and really should not, leave Graham. What else was Croften to do?

He turned and left. He knew it was a shitty thing to do. He didn't want to make it seem like he would only hang around Ainsley if they were together. But Ainsley had just admitted to wanting to be with him. And that was something he would never be able to ignore. So he removed himself from the equation.

Ainsley called after him, chased him to the front door, but ultimately let him leave. And for that Croften was thankful. He was going to go home, and he would forget about Ainsley and this stupid town he had let himself fall in love with. He didn't even want to go back to Mara's and Ursula's. It was getting late, but he would just sleep at the train station. They might find a way to get him to stick around, and he was not having that.

No one was on the streets to bother him. He shoved his hands in his pockets, the cool air of approaching fall chilling him a bit. He only stopped when he remembered that he had left his art case in his room. He stood in the street at the entrance to the town and juggled the options in his head.

He could go back and get it. Could sneak in and out before they caught him. He would have to. The only other option was to ask Mara to mail it to him, which she wouldn't. She'd hold it hostage to get him to come back, and he couldn't do that.

Croften turned around and felt something sharp in his stomach, just below the ribs. Someone was standing before him, holding his shoulder and digging that sharp thing into him.

"Sleep with my wife, will ya?" a voice grumbled in his ear.

He knew that voice. He had heard many a husbands' and wives' voices as he snuck out of various homes. This particular one was attached to the memory of wiggling out of Madam Lacy's window.

The man left. Croften looked down. The hilt of a dagger stuck out of him. And his shirt, once gray, was now quite red. Breathing hurt. And his head was getting light. Croften took a step forward but fell to his knees. Then his side. Lying in the street.

He always knew it would end like this, alone and in the gutters. He just never figured it would be so soon.

18

Recovery

It was always an ordeal waking up. But it was particularly difficult for Croften that morning. His side hurt, just under his rib. He was in a bed that he did not recognize, in a room totally foreign to him. He blinked, and closed his eyes again, hoping to just ignore life and go back to the blissful ignorance that is being unconscious.

But that pain in his stomach was not going away and he was really thirsty. He groaned and forced his eyes open again. He was wearing pajama pants, but no shirt. He reached down and touched where it hurt. There was a bandage of sorts wrapped around him. When he touched the spot it hurt more, and he stifled a groan.

Oh yeah. He had gotten stabbed. Well that explained the pain. He was probably out for a while too, which explained his thirst. The only thing he was having trouble figuring out was the room he was in. And he was really curious. It was too fancy and big to be one of the houses in the town. And it wasn't the room he had had at Mara's and Ursula's.

He forced himself to his feet, the pain stabbing at him. But if he pressed against the source of it, it didn't hurt as bad. He leaned over, shuffling his way to the door. He pulled it open and squinted. This hallway looked vaguely familiar. He stepped his way along the hall, trying to figure out why it looked so familiar.

The steps creaked as he descended them, holding onto the railing for support. Turns out that getting stabbed makes balance a little difficult. He stopped half-way down when he spied a painting hanging in the hallway on the floor below him. One of his paintings. He knew exactly where he was, and now he was panicking.

He figured his best course of action was to go back to the room and climb out the window. He was good at that kind of stuff and really, a little stab wound in his side couldn't make escape that much more difficult.

Croften nodded at his decision and slowly spun around, steadying himself before climbing back up the steps, much more painful and annoying than going down them.

"What do you think you're doing?" Ainsley's voice cut through the air, and

Croften winced. He didn't dare turn around. He stood, frozen, as Ainsley climbed up to him.

Then Ainsley's hands were on him, and Croften was shaking. He was just weak from the stab wound, was all.

"You should not be out of bed," Ainsley chided. Then he bent down and hooked one arm under Croften's legs, lifting him up with a soft grunt.

Croften's excitement overcame his fear. He looked at Ainsley with wide eyes as he was carried bridal-style up the steps. "Why are you so strong?" he asked.

Ainsley's face remained hard-set, stoic...tired. He had bags under his eyes and his forehead had little wrinkles running over it. He said nothing, carrying Croften back to the bed and setting him down. Then he turned his attention to the bandage around Croften's body, fingers touching over the spot of the wound. "If you've opened your stitches…" His voice warned that Croften better not have.

Croften flinched at the touches. He was uncomfortable both with the pain and the closeness of Ainsley. Satisfied with what he found, Ainsley sighed and dragged a chair over, sitting next to the bed. He fixed Croften with a steady gaze.

Croften gulped and couldn't look away. "Where's the knife?" he asked, because he couldn't say anything else.

"What?"

"The knife. That was in me. Where is it? Is it cool looking at least?"

Ainsley shook his head, eyebrows furrowing. "I don't know. I assume the doctor threw it away."

Croften frowned. "Damn shame."

"Croften," Ainsley said, practically hissed, voice laden with distress. "You were stabbed!"

"Yeah, I know. Least I could do is get a cool knife out of it."

Ainsley's face twisted into a mix of disgust, fear, and concern. Usually, it was the kind of face that Croften liked to get from people. But it worried him on Ainsley. He didn't ever want to make Ainsley feel any of those things.

"Sorry," he mumbled. He still couldn't look away and it was annoying. Because the more he looked into those blue eyes, the worse he felt. "Uh, so, what happened?"

"You tell me," Ainsley said. "All I know is that you were found lying in the street, bleeding out. Someone, thank God, found you and took you to the doctor before you had time to die!" What a shame, Croften thought. Ainsley was crying now and Croften felt even more guilty. "What happened?"

Croften gulped, really wishing he had a glass of water. Or alcohol. No, yeah, make it alcohol. "Uh, I was stabbed." He shrugged.

"By whom?"

Well, he certainly wasn't going to tell the truth on that. "Just some drunk guy. I don't know. I was just walking, and he came up to me and was like, all drunk and stuff. Stabbed me. I don't know, maybe he thought I was someone else."

Ainsley's eyes narrowed, thankfully not crying anymore. "Just some random drunk guy?"

"Yep." Ainsley didn't look totally convinced. "Why am I here, by the way?"

"What do you mean? You need a place to recover."

"Yeah. But why am I here." Croften gestured to the room. "In your house?"

"Oh. Well, they wouldn't let you leave the doctor's unless you had someone to take care of you during the day. And well, I don't work so I figured it made the most sense."

"Ursula doesn't work either."

Ainsley was actually blushing now, and he turned his head away, finally breaking the eye-contact spell. "Well...I didn't think that it would be a good atmosphere for recovery. She does have a tendency to be a bit...less than gentle."

Croften chuckled. "That's one way to put it." He stretched his shoulders a bit. The room fell into silence. Croften had never been terribly comfortable with silence. But the only other option was to talk about his feelings. He shuddered.

"I-" Croften started.

"We-" Ainsley started at the same time.

They both fell quiet. "You first," Croften said.

"No, no," Ainsley said. "Go ahead."

Croften sighed. They were staring at each other again. He was going to wait for Ainsley to start again. But he was taking too long.

"Sorry I just ran out," Croften mumbled.

"It's alright. I understand. I'm just so glad you're okay." He was starting to cry again. "I couldn't stand it if our last interaction was...that."

"Yeah," Croften agreed. Bile bit at his stomach, threatening his throat. He had intended for that to be their last interaction. But he had always figured at some point they'd meet again. But it's kind of hard to do that when you're dead.

There was a knock on the door and Benson stuck his head in. "I figured you might like some tea," he said.

"Oh yes!" Ainsley said. "Thank you!"

Benson walked in and placed a tray of tea on the table next to the bed. Croften started to sit up, reaching for one.

"Let me help." Ainsley stood up and grabbed Croften's sides, helping him to sit against the headboard. The touch of Ainsley's fingers against him made Croften's skin hot.

Croften took the teacup he was offered and held it to his mouth, a small attempt to hide his blush as Ainsley positioned the covers around him, tucking him in.

"The tea's supposed to help with the pain," Ainsley said. He settled back in his seat with his own cup.

Croften took a sip and tried not to look disgusted. "What's in it?" he asked, his voice betraying him.

"Ginger," Ainsley said.

"Is that it? Is it just liquefied ginger?" Croften had never been a fan of the taste of ginger in the first place. This was torture.

Ainsley took a sip. "It's not that bad. Don't overreact. You need it to heal."

"Can't I just knock back some drugs and pass out until I'm better?"

"Absolutely not!"

Croften sighed and suffered his way through the cup, glad at least to not be thirsty anymore. And thankfully Ainsley didn't seem to want to talk as they drank their tea. Of course, tea couldn't last forever.

"Why did you leave?" he asked. Croften's cup was empty, but he kept it held to his mouth. "I can understand you were upset but...I just have to know why."

"What do you mean why?" Croften asked. As if it wasn't entirely obvious.

Ainsley looked down at his hands in his lap, fingers fidgeting. "I just...I," he took a deep breath, "I know that it's probably ridiculous, but I just wanted to be sure."

Croften shook his head. "Be sure of what?"

"Be sure that you didn't...well...it sounds a little silly saying it out loud, but that you didn't hate me for what I did. For running away the night before my wedding with some...you know."

Croften's eyes went wide because how could Ainsley even think that? Who on earth would hate him for that? Well, maybe Graham at first. And their families. And apparently all of the other snooty uptight bitches in the world. Okay, it actually made sense that Ainsley would think that, and now Croften felt even worse for just leaving.

"Of course not," he said. Ainsley looked up, uncertain. The only way Croften could convince him would be to tell the truth. Which he wasn't a fan of. Truth, in general, was unsettling. "I left because..." He really didn't want to admit it. It made him sound like such a jerk. "Because I knew you would never be with me and I couldn't handle that." He shrugged, like that would help.

Ainsley sighed. "Oh, good. I was worried you...thought less of me."

"Never," Croften said. "Nothing you could do would make me think any less of you." Ainsley smiled and Croften chose instead to notice how dark it was outside. "Hey. It's pretty late."

"You are staying here," Ainsley said. "I don't want to hear any arguments. You need to rest, and I'm keeping you right where I can keep an eye on you."

"I was going to ask where Graham was." Not that Croften particularly cared. He was just curious.

Ainsley blinked and looked out the window. "Oh. I hadn't realized." He frowned. "I didn't hear him come in... I hope he's okay."

"Maybe he's just working late on something?"

Ainsley nodded. "I'm sure that's it. Yes." His face grew ever more worrisome.

"He's not...like upset I'm here, is he?" Croften really didn't want to drive them apart. Curse his bleeding heart.

"Oh no." Ainsley looked at him. "It was his idea, actually." Croften ignored the weird feeling in his stomach. Different from the guilt. "But he was rather upset at what had happened as a whole. I'm worried he might do something drastic."

"Like what?"

"Like punching Henri at a party for being rude to you."

Croften gulped. Graham could never know the truth of who had stabbed him. He wasn't going to be responsible for a murder. Even if the victim had tried to murder him first. He had kind of deserved that.

"I'm sure he'll turn up soon." Ainsley said. He smiled but it didn't reach his eyes. "You should get some more sleep."

"I feel like I've been asleep for ages." But all that talking about things did take a lot out of him.

Ainsley stood up and helped Croften shift so he could lie down. He adjusted the covers, tucking Croften in so tight he could barely move. Then he placed a gentle kiss on Croften's forehead. He pulled back and they stared at each other, both equally surprised by the show of affection.

"I'm sorry," Ainsley said, clearing his throat and standing up straight.

Croften blushed and slid down, hiding his face under the blanket. He remained under there even as Ainsley turned off the lights and closed the door. He tried to curl up but the pain in his side stabbed at him and he straightened out. He really wished

he had some drugs.

Graham did, eventually come home. But it was much later, and Ainsley was already asleep. He woke up with Graham, though, making sure he would be awake before Croften. Graham was half dressed when Ainsley shuffled into their dressing room.

"Good morning," Graham greeted.

"Where were you last night?" Ainsley asked. He didn't mean to be accusatory, but it came out like that anyway.

"Work."

Ainsley huffed. "He woke up yesterday." Graham looked over at him. "He doesn't know who it was, so you can call off the search."

"He doesn't know?"

"Said it was just some random drunk guy." Ainsley shrugged and started getting undressed.

"And you believe him?"

"Of course not. But we can't force him to tell us."

"Maybe you can't, but I'm sure I could." Graham paused for a second. "Or we could just let Mara and Ursula have a few minutes with him."

Ainsley gave him a stern look. "Don't you dare. You heard the doctor. He needs his rest, and you going in there and yelling at him for information is not going to help him. I know you're angry. I am too. But all we can do now is help him recover."

"No. We can find who did that and return the favor." There was a slight growl to Graham's voice, and Ainsley had to take a steadying breath.

"We don't know who it was, and we aren't going to find out. So, I really think it's best if you just let it go."

"I agree with Ainsley."

Graham and Ainsley both startled and turned towards the door. Croften was leaning against the door frame, a smirk plastered on his face, arms crossed. His eyes were bouncing between the two of them, in different stages of undress.

"Croften!" Ainsley chided. He grabbed his shirt and held it over his body. He was one part worried that Croften was walking around again, and even more flustered at being seen so revealed. Especially to Croften.

"Sorry. Heard some commotion. Wanted to come check on things." His eyes settled on Graham, who had made no such effort to cover himself. He at least had his trousers on.

The two made eye-contact and Ainsley held his breath. Graham may have been the one to invite Croften into his home, but Ainsley wouldn't be surprised if this particular incident changed his mind. After all, the longer Croften was in their house, the more likely this was to happen again. And next time it could be worse. Ainsley could be completely naked. Or the two of them could be alone. Ainsley blushed at the thought.

"Feeling better, I see," Graham said. He hadn't shooed him out of the room.

Croften shrugged. His eyes flicked back over to Ainsley. "Starting to."

"You really should be back in bed," Ainsley said, starting to worry at how at ease Graham was with him standing there. Graham just sighed and went back to getting dressed.

"Don't think I can walk. You're gonna have to carry me." Croften smiled.

Ainsley frowned.

"I can assist you with that," Graham said, stepping towards him.

"Suddenly it's not that bad!" Croften turned and left, Graham still following after him.

Ainsley quickly tossed some clothes on and chased after them, worried that Graham might do or say something drastic.

They were sitting on the bed. Croften was leaning to the side a bit, the bandages unwrapped and laid in a pile on the bed behind him. Graham was dabbing a medicated cloth over the wound on his side.

"Oh! No, let me! You have to get ready for work." Ainsley rushed forward. After all, he had offered to take care of Croften. And cleaning his wound was part of that.

"It's fine," Graham said. "I have time."

Croften was looking away. His face was almost as red as his hair. Ainsley sat on the other side of him, a little mesmerized. Croften's eyes were screwed shut, his body tense as Graham tended to him. But it didn't look like an uncomfortable kind of tense. More like an embarrassed one.

Ainsley placed a hand over Croften's and mused over that. Something was different. He could tell. Graham had not tried to kill Croften for his cheek with Ainsley. And Croften was accepting Graham's help. Ainsley wasn't really sure what had made both of them mellow out. But he was glad for it. Made his life infinitely easier.

19

Reprise

It wasn't as weird as Croften thought it would be. Granted, he did tend to overthink and expect the worst. But what happened as he recovered at Ainsley and Graham's house actually turned out to be the best. He got to spend the whole day with Ainsley's, usually undivided, attention, and when Graham came home, he wasn't as intimidating or angry as Croften thought he would, or should, be.

Sometimes Ainsley would fall asleep in his chair

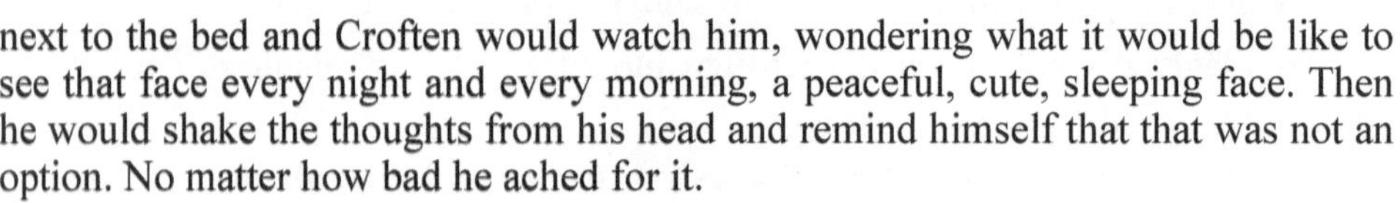

next to the bed and Croften would watch him, wondering what it would be like to see that face every night and every morning, a peaceful, cute, sleeping face. Then he would shake the thoughts from his head and remind himself that that was not an option. No matter how bad he ached for it.

"I hope you don't mind," Ainsley said one day as Benson brought Croften a tray of food for breakfast. Croften insisted he could get up and sit at a table, but Ainsley was convinced he'd open his wound more, and commanded him to stay in bed. "I've asked Graham to keep an eye on you today."

On cue, Graham filed into the room behind Ainsley.

"I've got some work to get done, you see," Ainsley said.

"Right. Editing cookbooks," Croften said, smirking at him.

"What?"

Croften's eyes slid over to Graham. Ainsley followed his gaze. Graham's eyebrows rose slightly at Ainsley, and he nodded.

"Ah, yes, editing...cookbooks," Ainsley said. He shook his head at Graham and left, Graham taking a seat in the chair by the bed.

Croften huffed, ignoring the tray on the bedside table. "I don't need someone to look after me," he said. "I'm not a child."

"Could have fooled me," Graham said, a small smile on his face. If Croften didn't know any better, he would have called it fond.

But Croften did know better, so he crossed his arms, pouted, and slid down the headboard. If Graham wanted to believe he was a child, then fine, he would be one.

"You should eat something," Graham said, looking out the window. "Ainsley would be awfully upset if you didn't."

Croften grumbled. He did not want to do as Graham suggested, but more than that, he did not want Ainsley upset with him. Not just because he would get that angry/hurt face. Croften had found that Ainsley's worried words and actions could hit harder than any of Ursula's smacks. He pulled the tray over and bit into the eggs with a growl.

Graham chuckled but did not look back, his attention focused on the tree outside the window. In a few days it would start to change colors. Croften imagined it would look rather beautiful, all red and orange and yellow. Maybe if he could raise his arm without the stinging pain, he would try to paint it.

Graham made a small noise. It sounded a bit like he was thinking about talking, but not actually doing it. Croften knew the feeling and the sound all too well.

"Something on your mind?" Not that he particularly cared.

Graham looked back at him, shaking his head. "No."

Croften bit back the comment about how there was probably never anything on his mind because he was empty headed. "You definitely have something to say. Out with it."

"I've been instructed not to say anything about it," Graham said.

Croften laughed. "Ainsley really has a hold on you, huh?" Not that Croften could blame him. Ainsley had quite the hold on him as well.

"I suppose he does," Graham confirmed. "But he is usually right about these things."

Croften leaned over, dropping his voice to a whisper. "I won't tell him you told me."

That same totally-not-fond smile appeared on Graham's face again. "You really wouldn't want to hear it," he said before turning to face the window again.

"Oh, but that just makes me want to hear it even more." Croften set aside his tray and stared at Graham, hoping the intensity of it would burn a hole in his skin.

"If you insist." Graham adjusted his seat, so he was facing Croften fully. "It's about Henri."

Croften barely managed to stifle his groan. "What now?"

"That mural he did got him a lot of attention," Graham said.

When he didn't continue, Croften rolled his eyes and said, "Yeah, no kidding.

Tell me something I don't know."

"He's been hired for the city's Fall Fest."

Croften's mouth hung open. He managed to spatter out a few starts of sentences before the champion thought of all rung out. "He doesn't even like the Fall Fest!"

Graham shrugged. Croften let his head fall back. He groaned as he ran a hand over his face. Of course. Of fucking course. Croften's recent injury, and general lack of preparedness, meant he hadn't been able to get his application in this year. The Fall Fest was the *one* job, the *ONE JOB*, that he could always count on beating Henri on. The Fest had a certain flavor to it, one that Croften's style matched perfectly. The money he made from that job alone was enough to last him a whole year if he planned right, which he rarely did.

"Talk about rock bottom," Croften mumbled, slipping further into the sheets. He had lost all hope of winning Ainsley, and now he had lost his best paying gig. The year had started out on a bad note and was ending on a worse one.

"I told you you wouldn't want to know," Graham said. Croften glared at him from the sheets. He looked uncomfortable.

"No," Croften replied. He slid back up and looked at his discarded food. He wasn't sure if he could stomach any of it now. "It's good you told me. Uh, thanks. And look, you really don't have to sit here all day. I'm not going anywhere. Go do something."

Graham's head shook. "No. Ainsley would be upset. He won't be able to relax if you aren't being looked after."

Croften frowned. The guy really did just do whatever Ainsley wanted to make him happy, didn't he? Which begs the question, "If you're all about making Ainsley relaxed, why do you drag him around to all these parties and stuff? Clearly, he's happier not being ignored. And you certainly seemed more at ease." Until he punched Henri. But Croften was certainly trying very hard not to think about that.

"It's not like I want him to go," Graham said. Croften squinted at him. "He insists on going."

Croften's growing glare fell. "You're lying. Who would willingly put themselves in that kind of situation?"

"An idiot," Graham said.

Croften gasped. "Ohh, I'm telling Ainsley you called him an idiot!"

Graham chuckled. "He knows I think that. Because he knows that wanting to go to those parties is idiotic."

"So why do you let him?"

Graham raised an eyebrow. "Are you suggesting I order my husband around?"

Croften opened his mouth but then snapped it shut. He could sense a trap coming. "Why does he go then?" he asked instead.

Graham took a deep breath, looking back out to the window on the exhale. "Ainsley thinks that if he doesn't go that it'll be worse."

"Worse how?"

"I'm not sure. He's convinced that by him not going people will just talk and speculate more."

He wasn't totally wrong. Croften had been dragged around to enough parties, especially lately, to know where Ainsley was coming from. If someone's wife or husband didn't show at a party, there were a million questions. And if the answer was anything other than 'they're sick' then there were a million rumors. But Croften suspected no one would even notice if Ainsley wasn't there, as they certainly didn't notice when he was.

"I've told him I'll stay with him," Graham continued. "But he still insists it's worse if neither of us are there."

That was even more accurate. Short of being on their deathbed, anyone who doesn't go to an invited party in the rich world was practically digging their own graves. But it was starting to become clear to Croften that Graham didn't particularly care about that. Maybe he had at one point or did a little bit still. But he was much more interested in Ainsley's happiness. Ainsley was the one pushing for all of this. And Croften wasn't sure why. If he had a rich, hot guy that would blow everyone off to hang out with him, he'd never turn that down.

Not that Graham was hot.

"Have you tried lying?" Croften asked. "I mean, I know you said you're not a fan of it or whatever. But you could just…not tell him about them."

"I tried. Unfortunately, Benson seems to be on his side. He always tells him about them. Can't distract him from them either."

"Clearly we need to have a talk with Benson," Croften said.

"Good luck."

Graham turned his attention back to Croften. There was something in his eyes that made Croften want to help him. He wasn't sure why. It must have just been the pity. Yeah. He pitied Graham. He was just trying to have a good marriage and make Ainsley happy. Croften could respect that.

"I think you should put your foot down," Croften said.

"Put my foot down?" Graham's eyebrow rose again.

"Yeah. He can't force you to go to those parties any more than you can force him. So next time just don't go. If he wants to go, he can go alone."

"He would," Graham said. His face turned worried. "He can't be out there alone."

Croften rolled his eyes. "I know he's a softie, but he's not completely defenseless. It's not like someone's going to openly attack him or anything."

"They did once," Graham said, looking down.

"What?"

"Before we moved here. Someone attacked him."

Croften jolted up. "Who the fuck?" His side not-so-kindly warned him that it was stabbed recently, and he grabbed it, finding each breath a little more difficult than the last.

Graham stood up and grabbed his shoulders, pushing him back down. He moved Croften's hand and examined the bandages, making sure he wasn't bleeding through them.

"Who the fuck attacked him?" Croften asked. He wanted names, and he wanted weapons.

"It doesn't matter," Graham said, satisfied with Croften's wound and sitting back down. "It happened. It was dealt with."

Croften ignored the perk of interest he had at 'it was dealt with'. "I'll tell you mine if you tell me yours?"

"I'm sorry?"

"You tell me who attacked Ainsley, and I'll tell you who stabbed me."

Graham frowned at him. "So, you do know."

"'Course I know."

"So, tell me."

"You first."

They stared at each other, neither backing down. Croften grabbed at the blankets around him, toying with them as he tried to be okay with the silence. Graham was stiff as a board, and about as unmoving. Even his chest seemed still as he breathed.

"Ugh." Croften crossed his arms and looked away. Clearly, he wasn't getting anything from Graham. And he certainly wasn't going to give up his information first.

"Oh, yes," Graham said, getting up. "I almost forgot." He walked out of the room and Croften figured maybe he'd get the day off from constant surveillance. But Graham returned a few seconds later, holding a book in his hand. "I got you something."

Croften fought the blush that brought to his face as he reached out for it. There wasn't anything on the cover, just a simple design. He opened it, but the pages were blank.

"I couldn't find a journal in your room at Mara and Ursula's," Graham explained, retaking his seat. "So, I got you a new one. Figured you might want to work on your next novel while you were here." He was smirking.

Croften gulped. "Right. Yeah. That. 'Course. Why wouldn't I?" He put the journal down and fake yawned, stretching the arm that wouldn't agitate his wound. "But boy, am I tired. I should really nap."

He slid down the covers and hid himself under them. He heard Graham chuckle but thankfully he didn't say anything more about it. Croften did close his eyes. It would be easier to sleep the day away. But something was nagging at the back of his head.

"You guys should throw your own parties," he mumbled.

"I didn't know you talked in your sleep," Graham said.

Croften tossed the blanket down, blinking at the light. "I think he likes it, ya know. The whole party concept. You should only invite cool people and let everyone else overthink why they weren't invited to the party of the century."

"And who, exactly, do you suggest we invite? There are not many cool people around here."

"Well, there's me," Croften said. "And Mara and Ursula, but don't you dare tell them I said that."

"Quite the little party we have," Graham said.

"There's got to be some people you know who aren't total losers. I don't know, like a really crazy cousin or an old coworker that knows a lot of people."

Graham shook his head.

"Whatever. I still think you should."

Croften settled back down against the pillows and stared at Graham, who had turned his attention back to the window. Croften felt unusually hot. All he could think about was the other day, when Graham had cleaned his wound up for him. He had practically forced himself onto the bed and was removing the wrappings before Croften could say anything.

He had been expecting a rather harsh time of it, Graham agitating the wound as a way to punish Croften for taking in the sights. (And what sights they were). But Graham had been rather soft. His touches had been, dare he say, tender. And his fingers had been warm, touching across Croften's skin.

Croften blushed at the memory and slid back down under the covers. It was certainly a day to sleep instead of think.

The doctor had warned them that Croften would be sleeping a lot, especially in the first few weeks of recovery. It was the body's natural way of healing itself. It was actually a blessing. Croften got his rest, and Ainsley got to write. He sat next to the bed, journal on his lap, and wrote. He had finally figured out how to end the next book, and the words came easily.

"Dear diary," Croften said, his voice slurred with sleep. "I love Graham so much. He's just the hottest guy at the ball."

Ainsley smiled and closed the journal. "Have a nice nap?"

Croften nodded. "Could I get something to drink?"

"Of course."

Ainsley got up and placed his journal on the dresser by the door, away from Croften's curious eyes. He went downstairs and got Croften a cup of ginger tea and some water since he continued to insist on being a child about the taste of the tea.

He nearly dropped both cups when he returned to the room. Croften was sitting on the bed, holding his side with one hand, and perusing through the journal with the other. Ainsley put the drinks down and snatched the journal out of Croften's hands, holding it close to his chest.

A beat of silence passed.

"Uh," Croften said. He looked up at Ainsley.

Ainsley had to think about how he should react. Croften was pretending to be Raleigh Mayans. And he had just found Ainsley writing stories about them. Therefore, Ainsley should be embarrassed.

"Just something to pass the time," he said.

Croften stared at him, unblinking. "You're him, aren't you?"

Ainsley gulped and nodded. He didn't know why he was so nervous for Croften to find out. He knew it wasn't like Croften would tell anyone. But what would Croften think? Knowing that Ainsley wrote such things? Had kept it from him for so long?

"Right." Croften laid down and pulled the covers over his body and head, hiding. "If you need me, I'll be dead."

"Oh dear." Ainsley leaned over and tried to pull the covers away, but Croften kept a tight hold. He sat on the edge of the bed and placed a hand on Croften's body. "It's really alright."

Croften's head shook under the covers. "Why didn't you say anything?" He was hissing slightly with each word.

"I was worried...well I was worried you might, well, that you might do something."

"Do something?"

"Well, I didn't know you all that well. So, I figured if you knew I was the author, you might do something stupid, like you're known to do."

Croften tossed the covers down, staring at Ainsley with a beat red face. "Why did you let me go on like I was you?" he asked.

"Well, it was rather funny." Ainsley chuckled softly at the memory of it all.

Croften frowned and pulled the covers back over his face. Ainsley laughed and sat further up, pulling them back down. "There's nothing to be embarrassed about, dear. It's quite the compliment, rather."

Croften pressed further into his bed, trying to hide. But Ainsley wasn't going to let him do that. They were friends, and friends were open and honest with one another. Croften looked to the side. "It's dumb," he said. "I just...I talked about them so much." His eyes screwed shut.

"I enjoyed that, actually. I don't get to meet many fans, you know. It's nice to hear what people like, what they think."

Croften's face was still flushed, but it had calmed down a bit. "Why the secrecy?" he sat up a bit. "Ainsley, did you ever think maybe these snooty bitches would actually talk to you if they knew?"

"Of course not! Croften! You've read those books. That's the last thing that's going to make them like me."

"Those books are crazy popular," Croften argued. "You never know who might like them. Ursula for instance."

Ursula liked his books? Ainsley smiled. Then he shook his head. "It doesn't matter. For every one that does like them, there's two that won't. And they tend to be louder. It's best to just keep quiet and avoid attention."

Croften squinted at him.

"What?" Ainsley asked.

"Keep quiet and avoid attention?"

"Yes."

Croften huffed at him. "You really are an idiot. Living like that isn't going to make anything better. You can't just sit back and take this kind of abuse. You gotta fight back."

"But I..." Ainsley sighed. He couldn't bring himself to say it.

"You don't deserve this, Ainsley," Croften said, reading his mind. And oh, how he wanted to believe him. But he did deserve it. He made the choice to leave Graham and run off with that man. He made the decision to run back home. He made the choice to still marry Graham, putting unnecessary stress on him because Ainsley was afraid of what would happen otherwise.

"Hey." Croften sat up more, face level with Ainsley's. And very, very close. "You don't deserve it." And there was such truthfulness in his eyes that Ainsley almost believed him. Croften's hand came up, resting warm against Ainsley's cheek. "You deserve happiness," Croften continued, face even closer now. "And fuck everyone else."

Croften's head tilted. Ainsley knew that tilt. He didn't move away. But Croften didn't move closer. He was waiting, eyes searching over Ainsley's face. Ainsley's mouth was dry. He couldn't. No. He was married. To Graham. He couldn't kiss Croften. No matter how warm he was, or how enticing his lips looked, or how very much he wanted to.

Their lips touched, every so softly. Ainsley felt a shiver run down his spine. He was hot and cold at the same time. And he wanted more. He pressed forward, increasing the pressure of Croften's lips against his, closing his eyes so he could enjoy the sensations.

Then the door to the room opened and Ainsley jumped back, standing up and feeling his heart beat wildly in his chest. He shook. He knew it was too early in the day for Graham to be home, but that's all he expected to see when he turned.

Ursula stared at them with a wide gaze. Ainsley really wasn't sure what to say. How much had she seen? Apparently, a lot, judging by the way she was looking at them, a shocked smile on her face.

"Well, I should...get to work."

Ainsley held his journal to his chest and rushed out of the room, Ursula stepping out of his way. He hurried to his room and shut the door behind him. He couldn't stop feeling the flutter of his heart against his chest.

He had kissed Croften. And he had liked it. He slid down to the floor, sitting against the door. What was he going to do? It was going to be much harder to ignore his feelings for Croften now that he knew what it felt like. He bit his lip. He couldn't kick Croften out. He didn't want to. He hugged his knees to his chest.

He had to tell Graham. He couldn't lie to him anymore. But what would happen if he did? Graham wouldn't hesitate to kick Croften out. And where would that leave them? Would Graham divorce him? Leaving him alone? Or would he insist everything was fine and go back to sleeping in his office.

No. Ainsley couldn't let any of that happen. Just one more lie, he told himself. Just this last one. He would talk to Croften. It was a mistake, it wouldn't happen again, and Graham would not find out. It was the only option.

20

Getting Even

Croften had said nothing about the kiss. And Ainsley was equally happy and disappointed. He had expected Croften to tease him about it, to hold it over him, to make jokes about telling Graham or something. He had been prepared for that. Had expected it. Had maybe looked forward to it. But Croften acted as if it had never happened. Which was what Ainsley wanted. So, really, it was a good thing.

"Are you sure you're okay?" Ainsley asked. He had one arm around Croften's waist, Croften's arm over his shoulders, leaning against him as they walked down the hall.

"I'm fine," Croften said. "I can walk on my own, you know?"

"I still don't think you should be walking at all." Ainsley had to catch himself before he started calling Croften dear again. He figured he had just been letting himself get too friendly with him. That's why it had happened, so he would be more reserved going on.

"You heard the doctor," Croften said, wincing a bit as they started to descend the stairs. "If I don't walk around and move and stuff I'll turn into a living skeleton." He winced again, free hand going down to cover his side where the wound was.

Ainsley tutted at him. "But really. You're in pain. You shouldn't be agitating it."

"I'm only in pain because you refuse to drug me," Croften said.

Ainsley glared at him. "Natural remedies are better. They've worked for thousands of years; you're just being stubborn."

"Right, right, sure."

They entered the dining room and Ainsley helped Croften into his seat, food already waiting for them on the table. Croften looked at where Graham would sit as Ainsley sat across from him.

"How does he stand waking up so early?" Croften asked. "If I did that every day, I'd probably die."

"If you did that every day, you'd get used to it," Ainsley told him. He laid his napkin on his lap and started to eat. "Now eat your food."

Croften grumbled but did as he was instructed. Ainsley smiled. This was nice. He liked having someone to eat breakfast with. And eating it at the table instead of his desk or in the room was even better. He wished he could do that with Graham every day, but he wasn't convinced himself that he'd get used to waking up that early.

"So, you guys been married six years?" Croften asked, rather suddenly, mouth half full.

"Chew your food and swallow before speaking," Ainsley said. Just to ignore the question.

Croften opened his mouth, "So you guys married six years?" he asked, chewing loudly on his food as he did.

Ainsley shook his head at him. He hoped that by answering his question Croften would suddenly grow better table manners. "Yes."

Croften did finish his bite, thankfully. But he didn't stop talking. "So, you were in that other town for five or so years?"

"Four and a half," Ainsley said. He took a large bite of toast, chewing slowly so he couldn't answer any more questions.

Croften placed an elbow on the table and leaned his chin on his hand. "So, you moved here when that guy attacked you?"

Ainsley startled and spat half his toast back out on his plate, choking a bit. He grabbed his tea and gulped it down, trying to calm his coughs. Croften only stared at him. "You-you know about that?" He had purposefully left it out of his story.

"Oh yeah." Croften leaned back, wincing slightly as he stretched. "Graham told me all about it."

Ainsley cleared his throat, finally calming his breath, if not his heart. "He did?" He didn't think that was the kind of thing Graham would say.

"Of course." Croften took another bite, continuing to talk as he chewed. "He didn't give me all the details as to how it was 'dealt with'. But I'm starting to suspect murder."

Ainsley smiled a bit. Croften really was a fan of violence. But Ainsley thought the way that it was handled was much more alluring than violence. "Well, murdered in a sense."

Croften dropped his silverware and leaned forward, elbows on the table. His eyes were wide and attentive, waiting.

Ainsley took a sip of tea. "Elbows off the table, dear," he said. He didn't even realize he had said dear. It was just second nature at this point. Croften complied, sitting back, still waiting. "Graham's a lawyer, you know. He deals mostly in insurance and all, but, well, he's really quite knowledgeable."

Croften furrowed his eyebrows. "What did he do?"

"He ruined them, of course." Ainsley tried not to smile. He hadn't entirely approved, thought it was a bit of an overreaction, but it still was impressive. "He found out everything about them and went after them no matter how small the infraction was. Eventually their family got tired of the time and money spent on it all, and they...well, I'm not sure where they went. But they did leave."

"Wow. You know, I was hoping for a little more physical intervention, but alright." Croften shrugged.

"Really, now. Not everyone needs to get stabbed to learn a lesson." Ainsley sighed. "At least I hope you did learn a lesson."

"What lesson is there to learn from a random drunk guy stabbing me?"

Ainsley gave him a look. Graham had told him that Croften admitted he knew who it was that stabbed him. He had said it in an attempt to get Ainsley to agree to let him interrogate Croften for information. But clearly Croften was going to go on pretending.

"Well, I would hope you'd learn not to just run out on your friends in the middle of the night."

Croften blushed and slid down in his seat. "It wasn't the middle of the night," he argued.

Ainsley felt himself blushing as well, but he bit his lip, trying to fight it. He had been right. Ignoring the kiss with Croften was only making things worse. Every time he helped him change his bandages or get adjusted in bed, any time he touched Croften really, all he could think about was that kiss. And how good it had felt, and how badly he wanted to do it again.

Ainsley tried to convince himself that it was just the difference of Croften that attracted him. Ainsley spent the majority of his life with people like Graham. Repressed, emotionless, cold. Not that Graham didn't have the capacity to be warm and loving, he just had trouble with it.

But Croften wasn't like that. He was crazy and chaotic. He acted on impulse and did stupid things because he felt his emotions so fully, he couldn't stand it. Ainsley was attracted to that. Had always been attracted to that. It was why he had been drawn to that gentleman's club in the first place. Maybe it was because he wanted to be like that. Either way, Croften was something he wanted, but couldn't have.

"You alright?" Croften asked. Ainsley realized he hadn't said anything in a while.

"Oh. Oh yes. I'm fine, thank you. Actually," he tapped his finger against the table, "might I be able to ask you a question."

Croften shrugged. "Sure."

"Why did you kiss me the other day?"

Croften smirked. "Uh, I didn't." Ainsley opened his mouth to argue but Croften continued. "You kissed me."

Ainsley huffed. Yes, technically he had kissed him. "But you initiated it!"

"Did I?" Croften's smirk widened.

Ainsley frowned at him because yes, yes, he did. He had leaned closer, had placed his hand on Ainsley's cheek, had tilted his head. Ainsley knew a request for a kiss when he saw it. So what if he had given in to that request? He wouldn't have had to if it wasn't asked of him.

Croften laughed, his chuckles breaking up Ainsley's thoughts. "You think too much," he said. "It was just a kiss." He shrugged. "Don't think too much about it."

"Don't think too much about it?" Ainsley asked. "Who are you and what have you done with Croften?"

Croften laughed again. "Ah, who knows. Maybe I did learn a thing or two."

Croften most certainly did not learn a thing or two. The only thing he learned was how to be a better actor. Obviously, it wasn't just a kiss. It was the best goddamn kiss he ever had in his life. But he wasn't a complete idiot, despite what everyone believed of him. He was dumb, but not an idiot.

If he played up the kiss like it was, he'd lose Ainsley for good. He knew that. He had actually been worried that Ainsley would do something stupid and tell Graham. But he hadn't, and Croften wasn't going to look a gift horse in the mouth. He was going to sit all day and dream about the kiss but that was it.

And oh, what dreams he could have. Ainsley's lips had been as perfect as he imagined. All plump and round and soft and warm. It had been the most perfect kiss in all of creation, and had he not been wounded he would have murdered Ursula for showing up when she did.

But she had made it up to him. She happened to be close, personal friends with the doctor, and had gone down on Croften's behalf to get him the good medicine that Ainsley had refused for him. He couldn't use it right away, obviously. Not with Ainsley hovering as he did. Granted, he was never going to complain about being around Ainsley. Although he was never going to talk about the books to him ever again.

But then he finally got his chance.

"I trust the two of you to behave yourselves," Ainsley warned, arms crossed in the doorway.

He had to go to London to turn in the manuscript for his newest book. And no, he had not agreed to let Croften read it early. Mara and Ursula were going there for something or another (Croften couldn't be bothered to remember) so he was going to travel with them, leaving Croften in the capable care of Graham.

"We'll be fine," Croften assured him. "Don't worry."

"I'll be back tonight," he said, as if it were another warning. "I expect both of you in one piece."

"It'll be alright," Graham assured him. "Have fun."

Ainsley gave them both a hard stare and then huffed before leaving. Really, what did he think the two of them were going to do?

"Alright," Croften said, once he heard the door shut downstairs. "He's gone, you can leave now."

"Leave?" Graham asked. He cocked an eyebrow in a way that Croften most certainly wasn't coming to find adorable.

"Yeah. Look, I'm basically fine." He raised his left arm, biting the inside of his cheek so he wouldn't wince at the totally fine amount of pain. "I don't need constant surveillance. You've got the day off so go take it off. Do whatever it is you do in your down time."

Graham shrugged. "I usually do whatever Ainsley wants to do."

"Wow. So you just have, what, no personality at all?"

Graham frowned at him. Croften sighed, resisting the urge to roll his eyes. He needed Graham to leave. He would tell Ainsley for sure if he knew.

"Look, just, I'm fine. You don't have to sit there all day. Go read or something. Or, I don't know, knit."

"Knit?"

"Sure! Yeah, it's fun. Very relaxing." Graham gave him a skeptical look. Croften groaned. "You're free! No work, no Ainsley. You can do whatever you want!"

"What if I want to sit here with you all day?"

Croften scoffed. "Sure. That'll be the day."

Graham stood up, hands on his hips, looking down at Croften. "You're not planning to leave, are you?"

"What? Why would you think that?"

"Ainsley will never forgive you if you do."

"Is that why he's been hovering?" Croften sat up, leaning against the headboard so he didn't have to look so far up to see Graham. "He's worried I'm going to run away?"

"You did once," Graham pointed out.

"Yeah, and it didn't end well." Croften sighed, running a hand down his face. "Look, I'm not going to leave, alright? So, you can go off and do whatever you'd like, and I'll be right here when he gets back. Okay?"

Graham stared at him, eyes squinted a bit, making a judgment call. Granted, he didn't have much faith to go on. Croften wouldn't trust himself either. But he relented, nodding. "I'll be in to check on you," he said.

"Don't worry about it. I'm fine."

Croften smiled as Graham left. Once he heard him downstairs, Croften turned over and reached under the mattress for the bottle Ursula had given him. He glanced at the directions and then knocked back a nice, big gulp. He slid the bottle back under and laid down.

A few minutes later he felt it kick in; the fog in his brain, the relaxation of his muscles, the warmth spreading through his nerves. Oh yeah. That was better. Pain, what pain? He could punch through a wall if he wanted to. Not that he wanted to. Because his eyelids were getting heavy and he was just too comfortable to think.

A thumb and finger pulled his eyelid open. "He looks drugged," a familiar, deep voice said.

"What?" a familiar, light voice asked.

The finger and thumb left, letting Croften try to return to his slumber.

"How did he get it?" the light voice asked.

"I don't know. I didn't give it to him."

"I wasn't suggesting that."

Clearly, the voices were not going to leave. Croften forced his eyes open. Graham was sitting on the bed next to him and Ainsley was standing a bit away, wringing his hands together. "Hey guysssss," Croften said. His jaw felt pretty loose, and it was hard to talk right.

"Croften! Oh, thank goodness! What on earth did you take?" Ainsley stepped closer, standing right next to Graham.

"The good shit," Croften said, smiling. Because he certainly did feel good. No pain to speak of.

"Where did you get it?" Ainsley asked.

"And where is the rest of it?" Graham asked. "If you didn't just take it all right away?"

"I didn't," Croften hissed.

"Where is it, Croften?" Ainsley demanded.

Croften laughed. "'M not an idiot."

"Clearly you must be to do something so stupid!" Ainsley took a step closer, but Graham held an arm out, keeping him back.

"Let's keep a level head," Graham suggested.

"Yeah, dude," Croften said. "Chill."

Ainsley huffed, his face red, his eyes ablaze with anger. He crossed his arms and started to pace the room.

"I kissed him, you know," Croften said, placing his hands on Graham's leg. Graham gave him one of those cute little eyebrow raises of his. Ainsley gasped and hissed out Croften's name.

Croften sat up, grabbing at Graham's clothes to pull himself closer, until his arms were loosely wrapped around Graham's neck. "I kissed your husband." His words slurred together but he was sure they still made sense. "But is okay, is okay." He pulled himself even closer, practically sitting in Graham's lap. "Cause, cause I'm gonna...gonna even it out."

Clearly, the only logical way to make up for kissing Ainsley was to kiss Graham. He placed his lips against Graham's. Just a quick one, he told himself. But oh, how warm Graham was. He tightened his grip, deepening the kiss. Not as good as Ainsley, of course, but still pretty damn impressive.

This could actually work, he thought. Yes, it could work just fine. They didn't need to fight. No, no. Ainsley, he figured, could just have *both* of them. And they could have each other. And wouldn't that just be lovely?

Hands touched his chest, pushing him away. Gentle, but firm. Croften frowned, letting himself be pushed from the kiss. Graham was staring at him with a strange expression. When Croften glanced at Ainsley, he had a similar one.

"What?" Croften asked. He hiccupped. "Now we're even." He shrugged, his head lulling to the side.

The hands on his chest were pushing him back to a horizontal position. "I think it's best you get back to sleep," Graham said.

"He's been asleep all day," Ainsley argued. "And we still don't know where the medicine is."

Croften let Graham tuck him in, snuggling himself into the warmth of the blankets, eyes closing instantly.

"He's going to be no use like this," Graham said. He stood up, and Croften grumbled at the loss of his pressure on the bed. "Let's let him work through whatever he's got and when he's sober, we'll properly interrogate him."

Ainsley huffed. "I can't believe he would do such a thing?"

"Really? You can't believe that he would do this?"

"Hey," Croften said. He tried to open his eyes, but he really was just overly tired. Best part about medicine, really, was all the sleep.

There was a pressure on the bed again and a hand grabbing his shirt. "You listen to me," Ainsley said. His voice was different and Croften forced his eyes to open. Ainsley's face was level with his, still just as angry as before. "You are in very big trouble. Now, if you tell me where the rest of it is, I might just have mercy on you tomorrow!"

Croften gulped. "'Sunder the mattress," he said.

"Thank you."

Ainsley released him and got up. He reached under the mattress and looked about until he found the bottle. He gave Croften a hard stare and then left, Graham close behind.

Croften sighed and closed his eyes again. He knew he'd probably feel all kinds of regret in the morning. But at that moment all he knew was that he wasn't in pain.

21

Repercussions

It was quiet in their bedroom. Ainsley tapped his fingers against his chest, worrying. Graham had not said much since the incident with Croften earlier. But he also hadn't gone to sleep in his office. So that was an improvement.

Ainsley turned his head to look at Graham. He met his eyes and jerked his attention back to the ceiling. He hoped that even though Graham had been staring right at him, he hadn't noticed Ainsley looking.

Graham chuckled, discounting that theory. "Ainsley, it's okay."

That was not what Ainsley had been expecting to hear. He looked back over, finding that Graham's expression was soft. "Y-you aren't mad?"

Graham gave a half-hearted shrug. "I'm a little disappointed you didn't tell me, but no, I'm not mad."

"Well. If I had known that I would have told you." Ainsley had, after all, wanted to tell him. It was just oh so very complicated.

Graham shifted, turning to lay on his side and stare more at Ainsley. "You remember what I said? About sharing?"

Ainsley's eyes opened wide. *Oh.* That had been what he meant. "Out of the question!" He rolled onto his side as well, back facing Graham, and pulled the covers up to his chin. To think. The very thought. Kissing both of them? It was outrageous.

Graham slid forward, his arms wrapping around Ainsley's waist and pulling him back. This was new. They had never held each other like this before. Ainsley placed his hands on Graham's arms. They were warm.

Graham kissed the back of Ainsley's neck. "This isn't like before," he whispered. "You aren't leaving me."

"I'm not," Ainsley said. He hugged Graham's arms tighter. "Never."

"And that doesn't mean you can't also be with Croften."

"This is ridiculous. You're ridiculous. We are not having this conversation!"

Graham smiled against Ainsley's skin. "Alright."

Ainsley huffed and settled back against Graham, enjoying the closeness this position provided. Graham was absolutely out of his mind. They were married. They had made vows. Didn't Graham care about any of that?

"What if I'm mad that he kissed you?" Ainsley asked.

"Are you?" Graham asked.

"I have a right to be."

"You do. But are you?"

Ainsley gripped the blanket, wringing it out before him in worry. Because he wasn't mad. Not even in the slightest. Confused and surprised, of course. But Croften wasn't exactly himself there. After all, he wouldn't normally go around kissing Graham. Of that Ainsley was sure. But seeing them kiss had been…

"Ainsley?" Graham nudged his nose against the back of Ainsley's head. "Are you mad?"

Ainsley sighed. "No. I suppose I'm not. But it'd be nice to think that I could be!"

"You're right. Next time Croften kisses me I'll be sure to assume you're mad."

"You'd better, because there will not be a next time." Ainsley dropped the blanket and crossed his arms.

Graham kissed his shoulder. "Of course."

Ainsley opened his mouth, but he didn't say it. He figured it would be a good time to do it. To admit to the biggest lie of their marriage yet, bigger than Croften and his kisses. But everything was still so confusing, and Graham was in the business of talking nonsense, so Ainsley decided maybe he'd wait for things to calm down before bringing it up.

The problem was he had been waiting for things to calm down forever. He certainly could not have brought it up back in their old hometown. It had gotten better when they moved here, and Ainsley had almost admitted it. Then Croften showed up and things were back to being hectic.

Ainsley turned around in Graham's arms and snuggled up against his chest. Maybe there was a way he could say it without words…

The next morning, he woke up and cursed himself when he saw that Graham was already out of bed. He hurriedly got dressed and raced downstairs only to catch Graham as he was putting on his jacket by the door.

Ainsley sighed, hanging his head a bit as he reached the landing.

"Morning," Graham said.

"Morning." Ainsley frowned. He had meant to have breakfast with Graham, was going to try and make it his routine. But he was just too used to sleeping in late.

"Everything okay?" Graham asked. He smoothed his clothes down and looked Ainsley over.

"Yes. I'm just," there was no need to embarrass himself by saying the truth, "worried about how to deal with the troublemaker."

"Would you like me to stay home and help?"

"Oh. Oh, no. Thank you though, that's very sweet." Ainsley stepped up to him and wrapped his arms around Graham's neck. "You go and have a good day at work." He leaned in, and they kissed. "I'll be alright."

"Okay."

Graham pulled back but Ainsley didn't let go. *Just say it.*

"Are you sure you don't want me to stay?" Graham asked, a small smile forming on his lips.

"Yes. I'm sure. I just…" Ainsley hugged Graham and deflated against his chest. He was never going to be able to admit it, was he?

Graham hugged him back. "I told you, you don't have to worry about either of the kisses."

Ainsley nodded. He wasn't terribly worried about them anyway. He took a deep breath and let go, stepping back. "I'll see you tonight."

Graham picked up his bag and smiled, looking Ainsley over. "See you."

Croften woke up with the headache he knew he was going to have. He rolled onto his side and reached under the mattress. But no amount of searching about was producing the bottle he had put there. He woke slowly, fingers still feeling around, just in case. He leaned over and looked at the floor. Maybe it had fallen? Had rolled under the bed?

He grabbed the edge of the mattress and slid forward, until his head was hanging over the bed. His sight was a little blurry, but he didn't see any bottle under the bed, either.

"Good morning."

It wasn't Ainsley's voice that brought Croften's head back up. It was Benson, carrying a tray with a plate of food and some tea on it.

"Master Ainsley figured you wouldn't be up to getting out of bed." He placed the tray on the table.

"Where is he?" Croften asked.

"He's downstairs. I do believe he's catching up on some reading." Benson gave Croften a suggestive look and then left.

Croften groaned and fell back against the bed. Great. Ainsley had found the medicine. So not only did Croften not have it to help with both his headache and the pain in his side, but now he also had Ainsley mad at him. What a day.

Croften rolled to his feet, stumbling and grabbing for the table as the pain hit him. He chugged down the tea, shivering at the taste, feeling like he might actually throw up. He couldn't easily get rid of the pain, but at least he could try to fix things with Ainsley.

He grabbed his side, noticing how the bandage was already fresh. He blinked at it. He didn't remember waking up earlier and having it changed. He didn't think it was particularly easy for someone to change it when he was asleep, especially not without waking him up. But he had been in a pretty deep sleep. So he wouldn't doubt it.

Croften stumbled his way downstairs. Ainsley was in the drawing-room, sitting on one of the couches, reading. He didn't even react as Croften stepped into the room.

"Uh, hi?" Croften said. Still nothing. "Silent treatment, eh?"

Croften pursed his lips. Well, not like he could get in that much more trouble. He sat on the couch next to Ainsley and laid down, muscling his way to Ainsley's lap.

"What are you doing?" Ainsley asked, standing up.

Only standing up pushed Croften forward. And he didn't have the muscle strength to stop himself from just rolling onto the floor, landing on his arm, elbow digging into his wound. "Ow."

"Oh, dear! I'm sorry!" Ainsley bent down and helped Croften to his feet, sitting him back down on the couch. He pulled Croften's arm away, examining the bandage.

"Why does everyone insist on physically attacking me when they're mad?" Croften asked.

"To be fair," Ainsley lowered Croften's arm and picked up his book, "you did just try to lay on my lap."

Croften frowned, watching Ainsley move to the other couch to sit down. "I'm in pain," he whined. "Is it really too much to ask for a little bit of comfort?"

Ainsley fixed him with a hard gaze. "Well, I'm sure you got plenty of that yesterday."

Croften grimaced and shrank down in his seat. "How, uh, how'd you find it?"

"You told me." Ainsley opened his book and studied the page before him.

Croften squinted and thought about yesterday. He remembered sleeping a lot. And that was pretty much it. He must have woken up at some point. But he didn't recall.

"I don't suppose there's a way to get it back, huh?" Ainsley glared at him over the top of the book and Croften gulped. "Yeah. Didn't think so."

He sat there, listening to the silence of Ainsley slowly flipping pages. He glanced at his stuff on the table. Ainsley had set him up with some reading and drawing materials down there for when he was strong enough to sit. But none of what he looked at seemed interesting. He just wanted to take more medicine and pass out again. What was so wrong about that?

"You're not my dad you know," Croften mumbled. "Or Mara. You can't tell me what to do."

Ainsley closed the book and looked at Croften, who crossed his arms and looked away. "I'm not telling you what to do," he said.

"Telling me what not to do."

"I'm not-" Ainsley huffed," I'm not telling you what not to do. I'm just saying that while you're here, you won't be having it, because it's not good for you."

Croften scoffed. "Fine. Then I'll go somewhere where I can." He stood up and stormed to the steps. As if Ainsley really knew what was good for him.

"Croften?" Ainsley called after him.

Croften let the anger in him fuel his movements, adrenaline blocking the pain. He was an adult. He could do whatever he damn well pleased, and he wasn't going to have anyone going around telling him how to live his life.

"What are you doing?" Ainsley asked, chasing him into the bedroom.

"I'm going back to Mara's." Croften picked up his suitcase and tossed it on the bed, popping it open.

"You are not!" Ainsley said. He tried to grab Croften's arm, but Croften spun out of the way.

He opened a drawer and pulled out a pile of clothes. "I sure am. You can't stop me. You don't own me."

"I'm not trying to say that I do!" Ainsley watched Croften dump the clothes in the case before he grabbed them out again, taking them back to the drawer as Croften went to another one.

"Well, you sure act like it."

Croften dumped another pile of clothes in the case and went back for the first pile Ainsley had taken out. When he turned back around, he smacked into Ainsley, who was taking out the other pile, his hands digging, of course, right into Croften's bad side.

No amount of adrenaline was going to cover up the pain that had caused.

"I'm so sorry!" Ainsley said as Croften crawled on the bed, holding the pile of clothes to his side. "I didn't mean to!"

"Yep," Croften croaked out. He fell forward, his face digging into the mattress, his knees still curled up, compressing the wound. "Ya know. Some medicine would be really great right about now."

Ainsley sighed. He moved the case to the floor and sat down next to Croften. "I'm sorry. If...if you want to go that's fine. I just can't stand the thought of you ruining yourself like that."

"Ruining myself?" Croften could not actually lift his face, so he talked against the sheets, drooling a bit.

"Yes. I know this stuff makes you feel better, but I've seen it destroy people as well. And I wouldn't want that to happen to you."

"Why?"

"Because I care about you, obviously."

Croften groaned, the pain not just in his side but now in his soul. "You shouldn't," he mumbled.

"Shouldn't what?"

"Care about me."

Ainsley sounded thoroughly offended. "Why ever not?"

Because I'm terrible, Croften thought. Cause I'm a disaster who's never going to have his life together, and I can't be satisfied just being your friend, which makes me even more of a jerk, and you only ever deserve people that will make your life easier, not worse. Croften didn't say any of that, of course.

"Alright. Come on." Ainsley grabbed Croften's hips and pulled him up, supporting him as they stood.

Croften didn't say anything as Ainsley walked him back downstairs. He didn't know what else to say. He acted out in a fit of passion as he always did. Which was exactly why he needed to remove himself from Ainsley's life. Ainsley deserved peace.

Ainsley sat Croften down on the couch and then disappeared. Croften juggled the options in his head. If his stomach wasn't currently trying to murder him, he might have decided to just make a run for it.

When Ainsley returned, he was carrying a spoon that had a familiar liquid in it. "Here." He held it up to Croften's lips. "This is a normal dose," he continued. "And it's all you get today, understand?"

Croften nodded and opened his mouth, drinking the spoonful from Ainsley. Ainsley nodded and left to return the spoon. Then he picked up his book and sat on the couch next to Croften.

Croften felt himself blush. He waited for the medicine to kick in, hoping it would knock him out so he wouldn't have to deal with his emotions. It did start to work, loosening his muscles and taking the edge off the pain. But it didn't even come close to making him sleep. He growled and leaned his head on Ainsley's shoulder.

Ainsley tensed under him but didn't move or push him to the floor. "I'm sorry," he whispered.

Croften frowned, because why the fuck was Ainsley always apologizing for nothing?

"I didn't mean to try and control you," Ainsley continued. Croften screwed his eyes shut, begging for the sweet, sweet relief of being unconscious. "I just want you to be happy and healthy. And I'm sorry if I took it too far and unintentionally caused you more pain."

Croften grumbled. "It's fine," he said, drawing out the word.

He's never really had someone who only wanted him to be happy and healthy. Certainly not his father. Mara and Ursula did, but it was different. They were more like his mothers, more of an overbearing figure of authority trying to keep him from getting in trouble. Ainsley genuinely cared for him and wanted not just what was best, but what would make him happy.

And Croften didn't know how to handle that. He didn't want to lose that by leaving. But how could he stand to have it without having it fully?

He groaned and turned, burying his face in Ainsley's arm. At least he had this. And this, he figured, was pretty good.

22

Falling

The tree was as beautiful in the fall as Croften imagined. And he was learning to get really good at painting with his right hand. Before, all that slab of meat could do was throw colors wildly about. But now? Well now it could actually make shapes! Not that they were the shapes Croften wanted it to make, but they were shapes all the same.

"Are you sure you're comfortable?" Ainsley asked from the chair opposite him. They had brought

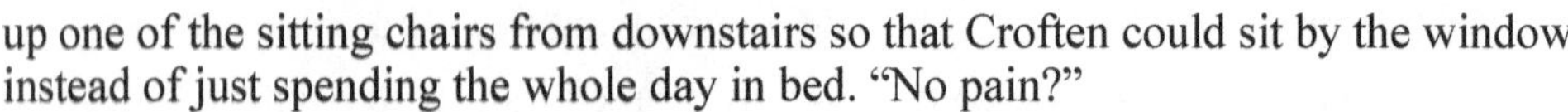

up one of the sitting chairs from downstairs so that Croften could sit by the window instead of just spending the whole day in bed. "No pain?"

"No pain," Croften confirmed. As long as he kept his left arm down, that is. As soon as he itched to reach up and paint like he knew he could then there was pain. "And perfectly comfortable."

"How's it going?" Ainsley leaned forward in his chair, craning his neck to try and get a look at the canvas.

"Not bad," Croften said. He turned the easel around so Ainsley could see. The expression on his face confirmed Croften's lie. "Okay, it's terrible." Croften sighed and dropped his brush, settling back into the cushions of the chair. "Leaves are gonna fall before I get the chance to actually paint them right."

Ainsley had a small smile on his face. "I guess you'll just have to give it a try again next year."

Croften smiled back. That idea was starting to grow on him. He hadn't let himself think on it much, because he was known to get hopeful over nothing. But things had settled down at the house. He and Ainsley were friends. Were friendly. And it wasn't nearly as incapacitating as he thought it would be. In fact, it was entirely possible that he was capable of being around Ainsley without the overwhelming desire to hold him and kiss him and love him.

As long as they didn't touch, of course.

"You know, I'd be knee deep in floats right about now," Croften said. The best way to avoid thinking about one painful idea was to think about another.

"Stop that," Ainsley said. "You can't change what happened. Ruminating on it isn't going to help you move forward."

Croften scoffed. "Move forward. That's a good one."

Ainsley gave him one of his patented disappointed looks and got up. He stalked over to the pile of discarded canvases and carried one back over. He held it up to the one on the easel and nodded at them. "What do you call that, hm?"

Croften shrugged. "I think I'd call that…useless once my side heals."

Ainsley groaned in frustration and dropped the canvas back on the pile. "You are such a stubborn pessimist," he said.

"Am not," Croften argued. "I'm an eternal optimist." Ainsley raised a challenging eyebrow. "A *self deprecating* eternal optimist," Croften added.

"Hm, yes. That I can believe."

Ainsley sat back down and picked up his journal. He had already started work on the next book, despite still not letting Croften read the previous one. Apparently, it would be a good lesson in 'delayed gratification'. But Croften was done with having lessons.

"So, what happens?" he asked, sitting forward as he watched Ainsley write.

"What's that?"

"In the next book," Croften said. "Just some highlights. Some good details to hold me over."

"No."

Croften scowled and sat back. "You're mean," he said. Ainsley just chuckled at him.

Clearly, he wasn't going to be getting anything from Ainsley, so Croften picked his brushes back up and studied the mess of paint on the canvas. Ainsley had been right, in a way. Crowley did need to stop thinking about the past and work on ways he could move on with his life. But he had always figured that his work at the Fall Fair *was* his way forward in life. So without it, he really wasn't sure what he was going to do.

No. He wasn't sure what he *wanted* to do. He wanted to paint. He wanted to look at beautiful things and record them on paper for others to see. He wanted to spend his days with Ainsley. Fuck it, he even wanted to spend his days with Graham now. He wanted to live in this town that had welcome him in like no other, even if the snooty rich people were boring as ever. He wanted to feel like he mattered. Like his life meant something, even if it was to just one person.

But Croften was used to not getting what he wanted. Maybe he was a pessimist, he thought, as he started haphazardly trying to control his right hand as he painted.

Or a realist at least. Either way, the longer he spent thinking about what he wanted in life, the less confident he felt he could get it.

"Stop worrying," Graham whispered in Ainsley's ear.

"No," Ainsley whispered back in defiance. He watched as Croften settled down on the bench, holding his side slightly. Ainsley knew he was mostly recovered, but he still didn't want Croften getting hurt. "We should bring him a chair. Something with a back so he doesn't have to support himself."

"He seems to be supporting himself just fine."

Croften turned and looked over his shoulder, the flames from the fire before him illuminating his skin. "He can also hear everything you're saying."

Ainsley blushed and the two of them joined Croften by the fire. It was the perfect fall night for such an event. It was just chilly enough to make one want to cuddle up around the heat, but not so cold that your back would freeze as you faced the flames. Ainsley sat down next to Croften, and Graham sat beside him.

"Are you sure you're comfortable?" Ainsley asked. "We can do something else if you'd like."

"I'm fine," Croften assured him. "Besides, when are we guaranteed a night like this again?" He looked up. Ainsley followed his gaze and smiled at the stars shining bright above them. "I mean, c'mon. It's gorgeous."

"It really is," Ainsley agreed.

Graham reached into the bag they had brought out with them and pulled out a blanket. He unfolded it and laid it across his and Ainsley's lap. Ainsley picked up the end of it. It was a large enough blanket that, if they squished together, Croften could probably fit in there with them.

"Oh, I see," Croften said with a laugh. "You want me to be comfortable but not warm."

"There's plenty of room," Graham said. He didn't look at them, however, as he picked up a stick and poked absentmindedly at the fire.

"Plenty may be a bit of a stretch," Ainsley mumbled. Croften looked at him expectantly, but he shook his head. They would have to practically be cuddling to all fit.

"Please?" Croften whispered. And for added effect, he wrapped his arms around himself and shivered.

Ainsley looked at Graham with a questioning gaze. Graham wrapped his arm around Ainsley and slid him closer, leaving more space for Croften. If Graham didn't seem to mind, then Ainsley wouldn't mind.

"Come on in, then." Ainsley held the blanket up and Croften scooted over, squishing Ainsley between him and Graham. He took the edge from Ainsley and wrapped it over his lap, tucking it under his legs.

It was now properly toasty, and Ainsley let that be the excuse for the blush on his face. "I haven't done this since I was a child," he said. "Thank you for the wonderful suggestion."

"You should learn that all of my suggestions are wonderful," Croften mumbled. His next suggestion was to lean his head against Ainsley's shoulder.

Ainsley glanced over at Graham, who was staring up at the stars. Either he wasn't aware that Croften had made such a move, or he was aware and didn't mind. Which still didn't make much sense. But it made more sense than before.

"I think he's falling asleep," Ainsley whispered, looking back down at Croften. His head was quite heavy on Ainsley's shoulder, and his eyes were closed.

"It's certainly a good atmosphere for it," Graham said.

"It was his idea; I think he'd want to enjoy it more."

Graham looked over and smirked. "Looks like he is enjoying it."

Ainsley's blush deepened. "I'm enjoying it, too," he said. Then he leaned his own head against Graham's shoulder. "With you, that is."

"And him," Graham said softly.

Ainsley sighed. He couldn't really argue that. Of course, he enjoyed all of his time with Croften. But he also enjoyed it with Graham. "What would it look like?" he asked.

"What would what look like?"

"That whole…sharing nonsense." Ainsley slid down a bit, half hiding his face in Graham's shirt.

"What would you like it to look like?"

Ainsley hummed softly and looked up at the night sky. He watched the stars twinkle gently and tried to picture it. "I'm not sure. I've never thought about anything like that before. I wouldn't begin to know how it looks. How it should work."

Graham shrugged, the movement of his shoulder sending a ripple of movement down to Croften's head. "I don't think it has to work in any one specific way. Just in whichever way it does work."

"Let's just…sleep on it for a while."

Graham nodded and turned his head, placing a kiss on Ainsley's forehead. Ainsley let his eyes close, enjoying the warmth of their shared heat. It was still a ridiculous proposal. But at least he wasn't as opposed to being open to thinking about it.

23

Christmas Cheer

Croften knew that he was in trouble when he hurriedly closed the door. Ainsley was standing in the hall, arms crossed, foot tapping on the floor. Croften adjusted the box in his arms, still a little out of breath from running so much. "I know. I'm sorry."

"Where have you been?" Ainsley asked. He took the box from Croften with a scowl. A few days ago, Croften had been given the okay from the doctor to not have to be all wrapped up. He still needed to take it easy, but he was generally free to move about. Not that Ainsley listened.

"I knew Ursula was gonna be out and I had to go grab something." Croften shook his head, reaching up to brush the snow from his hair. Fall had come and gone. Things settled into a comfortable routine between them, and even though Croften was not technically still recovering, he continued to occupy their spare room.

"You could have just asked one of us to go over for you." Ainsley led Croften into the drawing room. A lovely fire was going in the corner fireplace and Croften shivered next to it.

"Yeah, but it was easier if I went 'cause I knew where it was."

"Why didn't you ask them for it?" Ainsley sat down, sipping at his tea and eyeing the box on the coffee table.

"They can't know I took it." Croften rubbed his hands together and stepped up to the box. "It's Ursula's Christmas gift."

"You're going to give her something she already had?"

"Sort of." Croften reached in and pulled up one of the books, holding it out to Ainsley with a suggestive look.

"Oh. Oh no. I couldn't."

"Ah, come on." Croften sat on the couch, plopping the book in Ainsley's lap. He pulled the pen out of his pocket. "I'm a starving artist, I can't afford actual gifts."

Ainsley gave him a look, grabbing the pen from his hand with force. "You know, dear, if you need to borrow money-" he started signing books.

"I don't need to borrow money," Croften interrupted.

"I'm just saying. You're not exactly in the position to work right now. So, I thought I'd offer-"

"*I'm fine.*"

Ainsley nodded, continuing to scribble away. "So. What are you getting Mara then?"

Croften shrugged. "The utter joy of discovering that her wife is a huge dork?"

Ainsley sighed. "And what about me, hm? What do I get?"

"I can't tell you," Croften hissed. "It's a surprise."

"Do you have all of your gifts figured out already?"

"Most of them."

"Perfect. Then you can help me with my shopping tomorrow."

They traveled down to the town, Ainsley insisting they took the carriage even though it wasn't that cold outside. Croften helped Ainsley pick out a pair of matching scarves, assuring him Mara and Ursula would think it was adorable. Ainsley convinced Croften that, yes, he did have to get Mara an actual gift and no, it couldn't be that taxidermy bird they saw a few shops back.

As they walked along, running out of shops, Ainsley asked, "I don't suppose you'd be up to helping me with Graham's gift again, would you? Only the last one was so good, I'm not sure I can top it on my own."

Croften shrugged. He wasn't as opposed to it as he had been. Graham was, admittedly, a nice guy. He deserved a nice gift. "You don't have to get him something."

Ainsley huffed. "So no, then."

"I mean that not all gifts have to be physical. It can be an act of service, ya know? Like me letting Mara know how much Ursula likes the books." Ainsley shook his head and Croften sighed. "Maybe you could, like…make him breakfast in bed or something."

"Yes. Can you really see me getting up before Graham? I have a hard enough time waking up at the same time as him."

Croften chuckled. It had been a while since they went inside, and he was getting a little cold. He shuffled over, pressing against Ainsley's body, which seemed always warm. Ainsley wrapped an arm around him, pulling him closer to that warmth. Which helped in heating up his body in other ways.

"So, uh, yeah. You know. Just something like that," Croften said. "Not a physical thing that shows him you care, but a metaphorical one. Or whatever."

"I think that's an excellent idea, dear. And I think I know exactly what I'm going to do."

"Oh, please tell me it's something kinky," Croften begged. Ainsley gently nudged him with his hip, blushing a bit.

They finished looking through all the shops, but Croften insisted they found nothing better for Mara than the bird. Ainsley caved and they went to get it, insisting that he was not going to have his name attached to it.

They walked back to their carriage and Croften had a god-awful thought.

"Hey, Ainsley. Uh, do you know, I mean, do you suppose…" It sounded a little silly saying it out loud. Ainsley waited for him to continue. "Did Graham get me anything? Not that I care! Or that I want him to or anything! But, just, if he did, I should know. So, I can get him something so I don't look like a dick, ya know?"

Ainsley nodded. "Yes, I understand. I know he got you something but I'm not sure what. He was being rather secretive about it all."

Croften groaned. "Great. What the hell am I supposed to get him?"

"You don't have to get him anything, dear, I'm sure he's not expecting it."

"I gotta get him something. It's only fair."

Ainsley rubbed his arm. Croften bit his lip. There was enough time for...yes. That would be just perfect.

Ainsley woke up on Christmas morning feeling all warm and fuzzy inside. Graham was still in bed, and Ainsley snuggled up to his side, pressing his nose to the side of his neck. He pressed a lazy kiss there, too. "Good morning," he whispered.

Graham placed a hand on Ainsley's head, running fingers through his hair. "A very good morning, indeed." He kissed Ainsley's forehead and let out a little sigh.

Ainsley gasped, spying through the curtains. "It's snowing," he said. "Oh, how perfect."

Graham held him closer. "Not as perfect as you."

Ainsley blushed and buried his face in Graham's shoulder. The moment was ruined by a knock on their door.

"C'mon, lovebirds!" Croften shouted. "Sooner we eat, sooner we get presents." Then he was walking down the hall, stomping down the steps.

Graham sighed again, less content and more annoyed. But his voice almost sounded fond when he spoke. "Why is he still here again? Isn't he all better?"

Ainsley sat up, stretching a bit. "He may be better but he's in no condition to move all his stuff back to his town."

"Mhm. And the fact that you don't want him to move back to said town has nothing to do with it?" Graham sat up as well, leaning back on his arms.

Ainsley looked at him. "Let's not bring any of that up today, okay?" He wanted this day to be as happy and joyful as it could be.

Graham nodded and leaned over to press a kiss to Ainsley's shoulder. "Meant nothing of it. Let's go eat, shall we?"

Six years ago, Graham and Ainsley had their first Christmas together. The night before Ainsley had gotten quite weepy. It was his first Christmas without his family. And, as much as he disliked them, it was still just too much to handle. Graham had tried to take his mind off things by teaching him how to make these pastries he had learned about from one of his clients.

They hadn't turned out great. But they were an easy thing to make one night and eat for breakfast the next day. They had perfected the cooking technique over the years, so six years later when they shared breakfast with Croften, the pastries were rather good.

"These are delicious," Croften said, mouth half full. "I'd actually believe you edited cookbooks after this."

Ainsley smiled and shook his head. "Slow down. You're going to choke."

"But the faster we go the quicker we get to the gifts." Croften barely chewed and swallowed hard.

"We're only done when all of us are done," Graham informed him, taking a very small bite of his pastry.

Croften frowned and slid down in his seat. Ainsley couldn't help but be a little excited as well. Croften's emotions seemed to be contagious. And the longer they sat there the more Ainsley was buzzing with him to get to things. He squirmed in his seat a bit, trying not to add to the agitation that was Croften's huffing and shifting.

"Birds of a feather," Graham mumbled. He wiped his mouth on his napkin and stood. "Very well, then. Let's go."

Croften jumped up and raced into the drawing room. Ainsley took Graham's hand before following, giving it a little squeeze. Croften was already settled on one of the couches, two presents on his lap, rather clumsily wrapped.

"I wanna go first," he said.

"Sounds agreeable." Graham sat down on the other couch, Ainsley next to him.

Croften leaned over and handed them their gifts. Ainsley held his (which was obviously a book) in his lap and watched as Graham opened his own gift. It was a chunk of ivory, oval shaped, with a little stand attached to it. Painted on it was a miniature portrait of Ainsley, looking stunning in a soft light.

"For your desk," Croften explained. "Cause even if you do have something of him there you can always use another one."

Ainsley could not even begin trying to describe what he was feeling. Warm. And full. And happy. Croften had not just given Graham a gift, but one with meaning, one that wasn't selfish or an attempt to undermine him. He bit his lip.

"This is incredibly well done," Graham said, looking it over. "Thank you."

Croften shrugged. "Yeah. I know. I'm good."

Ainsley smiled and then turned to his gift. It was a book, as he suspected. But it wasn't full of words. It was filled with flowers. Flowers of different kinds and colors all pressed into the pages. And Croften had scribbled random facts about each one and drawn little sketches of them as well.

Ainsley realized he was crying when a little tear dropped to the page, smearing a bit of the ink. "Ah." He closed the book and rubbed his eyes. He could not be seen crying over Croften's gift. No matter how thoughtful it was. "Thank you. It's quite lovely." He cleared his throat. "My turn."

He got up and went to his desk, pulling the two gifts out of his drawer. He handed them to Graham and Croften and then sat back down, watching in anticipation.

Croften tore his open without a second thought. It was a set of brushes. He had had them made special from an artisan in Italy. They had Croften's name engraved in them and everything. Croften looked at them, eyes wide.

"I know. I'm sorry." He looked at his lap, at the book he had gotten. He felt a little sheepish getting Croften something so easy and impersonal when he had gone through all the time and effort of making the book.

"Sorry? Ainsley, these are great!" Ainsley looked back up, certain that it was some kind of joke. "This is probably the nicest gift I've ever gotten."

"You can't be serious?"

"Are you kidding me? Fusolli brushes? I've only wanted one of these for my entire life! And now I've got a whole set!"

Ainsley's face brightened up. "Oh? Oh, I'm so glad you like them."

"I fucking love them!" Croften ran his hand gently over them.

Ainsley smiled at them, but his attention was torn to Graham when he heard him messing with the package. He shook a little, biting his lip as he watched Graham reveal his gift, which wasn't the real gift anyway.

"I want you to read them," he explained, gesturing to the book Graham was holding.

"Are you sure?" Graham cocked an eyebrow at him.

Ainsley nodded. "I want to share this part of my life with you."

Graham smiled and leaned forward, kissing him. Ainsley smiled against his lips. He would have deepened the kiss if he didn't remember that Croften was there. He pulled back, blushing a bit. But Croften wasn't even paying attention, still looking over his brushes.

Graham stood up and left the room to get his gifts. He carried one in, rather large, and placed it on the couch next to Ainsley.

"Big gift," Croften mused as Graham left.

He returned with an equally large, though differently shaped, gift that he placed next to Croften. Graham sat in the armchair and crossed his legs, looking rather pleased with himself.

Ainsley and Croften exchanged a glance. Croften gestured to Ainsley's box. Ainsley carefully removed the wrapping, gasping softly. Graham had gotten him a typewriter. He ran his fingers over the keys. He had seen one of them in London when he had gone with Mara and Ursula. He hadn't even mentioned it to Graham. How did he know?

"Like it?" Graham asked.

Ainsley looked at him with a pressure in his chest that almost made him cry again. "How did you know?"

"Know what?"

"That I wanted one?"

"Oh. Well, I didn't. But I'm glad you did." He shrugged. "I just figured you'd like it. You always say your brain works too fast for your hand. And I understand this is to be faster."

Ainsley jumped up and raced over to Graham, leaning over and hugging him, pressing kisses to his cheek. He couldn't believe that he had such a wonderful and caring husband. One so attentive. One who knew him so well he could anticipate his wants and needs.

"You weren't lying when you said he was good at gifts," Croften said.

Graham pulled Ainsley into his lap, holding him close. "Your turn," he said, looking almost excited as Croften started to open his gift.

It was two parts. Part one was a framed painting. It was the one of Croften's mother that he had left behind. But that wasn't the part Croften was staring at. He was leafing through the other papers that had been wrapped together. A stack of paintings, mostly landscape and flowers.

"They're your mothers," Graham explained. Ainsley's eyes opened in tune with

Croften's. "I did some research, and I found her. Well, I found her name. Did some digging, managed to find a gallery in London that had a collection of hers."

Croften was making a very good effort at not crying as he looked through the paintings. He opened his mouth but all that came out was a dry squeak. Ainsley could imagine what he was feeling, being so close to the mother he never knew, learning about her through her art.

Croften gulped and turned his watery eyes to Graham. "Thank you," he said.

"You're welcome," Graham said, his voice soft. Soft in a way it had only ever been with Ainsley.

And Ainsley just couldn't stand it anymore, this electricity in the air. He stood up, wiping his own tearful eyes and cleared his throat. "Well. I'm going to go play with my present."

Graham chuckled softly as Ainsley carried the typewriter to his desk and looked it over. Croften just stayed on the couch, touching the paintings and doing his damned best not to cry.

24

New Year, New Outlook

Croften had been given a very special job. It was up to him to intercept the mail from Ainsley. Truth be told, he'd much rather help Graham with this 'special guest list' he was putting together. He had said something about 'Ainsley's friends' and Croften was all but itching to figure it out.

But Graham was nothing if not stubborn. Worse than Ainsley sometimes. Croften had pestered him for almost a week before Christmas to get the details.

But Graham had refused time and time again.

So, the day after Christmas, Croften followed Benson around as he cleaned, staring a hole in the back of his head. Turns out, everyone in this damn house was stubborn.

"How much?" Croften finally asked, because he was all out of arguments to give.

Benson gave him a coy smile. "More than you could afford, certainly."

Croften growled. He had been trying to convince Benson to give Croften the mail every day. Or at least filter through it to check for the letter Graham had warned him about. It hadn't come yet. And while Croften was very hopeful that it just wouldn't show up at all, he knew that if it did, it would be that day.

"Oh, come on, man!" Croften said. "You know this will be better for Ainsley! If he knows about the party, he's gonna be all weird about things! What he doesn't know won't hurt him."

"I am not employed to make decisions on Master Ainsley's behalf," Benson told him. "I will not withhold information from him."

"Nor deny his request," Croften finished, rolling his eyes. Because that was the same speech he had heard the last eight days he's brought it up.

Croften sighed and flopped to the couch as Benson finished dusting and left the room. Ainsley had taken his typewriter up to Graham's office. Well, their office now, as Graham didn't use it much during the day. Apparently, he had offered Ainsley to use it before, but he hadn't accepted until now. Which Croften was still trying to figure out. If he was quiet enough, he could hear Ainsley typing away at the keys.

Croften took out his sketch pad and started doodling just to get his mind working. He had to come up with a new tactic and he had to do it now. The mail would be here any minute and he had no idea how he was going to stop it.

He heard the backdoor open and close. But Benson did not go upstairs to the office. Croften sighed, sinking into the couch and focusing on his drawings. It was over. Not only was Ainsley going to make a deal of things, but Graham would also be upset with him. Not that Croften particularly cared one way or another if he was. He just knew it would harm his chances of being allowed to stay in their house forever like he planned. They didn't know that, technically, his place back in his old town was no longer his, and that he had sent Ursula to collect his things one day. That they were waiting in her house until he either got the okay from Ainsley and Graham or was forced to find a new place to live. He really didn't care about letting Graham down outside of that point. Not one bit.

More time passed and Croften busied himself with his art. He didn't even hear Ainsley walk up behind him. He just heard a voice, light and next to his ear that said, "I most certainly would not wear *that*."

Croften startled and slammed his book closed, hugging it to his chest. "A-Ainsley! Didn't hear you come in!

"Yes, dear," Ainsley said, moving to sit on the opposite couch with a smirk. "I figured. What were you drawing that for anyway?"

Croften gulped. The truth was much more embarrassing. "Uh. I was just, planning your next Halloween outfit is all. Is all."

Ainsley's smirk deepened. "Is that so?" Croften nodded. "So, I suppose it has nothing to do with the books then, hm?" Croften shook his head. "Good. Because I can assure you, dear one, that I would not look that good in adventuring gear."

Croften gulped. Dear one? That was new. "I wouldn't say that." His eyes glanced over Ainsley's body. His lovely, lovely body. "I think you'd look hot."

Ainsley chuckled and Benson entered the room, carrying a tray of tea, with a package and a bundle of letters under his arm. He gave Croften a look and placed the tray down.

"Your tea, sir," he said. He took the bundle, another look glanced in Croften's direction. "And the mail."

"Oh," Ainsley said. "It's rather late today."

"Indeed."

Benson kept looking at Croften as he slowly held the bundle out to Ainsley. Croften panicked. He threw his pencil across the room and stood up abruptly. "Oh no," he said. "My pencil!" He rushed forward, knocking into Benson's arm, spilling the letters and package to the floor.

"Oh dear!" Ainsley said, getting to his feet. "Are you two alright?"

"Perfectly," Benson told him.

"All good. Sorry about that." Croften dropped to his knees, gathering the letters while scanning each for the name he had been made aware of. He saw it, and stood up, compiling the others and shoving that one in his back pocket. "Here you are."

Ainsley raised an eyebrow at him as he took the stack. "What was that you took?" he asked, glancing down at the envelopes.

"I didn't take anything." Croften shook his head, holding his hands behind his back to make sure it was still there.

"Mhm." Ainsley said. He shook his head. Then he smiled, looking at the package. "Aha! Something you'll enjoy, I do believe." He handed it over to Croften.

Croften took it and tore it open. He gasped. It was a copy of the newest Dangerous Dan book. "Finally!" He opened it and scanned over the pages, flipping through for spoilers.

Ainsley laughed and then leaned forward, reaching around Croften's back and snatching the letter from his pocket before Croften even realized it, distracted as he was.

"Hey!" He closed the book and grabbed for the letter, but Ainsley spun out of the way, keeping the letter out of reach. "Give that back!"

"It's not for you, is it," Ainsley said, face prim as he opened the letter.

"It's not for you, either," Croften said. He immediately regretted it, however, because he knew exactly how sensitive that subject was.

Ainsley didn't seem to be troubled by it, thankfully. "I'm his husband," he argued. "It's my right."

Croften knew it was a losing battle, and he hung his head as Ainsley read over the letter. Now things would be difficult and weird, and Graham would be upset and really, Croften ought to just leave.

"Why did you try to hide this from me?" Ainsley asked. Then he huffed, shaking his head. "I can't believe Graham would employ you in his wild schemes!"

"It's not a wild scheme," Croften mumbled. "It's a surprise."

"Oh?" Ainsley put the letter down on the table and studied Croften. "Go on then."

"What part of surprise did you not understand?" Croften asked. Ainsley put his hands on his hips and stared at Croften, expectantly. He sighed. He just couldn't say no to that face. "Graham's been planning his own New Year's Eve party."

"What? He-he can't! No one would come! The Millers' party is an annual tradition! He can't throw a party that opposes it. Absolutely no one would be there!"

Croften shrugged. "Apparently, he's already got yeses. Said they were a bunch of your friends."

Ainsley furrowed his eyebrows. "Friends? Well, surely the list would be small. I mean, there's you. And I suppose Mara and Ursula, but I really can't see them snuffing the Millers. And I completely understand them not. Who does he mean?"

Croften shrugged again. "I don't know. I was hoping you'd shed some light on that."

Ainsley shook his head. "He's gotten rather creative, hasn't he?"

"Creative?"

"It's just another ploy of his! He's made up this whole fake party to trick me into not bothering him about this one! Oh!" Ainsley huffed and stomped his foot. "I can't believe him!"

"I don't think it's fake," Croften said. "He's been making all kinds of plans. Even gave Benson a menu and everything."

Ainsley scrunched up his face. "That surely can't be true. Who would he invite? That would say yes?"

A third shrug. "What? You don't trust me?"

"It's not you I don't trust, dear. But Graham."

Croften laughed, shaking his head. "You two really need to work on your communication and trust skills, ya know? It's not healthy."

"We are going to this party, and Graham needs to learn that he can't pull the wool over my eyes so easily."

Croften rolled his eyes. A house full of stubborn fools indeed.

New Year's Eve. A wonderful time of celebration and festivities. Ainsley woke up late, frowning. He had gotten pretty good at making sure that he woke up with or just after Graham. The early morning times were nice. Croften was usually still sleeping, and he and Graham could enjoy each other's company in the soft light.

But that day he had missed it. He sat up and blinked, rubbing at his sleepy eyes. He had to admit, however, that it was nice getting a full night's rest again. He didn't know how Graham operated on a daily basis.

He took his time getting dressed, looking over what he was going to wear to the Millers' that night. He figured it didn't matter a great deal, as no one would pay any particular attention to him. But he still had to look his best, lest he give them reason to jest at Graham.

When he went downstairs, Croften was at the table, eating. Ainsley's place was already set, and he sat down. "Why didn't you wake me, dear?" He asked, studying the half-empty plate before Croften.

"Wanted you to get your rest," he said, spewing a few crumbs on the table. Ainsley sighed at them. "You're gonna be up pretty late tonight, you know?"

Ainsley frowned and looked at the empty place at the head of the table. "Where is Graham? Surely he didn't go to work today? I thought they were closed."

"He's out," Croften said, not looking at him. "Had a few more things to prepare for the party, or whatnot."

Ainsley sighed. "Really. I can't believe you two are still keeping up with this whole charade."

"It's not a charade!" Croften cried. "How many times do I have to tell you! It's really happening."

Ainsley most certainly did not believe him. Even if Croften wasn't lying, he knew Graham was. It was just a new tactic to get Ainsley to stay home from a party. Graham must have spun quite the story to get Croften to believe him. But Ainsley was a professional when it came to dealing with Graham. And he knew the truth.

And so, he said nothing as he went about his day. Croften had devoured the most recent book and kept trying to sneak into the office to get a peak of the next one. Ainsley spent a few hours chasing him out before giving up and hiding the pages. Then he went down to get some reading done.

He started to get suspicious when the sun set, and Graham was still not home. Benson was even in on it, working that afternoon to make a variety of food and set up some decorations before finally accepting Ainsley's offer of having the night off. Ainsley even got himself dressed, determined he would just go to the damn party alone. He wasn't convinced that Graham hadn't just already gone without him.

"I'm telling you the truth," Croften said, watching Ainsley pace in the hall. He was going to leave in ten minutes with or without Graham. He had asked Croften to go with him, but he continued to insist on this party happening.

Before Ainsley could respond, the door opened, bringing in a rush of cold air as Graham stepped in, shaking the freshly fallen snow from his coat and hair. "Sorry we're late," he said.

"We?" Ainsley asked.

Graham stepped to the side, holding the door open as a small stream of people filed in after him. People that Ainsley knew. His friends. His old friends. Friends he hasn't spoken to since getting married. Friends he thought he would never see again.

"Hey there, Angel," Archer said, smirking that devious smile of his. A little similar to Croften's, now that Ainsley thought about it.

"Angel?" Croften asked, crossing his arms and leaning against the wall. Oh, they really could be brothers.

"Obviously," Jay said. "He's our little angel."

"Little and strong," Jordan added with a wink.

Ainsley blushed. He wished Croften wasn't here for this. Graham either. It's been five years since he's seen them all. He had spent a lot of his time at the gentlemen's club. He had gotten to know a lot of the men that worked there over the years. And here they all were. Standing in his foyer. Here to ring in the new year. Here at his husband's invitation.

"Aww," Sean said, smiling. "There's that adorable face we know and love so much!" He hooked an arm with Ainsley's, dragging him off to the drawing room.

Ainsley was still a little in shock to try and fight it. Not that he would if he was in the right mind. But he might have at least questioned it a bit. Sean sat him down on one of the couches, snuggled up to his side. Kai sat on his other side, grabbing his other arm. Jordan, Fink, and Jay sat across from them (after an incident in which Jordan tried to sit in Ainsley's lap and Fink pushed him off). Archer, meanwhile, did that circling thing where he was looking all around the room at stuff, the way Croften did. Ainsley wondered if they were maybe separated at birth.

"Oh no, kids," Archer said, pulling a book off the shelf. "We've got ourselves a danger boy." He held the book out to the others and Ainsley only blushed more.

"You naughty thing, you," Kai said, poking him in the side.

"You don't know the half of it," Croften said. He fell into one of the armchairs, legs hanging over the side. Ainsley was sure his face was about as red as Croften's hair.

"Oh?" Jay asked, sitting up to attention. "Do tell."

Graham, thankfully, walked in then, carrying a tray of drinks for everyone. Ainsley felt a little guilty that Graham was taking on the duty of serving, when he really should be. But he was sure that Sean and Kai wouldn't let him up even if he tried.

"So, how are you all doing?" Ainsley asked, eagerly grabbing a drink. If his face was going to be so hot all the time, he'd like for it to have a reason.

"Don't deflect," Fink said. He leaned forward, elbows on his knees. "We want to hear all the details."

Ainsley continued to deflect, choosing to just sip on his drink, as if he was thinking. He heard Croften chuckle, and he bit his lip. He knew he could trust Croften to not spill his secrets. But Croften would certainly make him pay for it.

"So, who exactly are *you*?" Archer asked, squinting at Croften a bit. He had always been protective of Ainsley, ever since they first met. He had nearly gone postal when Ainsley showed up that day after the incident. He had even been ready to fight Graham when he came to find him.

"This is Croften!" Ainsley said, interjecting Croften's start to that answer. "He's a painter. He's been staying in town doing some work."

"A painter, eh?" Jay asked. He leaned forward, looking past Fink to Croften.

Croften entertained their questions, but Ainsley wasn't really paying attention. He was looking for Graham, who had left after dropping off the drinks. He managed to squirm his way out of his friends' grasp, claiming he had to use the bathroom. He found Graham in the kitchen, arranging a plate of appetizers.

"What have you done?" Ainsley asked. He was a mix of pure happiness and guilt.

"I thought you liked cucumber sandwiches," Graham said. "But I'm sure I can put something else together if you'd like."

"No, Graham." Ainsley stepped up to him, wrapping his arms around his waist and leaning his head on his back. "What have you *done?*"

Graham kept working, moving Ainsley with him as he reached about the counter space. "I threw you what I figured would be a good New Year's Eve party."

"But…" Ainsley sighed. "You shouldn't have brought them here. I told you why I didn't want to see them again."

"Yes, you did," Graham agreed. "And I told you it was a very stupid reason that did not actually matter."

Ainsley sighed again, closing his eyes. He had made a lot of changes when he and Graham got married. The biggest one was to stop going to the club. Mostly because it was particularly important in the first few months that Ainsley didn't go out alone, especially when he was still in that old town. And then it had been because he was worried about Graham's reputation. He figured he could stop the 'prostitute' rumors if he wasn't there anymore. Clearly, he hadn't. For a while he just wrote to them. But even then, he was worried about someone finding out. He decided to cut all ties for the sake of his husband. Who had found out some time later and was decidedly unhappy about that decision.

"They're your friends," Graham informed him. "You're going to have a relationship with them."

"That sounds like a threat," Ainsley said with an airy laugh.

Graham turned around in his arms, hands cupping Ainsley's face. "It is." He kissed him. On the lips. On purpose. Ainsley smiled.

"Hey, lover boy," Archer said. He was standing in the doorway. "We've decided we're gonna kiss your husband at midnight."

"Have you now?" Graham asked.

"It's only fair." Archer walked up and grabbed Ainsley's arm, easily pulling him away. "You had him all to yourself the last five years, after all."

It turned out to be a lovely evening. Another drink in and Ainsley was no longer concerned with his or Graham's reputation. He talked and laughed and caught up with all his friends. They took rotations sitting on the couch with him. Even Croften seemed to be enjoying himself. Although, Ainsley couldn't help but feel a little jealous whenever he got too close to someone. Not that he would admit that. Must have just been the alcohol affecting him.

Then it was midnight. The clock rang out and six pairs of devious eyes were on him. Ainsley sank down into the couch, wary but excited. Kai and Jay were very chaste, pressing a kiss to his cheeks, one on each side, squishing his face together. Then Sean wiggled his way in, kissing the tip of his nose before flicking it softly. Jordan, predictably, got a little crazy, grabbing Ainsley's face from Sean and pressing a full-on kiss to his lips. Fink pushed him out of the way, rolling his eyes at him. He took Ainsley's face in his hands and leaned over, placing a gentle kiss on his forehead and whispering "It's going to be okay." Then it was Archer's turn. Ainsley watched him with the same nervous breath he used to watch Croften. But Archer behaved and just stood behind the couch, leaning over and kissing the top of Ainsley's head.

Ainsley sat, surrounded by his old friends, in pure bliss. But he hadn't been keeping track of how much Croften was drinking that night. He looked over, a little worried, and perhaps excited, that Croften was going to try something. He certainly was trying something. Just not with Ainsley.

Croften had tossed his empty glass over his shoulder (thankfully on the rug so it didn't break) and had grabbed Graham's face. They were kissing. And not like before. Graham actually seemed to be kissing him back this time. Somewhere inside him, Ainsley felt like maybe he should be jealous, or upset, or worried. But he just felt that same strange feeling he had before, only about ten times more intense.

It was an odd sensation. Like a warmth in Ainsley's gut, and a spread of love over his skin. Last time he just told himself it was the anger and frustration at what Croften had done. This time it was clearly the drink and the welcome surprise of his dear friends.

That was all.

25

Presentation

Croften really should not have been surprised when he woke up with a headache. It was alright for him to be surprised about waking up in his bed. Because he vaguely remembered falling asleep on the chair downstairs. Maybe Ainsley had carried him up again? That idea made the blood rush to his face, increasing the pressure of his headache.

Last night came to him slowly as he sat up, feet pressing against the floor. He remembered having a few drinks. And talking to Ainsley's old friends. He had gotten quite a few good stories out of them, and he knew he wasn't remembering all of them. He could still make fun of the few he held on to. Then he had a few more drinks. A few too many drinks, rather. And midnight happened. And Ainsley's friends had all kissed him. And Croften had loved seeing him so happy. But he had also seen Graham happy. Which was interesting. Because he had expected Graham to be upset, or angry, or jealous, or whatever he would be. But he was smiling. And then…

Oh no.

Croften had kissed him. He had kissed Graham. He groaned at the realization, burying his face in his hands. What was he going to do now? He certainly couldn't deal with this with a hangover. Nope. He certainly couldn't deal with this at all. He had to get out of that house.

Croften got up and flushed even hotter when he realized he was in his pajamas. Had Ainsley changed him? He didn't even bother getting dressed. He had to make a quick getaway, and fast.

He didn't hear anything when he opened his door, so he figured it was safe to use the front exit. He crept down the stairs, having already figured out where all the sensitive parts of the floor were, easily avoiding any creaks.

He peeked into the drawing room as he snuck past. Ainsley's friends were all still piled up on the couch. They had fallen asleep practically on top of him. And he was still there. Croften could see half of his face not obstructed by someone's arm, his hair all fluffed up. If he was still in the pile, then who had put Croften to bed last

187

night?

Croften did not want to think about who that could have been and the implications of that. He just grabbed his coat, tossed on a pair of shoes, and ran out the door, letting the morning chill cool off his thoughts as he raced over to Mara and Ursula's.

Mara was walking down the length of the hall when Croften used his spare key to sneak in. They stood still, staring at one another, the door still open.

"Close the door at least," Mara said, rolling her eyes. "You'll let all the heat out."

Croften complied, clicking the door shut with a soft tick. "Uh, you're up early. No big partying last night?"

"Could ask you the same thing," she said.

"Yeah, but ya didn't."

Mara shook her head, a fond smile on her face as she rolled her eyes. "Honestly. What did you do now?"

"Why do you always assume I've done something? Can't a guy just drop by in the morning to visit his friends?"

Mara anchored her hands on her hips. "Did you just stop by to visit us?"

Croften huffed, trilling his lips. "Okay, fine. Maybe I didn't. But you can't just assume it every time. I could genuinely just be visiting."

Mara laughed softly. She walked over and took Croften's arm, leading him over to the drawing room. Ursula was there, sipping on some coffee. She blinked at him. "What did you do?"

Croften rolled his eyes and let Mara push him to the couch, sitting next to him and holding him down. "He doesn't like to be assumed of doing things," she said, smirking at Ursula.

"But he always does things," Ursula argued.

"I kissed Graham!" Croften yelled out. He took a deep breath, the pressure in his chest lessening after he said it out loud.

"Again?" Ursula asked.

"What do you mean again?" Croften leaned forward, squinting at her.

"Uh." Ursula and Mara exchanged a glance. "Why don't you just tell us about when you kissed him."

"Last night," Croften hissed. "At midnight!"

"Oh, oh yeah," Ursula said, clearing her throat. "That's what I was talking about. Okay so just the once then." She nodded, sipping at her coffee and looking away.

Croften blinked at her because how the hell would they have known about it?

"Croften," Mara said, hand rubbing over Croften's arm, stealing his attention. "What happened? Didn't Graham and Ainsley kiss at midnight?"

Croften shook his head. "No. Ainsley's friends kissed him."

They exchanged another glance. "Okay, we are totally coming back to that later," Mara said. "But for now, let's keep the focus on you kissing Graham?"

"Yes," Ursula said. She set her mug down and stared, wide eyed, at him. "Tell us everything."

Croften sighed and hid his face in his hands. He didn't even remember it all properly. And the reason he had kissed him didn't make any sense. "I dunno," he said. "I was drunk." And Graham had kissed him back, he realized, blushing a hot red.

"Well that explains it," Mara said.

"All the best stories start with 'I was drunk'," Ursula agreed.

"There's no more to the story," Croften said. "It's just that. I was drunk and I kissed him."

"Hell of a story either way," Ursula said. Then she started laughing. "I'm sorry," she said, trying to catch her breath as they both stared at her. "I just...I just imagined it! It's too funny."

She laughed harder, her face turning red with the effort, wrapping an arm over her stomach as she bent over. Watching her, Mara started to laugh as well. She at least has the decency to cover her mouth and look away while doing it. Ursula, meanwhile, was falling onto her side, going into full hysterics.

"Glad to know my life is so amusing to you," Croften mumbled.

"Sorry," Ursula wheezed. "It's just...you used to...he was gonna kill...and now…!" Ursula started crying, both hands hugging herself now.

"Alright. I'm getting my stuff and I'm leaving." Croften stood up, but Mara went with him, continuing to hold his arm.

"Nonsense. You are going back to their house, and you are going to face this. You never know, something good might come of this."

Croften scowled at her. What good could come of kissing Graham?

"And take your mail with you while you're at it." Mara reached down, picking up a stack of letters and shoved it into his hands. "You don't live here. I'm burning any more mail you get."

"Yeah, yeah," Croften mumbled. He gave her a side hug. "Actually… I don't think I'll go back quite yet."

"Croften," Ursula chided. "You can't avoid them forever."

"I *know*. But I think I have a plan."

Croften hadn't been there when Ainsley woke up. He had opened his eyes to the tangled mess of limbs that belonged to his dearest friends. After successfully rousing them all, he made everyone some strong coffee with their breakfast and went to check on Graham, who was, predictably, hiding away in his office.

"Have you seen Croften this morning?" Ainsley asked as he set a cup of coffee down for Graham on his desk.

"Just barely," Graham said. He gestured out the window to the street before their house. "Saw him sneaking off earlier this morning."

"Sneaking off where?" Ainsley rushed to the window to see if he could spot Croften. But wherever he had gone, it wasn't in view. "He could be hurt!"

"He's mostly recovered," Graham said. "I'm sure he'll be fine. Besides, it looked like he was heading over to Mara and Ursula's. I wouldn't worry."

"Oh, but I always worry," Ainsley said. He gripped the drapes in his hands and wrung them together. "You don't suppose he's…worried about what happened last night?"

"Which part of last night?" Graham did a good job of feigning innocence, but that raised eyebrow of his was always a dead giveaway.

"The kiss," Ainsley said. He dropped the drapes and walked back to the desk. "Your kiss," he clarified.

"Not sure why he would." Graham shook his head softly and looked at the papers on his desk. "As far as I can tell we're all even now, right?"

"Even?"

Graham smirked in a playful manner. "He's kissed you twice and me twice." He shrugged. "Even."

Ainsley scoffed and sat himself on the edge of Graham's desk. He had been inebriated for most of the night, but he had done a decent amount of thinking. "You know…maybe it wasn't such a bad idea after all."

"I told you you would enjoy the party."

"Not that. Your…suggestion."

Graham sat back in his chair and studied Ainsley. "Which suggestion?" And his eyebrow rose again, making Ainsley pout. He knew exactly what Ainsley was talking about and he was still going to make him say it.

"That whole…sharing thing."

"Ah, that." Graham smiled and then shrugged. "I'm sure there's a way it could work out."

Ainsley crossed one foot over the other. "I know you enjoyed the kiss," he said. He stared Graham down. "Perhaps I'm not the only one looking to be shared?"

Graham held his gaze for a moment, then dropped it, looking down at his desk. "Perhaps."

Ainsley's stare softened. He hadn't expected Graham to outright admit it. He thought it would take a few weeks minimum to get that out of him. It seemed like Croften was having quite the effect on everyone.

"I'm going to take everyone to the station," he said. "See them off, but I won't be long."

"I can go with you, if you'd like," Graham offered.

"No, but thank you. Someone should be here in case the troublemaker decides to return." He laughed softly.

"You know, they're more than welcome to stay for longer if they'd like."

"I know." Ainsley nodded and looked down at his feet. In truth, he wished that they would. "But they need to get back. 'Tis the season," he added with a mischievous grin.

Graham got up and pulled Ainsley in for a hug and a kiss. "Give them my best."

"Are you sure you want to do this?" Mara asked, arms crossed as she stared at Croften gathering his things.

"Yeah. There's a very good chance this will end in disaster," Ursula agreed.

"I don't care," Croften told them. He shoved his large pad of paper under one arm and tried to pick up his easel with the other. It toppled, and Ursula caught it. "It's all I can do."

"I think there are several other options before this," Mara said. Ursula nodded, holding the easel for Croften while he tried to figure out a way to grab it successfully. "What are you going to do if they say no?"

"They won't say no," Croften said. They couldn't, not after what happened yesterday. Drunk or not Graham and Croften had kissed, and Graham had willingly let someone else kiss Ainsley. This was a good idea, no matter what Mara and Ursula said. "Besides, once I do this you don't have to listen to me complain about it all so, win-win."

"That is true." Ursula let Croften take the easel and then slapped him on the head.

"Ow! What was that for?" he asked, scrunching up his shoulders and trying to rub at the point of impact.

"I just feel like I haven't done that in a while," she said. "And I'm sure you deserve it."

"You are a menace to society," Croften mumbled, adjusting his grip and heading for the door, the two of them trailing after him. "Wish me luck!"

Mara opened the door and shook her head. "You're going to need it."

Croften gave her a look and braced himself before heading out into the cold. He had spent most of the day at Mara's, a good amount of time to stress and overthink the upcoming meeting. Croften nearly had himself talked out of it by the time he walked up to Ainsley and Graham's house, maybe ready to just turn around and head back. But then he saw Ainsley through the window, sitting on the couch and reading a book with a soft smile on his face and all fears melted away. This was where he was supposed to be, and he would not let himself leave.

He knocked on the door with his foot. They had given him a key, but he couldn't use it with his hands all full. So he just waited in the cold for Ainsley to come open the door.

"Croften!" he said. "There you are! I was worried about you!"

Croften blushed a bit. "Yeah. Sorry. Was working on a little project." He shook the papers in his arm, earning a curious look from Ainsley. "Graham around?"

Ainsley nodded. "He's in the office. Why?"

Croften nodded towards the stairs. "C'mon."

He didn't wait for Ainsley to respond, climbing his way up the stairs, almost losing the easel again. He heard Ainsley follow him slowly. He pushed the door to Graham's office open with his foot. Graham gave him a look but said nothing as he walked in.

"What's going on?" Ainsley asked. He stood to the side, fidgeting as he watched Croften attempt to open his easel with one hand. It wasn't easy.

"I have something to, er, ask," Croften said. He shouted in joy as he got the clip down, the easel resting on the ground easily. He placed the pad of paper on it, facing the desk, and gestured Ainsley over to Graham.

Ainsley gave him a wary look but followed his notion, moving over to stand beside Graham, one arm over the back of the chair.

Croften cleared his throat and pulled the pointer out of his pocket, folding it open and holding it before him, looking at the two of them. His body started to shake a little with all the nerves coursing through it. This was it. This was going to be it. The be all end all of his life. Either it went really well, and he was happy forever, or it went terribly, and he was back to being miserable. Either way, everything rested on this presentation, and he had to nail it.

Croften cleared his throat and lifted the first page of the pad, revealing the title card of his presentation. He slammed his pointer against the paper, moving it along each word as he read them out. "The twelve reasons you should date Andrew K. Croften, by Andrew K. Croften." He moved his pointer to his chest. "That's me."

Ainsley gave him a little encouraging smile, picking up on his nervousness. Graham just leaned back, hands folded before him. The very picture of a businessman in a business meeting. Croften gulped and flipped the paper.

"Reason one. He's cool. See exhibit A." He stepped away a bit, gesturing one hand over his body. He flipped the paper. "Reason two. He's hot. Refer back to exhibit A."

He gestured over himself again and Ainsley chuckled softly. He slid around, sitting down gently on Graham's lap, Graham wrapping his arms around him and holding him close.

Croften's body shook a bit more watching that. Because all he wanted to do was climb up into that embrace and be a part of it. And if he messed this up, he would never get the chance.

"Reason three," he said, flipping the paper. "He's good at cuddling." He very nearly just went over there to prove it, but he had to get through the rest of the reasons first. There was more to dating him than just cuddling, after all. "Reason four, he's fun company, as I'm sure you all know well." He winked. Well, he tried to wink but he was so nervous it came out more like a little face twitch.

He shook his head. Keep it together, he told himself. If he didn't, he'd lose them for sure. "R-reason five. He has soft hair." And here, below the words, Croften had drawn his hair in a soft pastel, because if he tried to let them touch his hair at that point he might actually just melt. "Reason six. He is talented."

To prove that, he had painted a few flowers around the page in a little border. Ainsley gasped softly, Croften waiting a bit as his eyes scanned over the page. Graham had transferred to a half-smile, still looking professional and business-like, but with a happy fondness in his eyes that stilled Croften's shake.

"Reason seven. He is a good kisser." He had originally planned to kiss them to prove it again, but he couldn't move. So he just said, "As I'm sure you have learned by now." Another throat clear. Just to give him a moment to fight the blush. "Reason eight. He is super romantic."

At this, Ainsley raised one of his hands. Actually raised it. Croften stared at it and the shake came back. "Uh. Yes?"

"Croften, may I just ask a quick question?" he said. Croften nodded, his neck stiff.

"Who is this presentation for?"

Croften opened his mouth, but Graham beat him to it. "I think he's propositioning both of us."

"Together?" Ainsley asked. Croften could only nod, his mouth gone dry. Ainsley smiled and shifted his seat a bit. "Do continue."

Croften licked his lips but his voice still came out a little dry and sticky. "Reason nine. He is not clingy."

Ainsley opened his mouth, one finger raised to argue.

"Please hold all further questions until the end," Croften said, cutting him off. Because yes, it wasn't entirely true as they knew him. But once he was actually in a relationship it would be different. Of that he was certain.

"Reason ten. He is dumb, but in a cute way," Croften continued, Ainsley's smile growing. "Reason eleven. He is super attentive." He stared them both down, eyes wide.

"And reason twelve?" Graham asked, with a voice that hinted at him not being entirely convinced.

Croften frowned, his body slumping a bit. He knew there was a chance this wasn't going to work. But coming face to face with that probability worried him. It really wasn't going to work. It didn't matter if Ainsley wanted this. If Croften wanted this. This was about the three of them, and Graham, it seemed, did not want it.

Croften halfheartedly flipped the paper over, not even able to muster the courage or energy to read the last page. It said: Reason twelve: He can and will murder anyone who hurts you, with a sketch of him hitting Alexander with a shovel. He just shrugged, hanging his head and waiting for one or both of them to kick him out already.

He heard some shifting about, a few whispers, more shifting. He closed his eyes, because he could feel tears stinging at them. He couldn't cry. Not now. He could hold it in, wait until he was back at Mara and Ursula's. Then he could lament about the loss of true love and how his life was worthless now, or rather, more than it was before.

Then there was walking, and a familiar warm hand on his chin, tilting his head up. Croften followed, looking up into Ainsley's blue eyes. He was smiling. "My dear," he said, his voice soft.

Croften's body stilled under his touch. He scanned his face for clues as to what 'my dear' meant. Was it a pitiful one, a 'sorry to have to do this but get out'? Or was it something else?

Ainsley's hand tugged, pulling Croften's face closer, their lips pressing together. His body shivered again, one, powerful jerk as a chill ran down his spine. Kissing Ainsley was like falling through a cloud. All soft and cool and wonderful. But it always ended too soon. Croften could kiss Ainsley for a hundred years and still need more.

He blinked at Ainsley when they separated, because he simply couldn't believe it. He still sort of expected this to end in disaster. For Ainsley to have meant that as a parting gift. But he didn't say anything about that. He just smiled, moving the hand up to his cheek, thumb brushing over his skin.

Croften's body flushed. It was really happening. Ainsley was going to be his. But it was more than that. It was more than Croften ever expected, ever wanted before. Because now, theoretically, *Graham* was also his. Nearly a year ago he never could have imagined wanting someone like him. And he was so incredibly happy that now he did.

"Guess it's only fair to make it even now, right?" he asked, eyebrows raising at Ainsley now that things had settled, had been settled, and he knew he was safe.

Ainsley glanced over his shoulder at Graham. He nodded. "Yes, rather. It does seem to work that way."

Croften nodded and steeled himself, his legs still shaking as he walked over to the desk. He felt a little ill, maybe some anxiety poisoning. Graham didn't move, just continued to lean back in his chair and look at Croften with an analytical eye.

Croften glanced back at Ainsley, to make sure this was okay. Make sure this wasn't just a Graham letting them be together kind of thing. Which would have been good. Maybe not as great as having both of them, but certainly something he would take. Ainsley just nodded, which did little to ease his fears.

Graham certainly didn't help, just sitting there, that half-smile on his face as he waited. What did they expect him to do? Just climb in his lap and kiss him? Not that Croften wouldn't have loved that. But maybe not *now.*

Instead, he held out his hand. Graham took it and Croften pulled him up, wishing the big idiot would wear some kind of emotion on his face. He could almost always tell what Ainsley was thinking, was feeling, but Graham was a lot harder to read. Croften always did like a challenge.

Croften tugged, bringing Graham closer, reaching a hand up to the back of his head, kissing him. It was the first time they kissed without Croften being inebriated, and it was a wonderfully strange sensation. Graham, as it turned out, was actually a damn good kisser. Croften could see, now, why Ainsley had married him.

And Ainsley was smiling when they pulled away. And his eyes were a little wet, a little teary, a little on the edge of crying.

"You okay?" Croften asked, genuinely worried. He wasn't sure if he would ever stop being worried. He wondered if he would ever feel confident enough to be secure in this...relationship. He was in a relationship.

Holy shit.

Ainsley sniffed and rubbed his eyes on the back of his sleeve. "Yes. I'm fine. I'm just...I'm happy. I... I can't believe that...that you, that we…" he chuckled, tears dripping onto his cheek.

Graham held his free hand out (Croften had not let go of the other), and Ainsley walked over, grabbing it. Graham pulled him close, until he was sandwiched between the two of them. Croften crowded closer, resting his head on Ainsley's shoulder. Because he too was so overcome with joy he worried he might overload on emotions himself.

He felt Graham's hands on his arms, reaching around Ainsley so he could hug them both close to him. Croften never figured he would end up with one person to love, let alone two. Let alone Ainsley. Let alone Graham. It was all so strange and weird and honestly, he wouldn't be surprised if he woke up and this was all a dream. He'd be depressed, but not surprised.

Because something as wonderful and as grand as this, couldn't be real.

26

Family Drama

Ainsley nearly slipped, reaching out to grab Croften's other arm. Croften just held him up, hands on his waist, giving him an encouraging smile. It wasn't fair. Croften could do this backwards, and Ainsley could barely even stand up without falling.

"You're doing great," Croften said.

Ainsley was sure the idiot was smiling, but he couldn't see. He was too busy looking down, watching his ankles struggle as he tried to find balance on the thin blades sliding against the icy lake beneath them.

"You actually do this for fun?" Ainsley asked, huffing out a laugh as he nearly fell again, Croften's hands on his body the only thing keeping him together.

"Once you get used to it," Croften said.

Ainsley finally looked up, his legs shaking from the effort. "I think I need a break."

Croften nodded and held on tight, maneuvering them expertly until they were at solid ground, where Graham was sitting on a blanket, watching them. Croften helped Ainsley down, letting him fall onto the blanket next to Graham.

"Having fun?" Graham asked. He smiled, almost a smirk, and handed Ainsley a thermos.

Ainsley smiled back, shivering a bit and drinking his cocoa with pleasure. Croften fell to the ground next to him, not even bothering with the blanket, just letting himself get covered in snow.

"Are you sure you don't want to give it a try?" Ainsley asked Graham. He had agreed to go with them to the lake but had insisted he wouldn't try to skate on it. He had gotten Ainsley a nice new pair of skates, however.

"I think I'm okay," Graham said. He placed his hand over Ainsley's, nice and warm on his skin.

"Ah, come on," Croften said. He leaned up on his elbows, looking over at them.

"It'll be fun." He waggled his eyebrows.

Ainsley chuckled. "Who knows, maybe you'll be better at it than me?"

Graham shook his head. "I'm certain I won't."

Ainsley shrugged and looked over at Croften. He did wish that Graham would give it a shot, he might actually enjoy it. And he was much more in shape than Ainsley, so he'd probably be better at it anyway. But he wasn't going to force it. He was just glad Graham had come to spend the day with them. He had actually taken Ainsley's suggestion to stay home from work for a few days, mainly so they could work their whole situation out. But now Graham was going back to work soon, and Ainsley had gotten quite used to his company.

"I know what'll get you out there," Croften said, delightful smirk on his face as he turned his eyes to Ainsley.

He reached over, leaning up on one arm and grabbing Ainsley's face, pulling him down into a kiss. It was warm and soft, and Ainsley closed his eyes, allowing himself to enjoy it.

Croften pulled away and winked at Graham as he struggled to his feet. "Gotta make it even, right?" He glided out to the middle of the lake, turning around expertly, hands on his hips, smiling at them.

Ainsley wrung his hands together. Croften had been very good at spending the last few days deflecting certain questions. Ainsley had tried to get him to sit and just go through everything: his expectations for this relationship, what he wanted, what he didn't want, everything one needed to know to function together. But Croften had not been agreeable.

Graham rolled his eyes.

"What's the matter?" Croften asked. "Scared?"

Graham shook his head. He looked at Ainsley, face exasperated. "Can I borrow your skates?"

Ainsley nodded, eager to see how Graham did. The skates would be a bit tight on him, but they still fit. And Ainsley slipped his feet into Graham's shoes, wiggling his toes in the warmth of them.

Graham did pretty well for himself. Ainsley watched in amazement as Graham slid over to Croften with ease, his legs and body straight and steady as he moved. Croften's eyes shot open wide when he realized that Graham could actually skate. He turned and zipped away, Graham sighing visibly before chasing after him.

Ainsley's amusement turned back to worry as he thought over what Croften had said. This whole 'even amount of kissing' was cute. And it had been adorable for a while. But Ainsley genuinely worried that Croften believed that was how it had to work. And it wasn't. He could kiss either of them as many times as he wanted, without having to worry about it. That was the fun of them being in a relationship. If only Croften would shut up for a few minutes and listen to him.

Ainsley would just have to wait. It would be easier soon. With Graham off at work, Ainsley could monopolize Croften's time and get the information out of him he needed.

Graham caught up to Croften, reaching out and grabbing his arm. This, of course, caused Croften to slip, falling down, pulling Graham with him. Ainsley jumped to his feet, watching them, waiting to see if they required any medical assistance.

But Croften was laughing, too busy doing so to move himself off of Graham. And Graham was smiling, so Ainsley knew they were okay. And then Graham grabbed Croften's face and claimed his prize, pulling him down into a kiss. They were all okay.

Croften was not an early morning person. He wasn't even a late morning person. No, he was the kind of person who thrived in the dead of night and spent the hours of the sun avoiding all human contact. But love can change a person, and having tired himself out yesterday with all that skating he had actually gone to bed early. And then he had woken up early. It was disgusting.

Croften grumbled and made his way downstairs. Graham was in the kitchen, reading a newspaper as he leaned against the counter. God, it was so early that not even Benson was here yet.

"You're up early," Graham said, not even glancing at him.

Croften mumbled a half response and slunk over to the counter on the other side of the kitchen. He opened the bread box and took a piece.

"Are you...going to toast that or anything?" Graham asked, eyeing Croften as he took a bite.

"Why?" Croften asked, spewing some crumbs on the floor. Graham just sighed and looked back at his paper. "Hey. When did I start getting mail here?" He picked up the envelope addressed to him that was sitting on the counter.

"You don't. You still get mail at Mara's. She dropped that off on her way out this morning. Said she was going to burn it but decided to be nice."

"What was she doing up so early?" Croften could barely keep his eyes open. He couldn't imagine having to actually be functional.

"It's hardly that early," Graham responded. He glanced out the window. "The sun is up."

Croften glared at him in the light blue of early morning. "Yeah, *barely*." The letter had an address return from the city, but no other identifying information. Croften shrugged and tore it open. Maybe, if he was lucky, it would be a notice about how terrible Henri had been at the Fall Fest and Croften hereby was pre-picked for all the years to come.

"Well, first gig of the new year," he announced as he read over the letter. "Family portrait." He didn't mean to sound so disappointed, even though he was. "I guess that solidifies my career as an official boring people painter."

"Are you sure you'll be up for it?" Graham asked.

"Mhm." Crowley's eyes scanned over the details of the letter. Apparently the family had just had their portrait done, but weren't very happy with the results. They were visiting friends in town the other day when they had seen some of his work and decided to hire him. "That was ages ago. I'll be fine."

"If you say so."

Croften hummed. "Weston," he said quietly to himself. Then out loud he said, "Weston. Why is that name so familiar?"

Graham shuffled his newspaper and gave him a slightly disappointed frown. "Because it's mine."

"Oh. *Oh. Oh shit.*" Croften practically giggled to himself as he danced in place. "Fuck yes!"

"Such an amazing revelation, I know."

"No, no, no!" Croften jumped over to Graham and held the letter up. "You said Henri does your family portraits every year, right?"

"Yes."

"Well, this year that weasel fucked up! And now I get to be the weasel! Ha-ha, take that!" Croften shoved the letter into Graham's hands and started dancing again.

"What's all the ruckus?" Ainsley asked, walking in with a yawn as he rubbed at his eyes. He was too adorable for his own good and Croften stopped dancing as his heart skipped a beat.

"Croften has received his first commission of the new year." Graham finally looked up from his paper, giving Ainsley a soft smile. But his eyes held a different look to them. "He's just celebrating."

"That is something to celebrate." Ainsley smiled wide and went over to give them both a hug and a morning kiss. Croften took the opportunity to really make sure his was a good one. He was celebrating, after all. "So, what's the job?"

"I'm redoing the *horrendous* portrait of Graham's family that Henri attempted to do.

"You are?" Ainsley looked over at Graham, worry clear on his face.

"Should I…not?" Croften didn't even think about how awkward this all would be for Graham. He didn't see his family, which meant he probably didn't get to be in the portraits. Which meant Crofton was kind of being a jerk right now.

"It's okay," Graham said. "It's good work, and you should go."

"As should you." Ainsley turned and dug around in one of the kitchen drawers, producing an envelope. He handed it, already open, to Graham with a slight blush.

Graham set his paper down and raised an eyebrow at Ainsley. Croften watched with a held breath as Graham read the letter.

"I'm sorry," Ainsley admitted. "I wasn't sure how you would react. I should have given it to you earlier."

"What is it?" Croften asked. He slid up next to Graham and peeked over his shoulder. He didn't get to read all of it before Graham had folded it back up, but it seemed that this year would be different in both painter and subject.

The room was quiet.

"W-well?" Ainsley asked. "You are going, aren't you?"

"I don't know." Graham shook his head. "I don't see what's changed since last year." He shrugged and handed the letter back to Ainsley. "Doesn't make sense why they would want me to go now."

Ainsley took the letter with a soft touch, holding Graham's hands. "Well, maybe they've realized that they were wrong, and that they love you and want you back in their lives," he suggested. He looked up at Graham through his eyelashes, an effective move that even had Croften ready to give into his every demand. "If there's still some hope of reuniting, don't you think you should give it a chance?"

Graham smiled softly. "Yes, dear," he said with a small sigh.

Then Croften got an idea. "You know. You guys are married," he said.

"We are?" Ainsley asked, fake gasping.

Croften rolled his eyes at him. "Yes. You are. And that means, you're technically in the family." He slid over, an arm wrapping around Ainsley's shoulder. "You should be in it, too." He waggled his eyebrows at him.

"No," Graham said, before Ainsley could speak.

"I wasn't talking to you," Croften said, giving him a look. He squeezed Ainsley's shoulder. "What do you say? They want me as their painter, they gotta have the *whole* family there."

Ainsley gulped. "Oh I-I don't think I could do that. It…it wouldn't be…they wouldn't like…I can't…"

"You can," Croften said. "And you should."

"I... I don't...well..." Ainsley looked over at Graham, and Croften sighed. He wanted to say that Graham really had nothing to say about it, it was Ainsley's decision, not his. But he figured that Ainsley was worried about the fact that it was Graham's family, and that he wanted to be respectful of that.

"It's not going to go well," Graham told him. "Don't put yourself through that."

Ainsley's body deflated a bit. Then it rose higher, smiling. "I think I shall," he said. "After all, Croften is right. We are married, dear. And whether they like it or not, I'm a part of their family now."

Graham's eyebrows rose up. "Are you...sure?"

Ainsley gave him a strong nod. "Absolutely." Then he smiled some more, going back to his tea making.

Croften looked over at Graham, who was giving him a look. It was a strange look. A wary look. It took all the elation of Ainsley's declaration out of Croften's soul.

The train ride had been rather comfortable. Croften spent the time looking out the window and scribbling things in the notebook Graham had gotten him in the fall.

He had decided to use it as a drawing journal, since he wasn't going to be writing any Dangerous Dan stories ever again, and it was nearly full already. Ainsley watched him with interest, and Graham read one of Ainsley's books. He was working his way through them rather quickly and had no lack of praise to give.

Even the carriage ride up to the house wasn't too bad. Croften was admiring his new brushes. He had been itching to use them but said he didn't want to waste them on some small thing. It had to be special. And this, he figured, was special.

But the closer they got to the house, the more agitated and worried Graham looked. He stared out the window, chin in his hand, frowning. His other hand opened and closed over his leg. Ainsley reached over and gave it a squeeze. He knew Graham's parents would not approve of Ainsley being there. But Croften had been right. Ainsley was a part of that family. And like it or not, they couldn't change it. And after seeing all his old friends, and reveling in the fact that they loved him, even after he had stopped talking to them, he was feeling more confident than ever.

They arrived at the house and stood behind Croften at the door. Ainsley was carrying some of his things, after trying not to laugh watching him struggle with it all. Graham had his eyes closed, preparing for whatever fight this would bring about. Croften knocked and Ainsley gave Graham a reassuring smile.

The door opened. The butler glanced over them.

"Uh, Andrew K. Croften," Croften said. "Painter."

The butler's eyes scanned up over Graham and Ainsley. He nodded and stepped to the side, holding a hand out for them to walk in.

Croften let out a low whistle. "Damn," he said. "Nice place."

And it was. Large and perfectly decorated in a tasteful fashion. The epitome of rich chic. The butler led them through to the fashionably furnished drawing room, where Graham's parents and brother were waiting.

Graham's mother looked at Ainsley and said, "What is *he* doing here?"

"We're here for the family portrait," Ainsley said, straightening his back a bit. His confidence was starting to fade, but he still had enough to go on for now.

"That would require you to be in the family," she continued.

"He is," Graham said. Ainsley's body shrank a bit, no longer feeling it so strongly in their presence. "I married him, and that makes him a part of this."

Alexander sneered at them. "Then you're not in it either."

Graham huffed. "So that's just it, huh?" He shook his head, hands on his hips. "Just going to pretend I don't exist, that I never existed? Are you going to get rid of all my stuff? Take away any pictures of me? It's as if I never happened, right?"

"You chose not to be a part of this family," his father said, frowning. "Do not get dramatic because we have accepted that fact."

Graham rolled his eyes. "No. You're right. I'm being dramatic. Just like Sarah was, right? Or do you even remember her?"

"There is no need to bring that up," his mother said. She pursed her lips, squinting slightly.

"Right. Because there's never a reason to bring anything up, is there?" He shook his head again. "That's fine. Go on with your painting. Let Alexander there carry on your great family legacy. I'm sure he'll handle it well."

Graham spun around and stormed out of the room, Ainsley hot on his heels. He walked right out, not grabbing his coat, so Ainsley grabbed it for him, chasing after him through the snow.

"Graham, wait! You'll freeze!"

Graham got a few more feet down the lawn before stopping, head hanging. Ainsley caught up, wrapping the coat over Graham's shoulder. He then pulled Graham into a hug, rubbing his hands over his back to both warm and soothe.

"I'm sorry," Graham mumbled, leaning his head on Ainsley's shoulder. "I didn't mean to snap like that."

"You call that snapping?" Ainsley asked. He chuckled softly. "I think that was rather tame." Graham shifted closer, wrapping his arms around Ainsley. "Graham, may I ask you a question?"

"Hm?"

"Who's Sarah?" Graham sighed and pulled away. "I didn't mean to upset you! You don't have to tell me, I was just curious."

"No. You should know." Graham rubbed the back of his neck, then shrugged his coat on fully. "I'm sorry I didn't tell you before. Sarah was my sister."

"You have a sister?"

"Had."

Ainsley's mouth opened slightly, and he felt a strange sense of guilt and sadness. "Oh, Graham. I'm so sorry. I... what happened?"

"She got sick. My parents didn't think it was that bad. Didn't want to get her a doctor. I didn't fight it and…"

Ainsley could imagine the rest. He shook his head and pulled Graham back into a hug. "I'm so sorry, my dear. I can't begin to imagine what that was like, to go through it. To...to have them…" The guilt and pain churned, transforming into a heat of rage. "I can't believe them," he said. "I simply can't."

"Yes, well, they are like that," Graham said.

Ainsley humphed. "They aren't getting away with it this time."

Ainsley released Graham and stomped back to the house, Graham waiting a moment before chasing after him. Ainsley didn't bother to knock the snow off his boots or take off his coat. He didn't even register Croften by the door, getting his own gear on. He just stormed right into the drawing room, face red and finger pointing at the family there.

"You despicable human beings," Ainsley said. The family looked surprised, but Ainsley gave them no room to talk. "I don't know how you can even stand to live with yourselves!"

"Ainsley," Graham interjected, grabbing his arm, Croften watching from behind.

Ainsley shook him off. "No! They don't deserve your time or your help," he continued. "Graham is the best man to ever live, and it's a wonder he came from such an awful family as you all."

"Now hold on-" Graham's father started.

"No! You hold on," Ainsley said. Every nerve in his body was alight with heat and electricity. "I can't believe I ever wasted so much time thinking about you all and worrying about Graham's relationship with you. But I see now that that was ridiculous! You don't deserve a relationship with Graham. You don't deserve my effort trying to fix it. I should have listened to Graham a long time ago and just been glad he wasn't here anymore. But I am now! So, you go ahead, and you push him out of this family because this," he gestured about to the room, "isn't even a family. And I'm taking him home with me, where we have a real family, and you can just sit here and be repressed all you want!"

Ainsley grabbed Graham's arm and pulled him away, grabbing Croften as well, dragging them both out of the house.

"Uh, Ainsley," Graham said, as he dragged them away, down the street.

"No," Ainsley said. "I've made up my mind. You were right and we are not going to waste a second more on them."

"I meant to say we have a carriage," Graham said, smiling a bit.

"Oh." Ainsley slowed to a stop, feeling rather warm. His body was still abuzz with adrenaline and excitement. "Right."

"That was hot," Croften said as they started walking back to the house, just to leave again. "I mean, damn. Remind me to find more reasons for you to yell, okay?"

Ainsley shook his head. He was glad he had done what he did, said what he said, but he shouldn't have yelled it. Graham grabbed his hand, smiling. Ainsley looked at him and smiled back. Because neither of them had to worry about that family anymore. And things would be better from now on. Now that Ainsley was no longer worried about Graham's relationship with them all. Now that he was glad Graham was no longer a part of that.

Only now there was a whole new relationship Ainsley needed to spend his time worrying over.

27

Specifics

Ainsley's plan wasn't particularly nice. But it would work. So, he didn't care.

"Croften, dear," he said, peeking his head into the drawing room. "Could you help me with something?"

Croften looked over his shoulder, putting his paper and pencil down. "Sure, what's up?"

Ainsley led him up to the office, pointing at the typewriter. "I think the ribbon got jammed, and I can't

get it out."

"Don't worry," Croften said, smirking at him. "I'll fix it for you."

Ainsley smiled back, shifting over to the pile of rope he had stashed. He waited until Croften sat down, his hands pushing and pulling around the typewriter as he looked for the snag. Ainsley took the opportunity and tossed the rope over Croften's body pulling it and him back, tying him to the chair.

"Uh, Ainsley," Croften said, testing the binds that would not break. "Not that I'm not totally into this but, uh, shouldn't we use the bedroom?"

Ainsley chuckled at him and sat himself up on the desk, arms crossed. He would not let Croften's cute ways sway him. They needed to talk. "This isn't about that."

"Oh?" Croften's face fell a little, then furrowed in confusion. "Then uh," he looked down at the rope. "What's with the rope?"

"I need to talk with you," Ainsley said. "And I need you to be honest and truthful with me."

"Don't those two words mean the same thing? Little redundant, don't you think?"

"Stop avoiding it," Ainsley said. He would not let Croften derail him. "This is important."

Croften gulped and his body deflated against the chair. "Yeah. Alright. Just make it quick."

"Make what quick?"

206

Croften sighed and looked away. "It was a mistake. You regret it. You want me to leave. I get it."

Ainsley frowned, his heart breaking for Croften. This is why they should have talked about it earlier. He shook his head and got off the desk, moving to sit on Croften's lap. Croften's head snapped to attention.

"It was not a mistake, I don't regret it, and I don't want you to leave." He placed a hand on Croften's cheek, turning his head for a kiss.

"You don't?" Croften asked as soon as Ainsley released him.

Ainsley shook his head. "Not even a little."

"Then uh...what did you want to talk about?"

"Well, for starters, I need you to know that you don't have to go kissing Graham now, okay? You can kiss each of us as often as you want without worry."

"As often as I want?" Croften asked. Ainsley nodded and Croften smirked, pressing forward and kissing Ainsley again.

Ainsley closed his eyes and placed a hand on the back of Croften's head, fingers curling through his hair. Croften really was a good kisser. But he pulled away reluctantly. There was still more to talk about.

"Stop trying to distract me," Ainsley chided.

"But I don't wanna talk," Croften argued. He kept trying to kiss him, so Ainsley had to be the bigger person and get up, moving away so he couldn't reach. Croften huffed. "You're mean."

"We need to figure out what all of this means, okay?"

Croften tested the chair, spinning a bit, probably trying to see if he could break it to escape. "Shouldn't Graham be here for this?"

"I've already talked to him about what he wants. What we need to know is what you want."

Croften squinted up at him. "What I want?" Ainsley nodded. "That...that's what this is about?"

"Of course. We're going to talk about our expectations and then come to a unanimous decision on how this will all work."

Croften looked him up and down. "That sounds like a rather healthy way to deal with a relationship. Who are you and what did you do with Ainsley?"

Ainsley chuckled. "I'm still me," he assured him. In fact, he felt more like himself than he had since the incident. "And I want to know what you want."

Croften took a deep breath. "Well, uh...you know. You. And-and Graham." He shrugged. "Do we really have to talk and figure this out? Can't we just...see how it goes?"

Ainsley sat himself back up on desk. "How would you like it to go?"

"Uh. I don't know."

"I think you do. When you think about the future, what do you see?"

Croften's eyes finally looked into Ainsley's. "I never really thought about the future before. But, uhm...I certainly want you there. Graham too. I dunno, I guess it's alright if Mara and Ursula stuck around. Although I don't think the future would miss Henri much."

Ainsley chuckled. Everything was so simple for Croften. He didn't think about how things would work; he just went with the flow. Ainsley would love to be able to do that. To not worry about how to organize dates and time spent together. To not worry about how things would work, just knowing that they would.

He got back down and reached behind the chair, undoing the tie and letting Croften get up. If he didn't have any expectations, Ainsley supposed that he would be okay with whatever they settled on.

Croften stood up, stretching a bit before grabbing Ainsley's waist and pulling him into a kiss. Ainsley rolled his eyes and let them kiss. There was plenty of time to figure out the future. In the future. Today he was going to live in the present with his husband and their new boyfriend.

That night, he lay in bed next to Graham, thinking about how Croften was just down the hall. It was a thought that excited him. It was a thought that wasn't nearly as exciting as if Croften was sleeping next to them. Said thought made him uncomfortably hot and he carefully folded the covers over so he could cool off.

"You okay?" Graham asked. He shifted, turning on his side.

"Sorry," Ainsley whispered. "I didn't mean to wake you."

"I was still up." Graham shifted again, sitting up in bed. "Can't sleep." He slid back, resting against the headboard. Ainsley moved up to sit next to him.

"Oh?" he asked. "What's on your mind?"

"Nothing specific."

Ainsley leaned his head on Graham's shoulder. Graham kissed the top of his head.

"What about you?" Graham asked. "What's got you so bothered?"

There were many things that bothered Ainsley. But chief among them was his feelings. Because truth be told, he loved Croften. But he couldn't say that. He couldn't tell anyone. Not until he came to terms with his other feelings of love first.

"I have something to admit to you," he said. He closed his eyes. He knew he needed to do it. But it was still hard. A little easier than he anticipated, but still difficult. Probably because of how long he's been putting it off.

"What's that?"

Ainsley took a deep breath. Best to just say it and get it over with. "I've been lying to you. For a long time now. A few years." Graham didn't say anything which made it worse and better. On the one hand, Ainsley was able to continue without interruption, on the other, he had no idea how Graham felt about this admission. "The truth is...I love you. And I have. For...a while."

He kept his eyes closed but he could feel Graham move. An arm wrapped around his shoulders and Graham pulled him closer.

"Ainsley," he said. For a moment Ainsley steeled himself for the worst. For anger and resentment. But all there was was a kiss to his head. "Thank you."

Ainsley pulled away, sitting up straight so he could look at his husband in confusion. "Y-you're welcome? I'm sorry, why are you thanking me?"

"All I've ever wanted to hear you say were those words." His smile was so soft. He reached out, a hand brushing across Ainsley's cheek. "And now you have."

"But-but aren't you mad? I lied to you! For years! I should have told you the second I knew but I didn't!"

"When exactly did you know?"

"I'm not sure, but it was a long time ago!" He knew exactly when. It was a few weeks after they had gotten married. Ainsley spent most of his time in their little apartment they had rented out, a steppingstone until they could afford a proper place to live. He spent his time alone and sad. It wasn't a particularly good time in his life.

But one day Graham had come home with a gift for him. His first journal. Because Graham had recalled how Ainsley mentioned wanting to maybe write, back when they were courting. And Graham figured he should. And it would give him something to do all day.

Literature was Ainsley's life force. It was what kept him going, what kept him alive on the worst of days. And Graham had just handed him the key to it all. And how was Ainsley not supposed to love him after that?

"I should have told you," he repeated. "And I'm sorry."

Graham pulled him down, kissing him softly. "I don't care that you didn't say anything, Ainsley. I'm just glad that it's true."

"It is true," Ainsley said. He kissed him again. "Truer than anything. I love you so much." He felt a swelling in his chest, a great rush of relief at saying it. And being able to say it without hesitation. He leaned over, body twisting oddly as he hugged Graham tight, tried to prove it by pressing against him with all his strength.

"I love you, too," Graham said. Even though he didn't need to, because he already had. He hugged Ainsley back, hands rubbing over him in a soothing motion.

Ainsley relaxed against him. Even the best-case scenario hadn't been this good in his head. He had expected Graham to be at least upset a little. At least at the fact that Ainsley had lied. Had held back. Had not given him the very thing he needed all those years.

And how good their life could have been if Ainsley had just admitted it. If he had just said 'I love you' and kissed Graham right then, the notebook still in his hands. How better would their relationship be if he made Graham more secure in his loyalty.

How different, he wondered, would things have gone with Croften?

"You're thinking too much," Graham said, placing a kiss on Ainsley's forehead.

"I always am," Ainsley said. "Graham, may I ask you something?"

"You can ask me anything you want, whenever you want."

Ainsley smiled, though he didn't dare pull himself away. He could not stand to look at Graham while he said this. "Do you think...I mean...do you suppose it would be alright...could we maybe one day…" he bit his lip. He thought this would have been easier than saying 'I love you' but clearly the flip of his stomach proved him wrong.

"You want to sleep with Croften," Graham guessed. Correct as per usual.

Ainsley gulped, his body heating up again, the closeness of Graham certainly not helping. He nodded.

"Well," Graham said. "As long as we're being honest…" Graham cleared his throat and Ainsley felt him tense under him. "That was sort of what was keeping me up, too."

Ainsley didn't know if he should laugh or not, but a chuckle escaped either way. "I think in that case, we'd better go get him, huh?"

28

Trouble Brewing

Croften was rarely happy when he woke up. The idea of still being alive in the morning usually filled him with dread. The last couple of weeks only left him feeling indifferent about the whole 'existing' thing. But that day, waking up with his arms around Ainsley's waist, nose pressed to the back of his neck, both of their heads resting on Graham's arm; happy didn't even come close.

He snuggled in closer, breathing in the scent of Ainsley as the early morning light filtered blue through the curtains. He peeled his eyes open and looked over at Graham, who was looking right back at him. He jumped a little on the inside, careful not to wake Ainsley.

"Good morning," Graham said, his voice a whisper over Ainsley's head.

"Hey," Croften said. He still felt a little bit like maybe this wasn't real. Or that Graham would change his mind. Or that Ainsley would. Or that Croften would do something dumb like he always does. He gulped. "Has your arm been there all night?"

Graham nodded. "Can't feel a thing," he said.

Croften chuckled. "Here, let me help." He carefully slid his arm out from under Ainsley and leaned up on his elbow, arm tingling a bit at being free. He reached up and gently grabbed Ainsley's head. He lifted it up a bit so Graham could squirm his arm out. Croften lowered Ainsley's head to the pillow while Graham rubbed his arm to get the blood flowing again.

"You got work today?" Croften asked. He knew that Graham did, but he was kind of hoping he would take off again. Which was funny. Because Croften used to wish he was at work all the time. And now he wanted him to quit.

"Yes," Graham confirmed. He looked down at Ainsley, his good hand moving over to brush gentle fingers over his cheek. "But I'll go in late. We should both be here when he wakes up."

Croften nodded and settled himself back down behind Ainsley, pressing soft kisses to the skin of his shoulder. "Do me a favor," he whispered up to Graham. "Lie and tell me this wasn't a one-time thing."

Graham's smile was soft and cute. "Can't lie about the truth."

Croften blushed and pulled himself closer, burying his face in Ainsley's neck. He had hoped, of course, that it wasn't a one-time deal. But hearing it actually confirmed was a bit much. He felt the bed shift as Ainsley mumbled and shifted beneath him. Croften pulled back a little, but Ainsley was already awake.

"Good morning," he mumbled, his voice slurred and muffled. He sighed and shuffled closer to Graham, nudging his head against Graham's shoulder.

"Good morning," Graham greeted. He leaned down and pressed a kiss to Ainsley's forehead.

Ainsley smiled and rolled onto his back. He turned that smile to Croften, and he swore he could die right then and there as the happiest man alive. "And good morning to you, too," Ainsley said.

Croften couldn't even talk, because all he wanted to do was wrap himself around Ainsley and kiss him. So that's exactly what he did. They only parted when the bed dipped beside them, Graham climbing to his feet.

"Hey," Ainsley said, reaching out but unable to grab him. "Where are you going?"

"I have to get ready for work," Graham said.

Ainsley frowned but said nothing more as Graham shuffled off to the dressing room. He rolled to his side, pressing his face to the side of Croften's neck.

"Yeah," Croften said, holding him close. "I agree. He should totally quit his job."

Ainsley laughed softly and snuggled closer. "We should get up," he said. "Go eat with him."

"Yeah, but will we?"

Ainsley made a noise and shook his head. Croften kissed him and closed his eyes, enjoying everything he ever wanted. Then the door opened again and everything he never knew he wanted returned, dressed and ready for the day. Croften groaned. How did Graham ever manage to be so awake in the morning?

"Have a good day," Graham said.

Ainsley rolled away from Croften's embrace and sat up a bit. Graham ran a hand through his hair and then leaned down, pressing a gentle kiss to his lips. Ainsley laid back, smiling at him as he turned to leave.

"Hold up," Croften said, sitting up himself, glaring a bit because how dare he. "What? I gotta marry you to get a good-bye kiss?"

Graham stared at him for a moment, a little surprised. "Oh. Sorry." He walked back over and as soon as he was within reach Croften grabbed his face and pulled him into a kiss. He made sure it was a good one, too. He had all day to kiss Ainsley, but he'd have to wait hours to kiss Graham again.

Graham's face was slightly red when Croften let him go. And he cleared his throat as he stood up. "Don't cause any trouble," he said, looking pointedly at Croften before leaving.

Croften laughed and fell back to the bed, pressed against Ainsley. "This is gonna be fun," he said. Ainsley smiled and shifted so he could lay his head on Croften's shoulder. Fun indeed.

Ainsley had gotten his pep back in his step. Whether it was his newfound relationship with Croften, the stronger than ever relationship with Graham, or the fact that he had finally told Graham's family off, he didn't know. And it didn't matter. All that did matter was he finally felt like himself again.

"I don't think this is a good idea," Croften said. He was watching Ainsley from the entrance to the drawing room, arms crossed. "I should go with you."

"Oh, please," Ainsley said with a huff. "I'll be fine. It's hardly that far of a walk into town and I know exactly what I'm getting."

"I'm going with you," Croften insisted. He stepped forward to grab his coat, but Ainsley stopped him.

"I appreciate your concern," he said, softly so Croften knew it was true. "But… this is something I *need* to do. It's not like I'm going into the city, or anywhere remotely crowded. I'm just popping into town to buy a new journal is all." The typewriter was perfect, of course, but not very conducive to writing on the go.

Ainsley had been hard at work on the next Dangerous Dan novel. The last one had been quite the hit, and ending it with Dan calling the prince by his real name before kissing him really made the demand for a follow up rather intense. Despite Croften's constant interruptions, he was actually moving along rather well.

"But what if something *does* happen?" Croften looked at him with worried eyes. They almost made Ainsley change his mind.

"I'll be alright." He placed a hand on Croften's cheek and kissed him. "I can handle myself." And he needed to handle himself. He was done playing the scared victim. It didn't matter what anyone did or said, he was finally going to live his life. And he was going to do it without fear.

"Promise?" Croften asked.

"Promise." Ainsley kissed him again and successfully managed to slip away.

Ainsley left the pouting Croften behind and started on his solo journey into town.

Honestly, what was he ever really worried about in the first place? The higher class around here may dislike him, but the town and the people who lived there had been nothing but welcoming. He may run into some trouble on the path down, but he didn't anticipate much to worry about.

Humming a jaunty toon, Ainsley arrived in town and took a deep breath in. Not even the cold could dampen his spirits. Ainsley walked the familiar path to the bookshop and smiled at the other few brave souls out in the early evening. He only made it a few steps before he spotted Alexander on the other side of the street.

Graham's brother was leaning against the side of one of the shops, huffs of smoke curling around him as he smoked. In the past, Ainsley figured he would have felt some apprehension or fear upon seeing him. But he was still riding the high of the other day's antics, and decided he wasn't quite done with them.

"What are you doing here?" Ainsley asked as he crossed the street.

The smile that Alexander gave him was unsettling, but Ainsley was determined to see this conversation through.

"Just here on some important business." Alexander looked down, watching as the ash of his cigarette fell with each tap he gave it.

"What important business could you possibly have here?" Ainsley crossed his arms and gave Alexander a good stare. "Graham is done with you."

Alexander smiled, more to himself than Ainsley. "I'm not quite done with him yet, is the thing."

"Whatever you're planning, it won't work." Ainsley was more positive than ever that Graham belonged far away from all of them. How he had been close to them at all was impossible to imagine.

"I already had everything planned out, you see." Alexander took a drag of his cigarette and finally looked up at Ainsley. "But you of course had to ruin it."

"What supposed plan did I ruin?"

"My plan to finally get Graham home. To get you out of the picture."

Ainsley shook his head. He figured if Alexander really wanted to get Graham home, he'd come to realize that it was a packaged deal. If he wanted his brother back, he would have to accept Ainsley, not get rid of him. "Are you talking about that day you came to visit? I wouldn't really call that a plan by any stretch of the imagination."

"Not that. The family portrait."

Ainsley shook his head. "I don't understand."

Alexander sighed, as if he was explaining basic education principles to a child. "With Graham coming over for the painting, we would have been able to convince him that you weren't worth it. And when he went home to discover you had run off on him again, he'd finally realize it."

Ainsley scowled and stepped closer to Alexander, the fuel of a fight returning. "But I would never run off on him! Never!"

"Not willingly, perhaps," a sickly voice said.

Ainsley gasped and spun around, facing Henri as he emerged from the shadows. "What are you doing here?"

Ainsley hadn't seen much of Henri, but when he did, Henri was always wearing a smirk or smile of some sort. It was like he got some joy out of being a bully. But standing in that alley, staring Aisnley down, the glint of something sharp in his hand, he didn't look so joyful.

Alexander stepped up to Ainsley's back. He could hear the twisted smile on his face. "See, Henri here was integral to plan A. I knew you would never be alone, not with that other painter about. But if *he* were there, too…"

"You ruined the painting on purpose," Ainsley said. That would explain why he looked so glum.

"Might have," Henri replied.

"And since that didn't work, he's been employed to help with plan B."

Ainsley wasn't missing. That was a fact. At least, that was the fact Croften told himself as he ran back up to the house. Croften had given Ainsley enough of a head start that he wouldn't get suspicious, then he had raced after him to keep an eye on things. But Croften hadn't been able to find him. Ainsley wasn't at the bookshop where he should have gotten his journal (and the owner mentioned he never came at all), and he wasn't at any of the other places he would want to go.

The only logical conclusion was that Ainsley had forgotten something at home or decided he didn't want to go out alone at all and they had just missed each other in the streets somehow. It was the only thing that made sense.

Croften nearly ran into Graham, who was shedding his coat by the door.

"Slow down," Graham said, reaching out to steady Croften as he teetered to a stop. "What's the hurry?"

Croften looked at Graham and didn't know how to say it. What was he thinking? There was nothing to say. Ainsley had to be here.

"Ainsley!" Croften called out, racing up the steps to the office where he was certain he would find Ainsley at his typewriter.

But Ainsley wasn't in the office. So Croften checked the bedroom in case he went to take a nap. But he wasn't there either. Clearly, he must have been in the kitchen, having a bit of a snack. Maybe he'd let Croften share it with him. But Ainsley wasn't in the kitchen.

His heart beating irregularly in his chest, Croften raced across the hall to check the drawing room. Ainsley wasn't there either and Graham was being not helpful as he stood in the foyer, staring at him.

"What's going on?" Graham asked.

Croften felt panic welling in his chest. He had let Ainsley go out alone and now he was missing. "He's gone," he said, his voice cracked and unfamiliar. "Ainsley's… gone."

Graham's eyebrows furrowed. "What do you mean he's gone?"

"Mara and Ursula!" He shouted, congratulating himself on a good thought. Ainsley had obviously ran into them and went back to their place.

"What about them?" Graham asked.

But Croften was already out the door and running down the street. He had to just be visiting with them. It was the only thing that made sense. Ainsley wouldn't just leave. Not by himself. And whatever alternative Croften's mind wanted to suggest made him sick.

The door was locked, of course, as good doors should be. And Croften's key he had never been asked for back was not with him. He banged his fist against the door, annoyed with how no one seemed to be waiting right next to doors these days. Graham was slowly walking up the lane behind him.

"What?" Ursula asked, throwing the door open, Croften's hand still knocking against empty air for a moment.

"Is Ainsley here?" Croften asked. He pushed his way in. "What am I saying? Of course he's here, where is he?" He didn't wait for an answer, strolling through and peeking his head in every room.

He nearly ran into the library, because if Ainsley was going to be anywhere it was there. He wasn't. But Mara was, pouring herself a drink and looking at him confused. "Croften?" she asked. "Was that you making all that racket?"

"Where is he?" Croften asked. He grabbed her by the arms, shaking her more from his own shake than anything else.

"What are you talking about?" Mara shrugged him off and stepped back.

"Ainsley's missing," Ursula said, entering the room with Graham in tow.

"What?" Mara asked. She looked between the three of them.

"He's not missing," Croften hissed at them. "He's just...out somewhere."

"Why don't you tell us what happened," Graham said.

Croften stood dejected in the center of the room as they all stared at him. How was he supposed to explain it? He gulped. "Ainsley wanted to go into town to buy a new journal. He wanted to go alone, so of course I decided to follow him. But...I don't know! I went to look for him and he wasn't anywhere!" His jaw started to shake, and he clenched it tight.

"Let's not jump to any conclusions," Mara said. She placed a steady hand on Croften's arm, calming him slightly. "Did he mention going anywhere else?"

Croften shook his head. "No. He said he would be quick. He promised he'd be alright."

"And I'm sure that he is," Ursula said. "Maybe he ran into a friend, went somewhere to talk?"

"Who?" Graham asked. "Everyone he knows is in this room."

Croften clapped his hands together because it made sense. He jumped up excitedly. "The party people!" he exclaimed. "Yeah! One of them must have come to visit, and they went out somewhere. They're probably still in town right now!"

Croften ignored the fact that he had checked every place that serves the kind of food Ainsley liked. He raced out of the room. Graham tried to grab him by the arm but too was slow to get a good grip, Croften slipping out of his hold. He didn't want to wait or sit around and theorize over things. He wanted to go out there and *find* him.

He heard the others following him a moment after, but he wasn't going to let them slow him down, determined steps leading him to town. And they didn't slow him down. They stopped him. Well, Graham stopped him, finally getting a good hold of his arm and pulling him back.

"Croften, you have to calm down," he said.

Croften struggled to pull his arm free, but Graham's grip was too tight. "I am perfectly calm," he said through clenched teeth. "You're the one who's not calm. Why are you so calm!?"

"Panicking is not going to help," Graham said, his voice even and tempered. "If we're going to find Ainsley, we need to keep a clear head."

Croften didn't know how he could be expected to stay calm and levelheaded when the love of his life was missing, and they had no idea where he could be, and any number of terrible things could happen or be happening to him and-

Graham pulled Croften over, wrapping his arms around him in a hug as tears slipped their way out. Croften balled his hands into fists and shivered, biting the inside of his cheek so he wouldn't cry more.

"We are going to find him," Graham whispered.

"Yeah," Croften croaked out, nodding. "I'm sorry. I should have been here with him. I shouldn't have let him go alone. I promised I would always be there, and I wasn't."

"Stop," Graham said. "This isn't your fault. You know as well as I do how stubborn he can be. If Ainsley wanted to go into town alone, he was going to go into town alone."

Croften sniffed and nodded. Graham was right, but that did nothing to take away the guilt that pooled in Croften's stomach. If anything happened to Ainsley, he would never forgive himself.

"Hey, idiot," Ursula said, leaning out of the carriage that she and Mara had just pulled up in. "Get in."

Croften dried his eyes on the heel of his hands and climbed in after Graham. He kept his eyes on the road in case they saw Ainsley walking back towards home. His leg bounced and Graham placed a reassuring hand on his knee. It didn't help.

29

Dramatic Climax

Ainsley's hand shook as he poised the pen over the paper. He was trying to think, which was a bit hard, with Alexander pacing behind him, footsteps heavy on the creaking floor.

"I haven't got all night," Alexander said.

"Sorry," Ainsley whispered. "I'm just having trouble finding the words."

"Honestly. It's not that hard." Alexander stopped his pacing and strode up to the desk, arms crossed as he stared down at Ainsley. "Dear Graham, I don't love you, I'm leaving, yada yada yada go home, Ainsley."

"You said you wanted it to sound authentic," Ainsley said, avoiding looking up at him. "I need time."

Alexander huffed and walked away, sitting down on the bed. They were at one of the inns in town, and Ainsley shivered as he looked back down at the paper before him. Alexander hadn't been entirely cruel. All Ainsley had to do was convince Graham that he was gone and to return home, and Alexander would continue to keep him comfortable in this room for the rest of his life.

A tear slipped down the side of Ainsley's nose, dropping onto the paper, staining it with a splash. He sniffed and continued to work out his problem. He had to find a way to say in his letter what he needed to say while making it seem like he was doing what Alexander wanted. He had to think up some kind of code that would alert Graham and Croften to his predicament without letting on to Alexander that he was doing such a thing.

But he was way too stressed to figure it out. All he could do was panic. Panic at the concept of losing them. He had finally been having a good life, and now it was all at risk of ruin. And it was up to him to fix it, to come up with an idea that would get him out of this scrap.

He looked up at the window, wishing the blinds weren't drawn so he could stare out at the town and help calm his mind.

"That doesn't look like you're writing," Alexander said, a threat unspoken in his voice.

Ainsley shivered again, nodded, and started to write.

"Okay," Mara said as they all got out of the carriage. "Croften and I will check the West, you guys head East, okay?"

They nodded and split up. Croften hurried along, doing his best to keep the calm mind that Graham insisted he had. But it was hard when every building they checked didn't have Ainsley in it. He just got more and more worried.

"What if he's not in town?" he said, hopping across the street to peer into the window of a closed store. "What if, like, I don't know. What if he got on a train or something?" There were a hundred reasons Ainsley would have done that, and they all terrified him.

"I don't think he would," Mara said. "He didn't take anything with him when he left right?"

"No. But that doesn't mean he didn't get on a train. There are plenty of places you can get to and back in a day."

"Any that he would go to?"

Croften stared at her with a frown. She was right. The only place Ainsley would theoretically go on his own was the city. But if he wasn't on his own…

"Croften," a thick, lecherous voice said.

Croften growled and turned around. Léon stood on the street, face passive.

"Not the time," Croften said. What the hell was he even doing back in this town anyway?

Léon held up a hand. "I know where Ainsley is," he said.

Croften's body went numb. "What?"

Léon rolled his eyes. "He's at The Silver Lion. With Graham's brother."

"*What!*"

That was on the other side of town and he had to haul ass if he was going to get there anytime soon. Mara called after him, but he ignored her. It didn't even cross his mind that Léon was lying to him, which was completely in the realm of possibility. All he knew was he had a lead on where Ainsley was, and he was going to find him.

The quiet in the room was only amplified by the roaring voices that filtered up through the floorboards. It was well into the night now, and the room below was filling up with nightly guests. They would all be sharing a drink and a laugh with their friends while Ainsley sat alone in this room.

Alexander had just gone out to send Ainsley's letter. It would arrive tomorrow morning, and then Graham and Croften would know where to look for him. All he had to do was wait.

But what if they didn't know where to look? What if they couldn't figure out his code? What if they were already out looking and missed the letter completely? Ainsley sighed and sank into his chair. What would he do then?

"I have to escape," he whispered to himself. And it was true.

He wouldn't be able to just leave through the door. Not with Henri standing guard outside until the business was done. Ainsley got up and opened the window. He poked his head out into the cold night's air and looked around. There wasn't much he could use to climb down. But surely the drop wasn't so far, not if he lowered himself down as far as he could first. He might risk a rolled ankle, but it was certainly better than any alternative.

Ainsley carried his chair over, careful not to make too much noise and alert Henri's suspicions. He used the chair to steady himself as he perched up on the windowsill. If Croften could climb a tree up to his window, Ainsley could surely climb himself out of this one.

"Just don't look down," he told himself as he grabbed the sill tight and began to lower himself. His arms shook with the effort. When he did, inevitably, look down, he discovered he had misjudged the distance, or rather his own athletic abilities. Ainsley tried to pull himself up, but he lacked the strength. He would have to fall.

Wood splintered from within the room with a loud crack. Ainsley's head snapped up, searching for any damage along the window. Heavy footsteps raced into the room, and he held his breath, expecting Alexander's head to come poking out looking for him.

"Where the hell is he!?" Croften shouted.

"He was in here a minute ago," Henri replied.

There was a thump, and Ainsley could only assume Croften had pushed Henri against the wall. The growl in his voice only confirmed that suspicion. "Where. Is. He?"

"Croften," Ainsley tried to shout, but only a weak whisper escaped. His lungs were too tired from the effort it took to keep his arms working.

"The window's open," Graham said. And Ainsley counted his lucky stars that his husband was so observant. A few seconds later Graham's head emerged from the

window, immediately looking down.

Ainsley gave a small smile. "Hello," he wheezed.

Graham grabbed Ainsley's arms and started to pull. Reinvigorated with the help, Ainsley found the extra strength needed to pull himself back inside.

"You tell me where he is right now!" Croften said, still threatening Henri. The bruise forming on Henry's cheek told Ainsley that the threats had already been made real.

"Croften, dear, it's alright," Ainsley said. He held tight to Graham's arm as he recovered from his window hanging journey.

"It is not alright!" Croften turned to him with a dark look. "You're missing, damn it!"

"Am I?"

Croften opened his mouth to yell again, but then he finally realized that Ainsley was standing right before him. "Ainsley!" He rushed over and wrapped his arms around Ainsley's waist, holding him tight and burying his head in Ainsley's shoulder. Graham expertly removed his arm, wrapping it around them instead.

"I was so worried," Croften continued. He shook his head and Ainsley could feel wet spots forming where his tears fell.

"I know, my dear. But everything is okay now." Ainsley closed his eyes and hugged Croften back with equal force. He, too, had been worried. Worried he would never feel the embrace of his two loves ever again. He never wanted to let go.

Graham's arm was gone from them in an instant. The air around them wavered as he rushed out of the room.

"Where the hell is he going?" Croften asked. He perked his head up and swiveled it to stare at the broken-in door.

Ursula was standing in the hall, leaning against the wall with heavy breath. "Alexander showed up," she explained. She pointed down the hall. "They went after him."

"Hope they catch him," Henri mumbled.

Croften growled and spun around in Ainsley's arms, glaring at Henri. "*You.*"

Ainsley increased his grip, hoping to stop any further conflict. "Let's just go," he whispered in Croften's ear. No more fighting. No more pain or worry. Just the peace and tranquility their life deserved.

30

Ready

Ainsley woke up to comfort. Last night had been a bit of a blur. Croften had wanted to take Ainsley straight home after finding him, but Ainsley insisted that he go to the station and give a statement. He wasn't going to let Alexander get away because he was too worried or afraid to say anything. Graham had assured him he would 'take care' of it, and secure in the knowledge that that was true, Ainsley let Croften take him home. They had gone right to bed,

Croften holding Ainsley in a tight hug, his body curled around him. And he was still there when Ainsley woke up.

Ainsley's body was a little stiff from not moving at all during the night. He wiggled slightly, trying to straighten out and stretch. Croften startled awake, his body jolting as his eyes snapped open. They immediately focused on Ainsley.

"Are you okay?" Croften asked. He undid Ainsley's efforts, readjusting his grip and tightening his hold. His arms wrapped around Ainsley's shoulder and his legs tangled up with his as well. He pressed their foreheads together, Ainsley's focus blurry as he tried to look at him.

"I'm okay," he whispered. He wiggled a bit. "Any chance I can get my arms back?"

"No." Croften just tightened his hold. "I am never letting go of you. Ever."

Ainsley chuckled and managed to move enough to look over his shoulder. The bed behind him was empty. "Where's Graham? He came back last night, didn't he?"

"I don't think he did, actually," Croften mumbled. Ainsley shivered. "I'm sure he was probably just working on the case and stuff."

"M-maybe he's in his office," Ainsley suggested. Either home or work. He had to be. Any alternative was too much to handle.

"I'm sure he is," Croften confirmed. He pressed a kiss to Ainsley's forehead. "He just wants to make sure everything is taken care of for you."

Ainsley nodded and buried his face against Croften's chest. He let himself be smothered for a little while longer, because he was worried and tired and Croften was soft and warm. They lay there in the quiet, the intensity of Croften's love pulsing in the hard beat of his heart that Ainsley could feel.

"I'm sorry," Ainsley mumbled. He rubbed his face against Croften's shirt and tried not to cry.

Croften was quiet for a moment, so Ainsley tipped his head back, checking to make sure he hadn't fallen asleep. "Sorry," he said. "I'm just having trouble figuring out what on Earth you could possibly be sorry about."

"I let him take me," Ainsley said, his body shivering at the memory of it all. "I didn't even try to stop him I-"

Croften had moved one arm out from the embrace. He pressed his hand to Ainsley's mouth and his eyes were the most intense he's ever seen. "You listen to me. This is absolutely in no way your fault. If I ever hear you say anything like that again I will...do something bad, trust you me."

Ainsley wiggled his own arms free and pulled Croften's hand away, placing it on his cheek. "Perhaps you're right."

"I am."

Ainsley smiled. Smiled because he knew Croften. And he knew exactly what he was thinking. "But you have to promise you'll understand that it's not your fault, either."

Croften grumbled. "Fine. But I'm still never letting go of you. Ever."

Ainsley laughed again and tried to pull free. "I think that'll make everyday activities rather difficult."

"Doesn't matter." Croften kissed Ainsley's forehead.

"What about my writing? And your painting?"

Croften shook his head. "This is our job now."

Ainsley smiled and closed his eyes. He would eventually need the use of his limbs, but for now he was content to let this be his life. He heard the door open and lifted his head to watch Graham slip in. His clothes were wrinkled, his hair distressed, and his eyes were heavy and surrounded by dark circles.

"Hey," Graham whispered.

His voice roused Croften, who looked over his shoulder and said, "You look like shit."

"Thanks." Graham shook his head and climbed onto the bed, hovering over Ainsley. "How are you?"

"I'm okay." Ainsley smiled as Graham bent down and kissed his cheek. "You do look awful. Did you get any sleep?"

Graham shook his head and fell to the mattress behind Ainsley. He snuggled up to him, arms snaking around him, pressing against Croften's. His legs tangled up with theirs as well, squishing Ainsley between the two of them. Ainsley squirmed and rocked and shifted until he managed to get himself turned around. He settled facing Graham with Croften draped over his back.

Ainsley even got one arm free, reaching up and placing his hand on Graham's wrinkled face. "Are you alright?" he asked in a whisper. He wanted to let Graham get some rest, but he was so curious about how it was all going.

Graham smiled, his eyes still closed. He nodded and rested his forehead against Ainsley's. "I am now that you're safe."

Ainsley smiled back and closed his own eyes, rubbing his thumb over Graham's cheek. "Get some rest, love," he said softly. "You've been working so hard for me."

Graham just hummed out a note of agreement and Ainsley watched over him as his breath became steady and he fell into a deep slumber.

"He shouldn't sleep in his clothes," Ainsley mumbled, careful not to wake him.

"Naughty, naughty," Croften whispered in his ear.

Ainsley nudged his leg back at him, trying not to laugh. "That's not what I meant."

"Sure it's not." Croften kissed the back of Ainsley's neck and made no attempt to move. Ainsley sighed and settled back down. Might as well try and get some more rest while they weren't letting him go.

It didn't matter how much Ainsley complained, Croften didn't let him go. Ever. It was really quite frustrating because he couldn't even go to the bathroom alone.

"Honestly, dear," he said, Croften wrapping himself around him on the couch. "I don't know what you think is going to happen, but you can let go."

Croften shook his head and rested it on Ainsley's shoulder. "Nu-uh."

Ainsley sighed and ran fingers through Croften's hair. "How am I supposed to write if you're all over me like this, hm?"

"Sit in my lap," Croften mumbled. "It's comfortable, look." He shifted up and pulled Ainsley onto his lap, both of them laughing a bit as they got settled.

Ainsley wrapped his arms around Croften's neck and kissed his cheek. "Yes, darling. You are quite comfortable but not very conducive to work."

"You shouldn't be working anyway," Croften mumbled. He buried his face in

Ainsley's neck, kissing it softly. "You suffered trauma. You need to rest."

Ainsley shook his head, about to argue, when Benson entered carrying a tray of fresh tea and the mail.

"Thank you," Ainsley said, taking the bundle from him. He flipped through them, tilting his head to the side so that Croften had better access for his kissing. He saw his own name in the upper left corner of one of the letters and huffed softly as he pulled it out.

"What's that?" Croften asked. He placed his chin on Ainsley's shoulder and looked down at it.

"Here." Ainsley handed it to him. Proud smile on his face. "Read it."

Ainsley waited eagerly, biting his lip as Croften opened the letter with one hand (the other resting around Ainsley). Croften read over it, furrowed his eyebrows, and then read over it again.

"Clever, isn't it?" Ainsley asked, wiggling a bit. He was too eager to hear Croften's response. It wasn't quite what he expected.

"Wow," he said, swallowing hard. "You must have been really upset to make this many mistakes."

"What?" Ainsley sighed. "No, no! It's a code!"

Croften gave him a look and then glanced back at the paper. Ainsley sighed and leaned closer, explaining how each mistake, when put together, told them what had happened. Croften's mouth opened, and he let out a long, "oh. That is clever."

Ainsley smiled. "I know it's a little silly, and I am so very glad you two found me so quickly. But, well, I was rather hoping I'd get to see it work out."

Croften chuckled and kissed his cheek. "You are adorable, you know that? You could always use it in a book."

Ainsley's eyes lit up because, yes! What a fantastic idea! "You're right," he said. He kissed Croften and smiled. "And I think I will."

He went in for another kiss but was stopped by the sound of the door opening. He jumped just a little, chuckling nervously at his reaction as Croften held him closer. It turned out to be nothing to fear, of course, as Graham walked into the room.

"Graham!" Ainsley greeted. He tried to get up to go greet him properly, but Croften wouldn't let him move. "You're home so early."

Graham nodded and sat on the couch next to them. "Just waiting for some paperwork to get shuffled around." He placed his hand on Ainsley's leg. "Thought I'd come by and check in."

Ainsley rolled his eyes. Honestly. They were both overreacting. "I'm fine," he said. "But I would be finer if you would tell me what's going on."

Graham just gave him that soft, slightly pitiful smile and patted his leg saying, "It's nothing you need to worry yourself about."

Ainsley huffed. "I demand to know what's happening with everything and I demand to know now!"

"Yeah!" Croften said. "We demand to know!"

Graham gave him a confused look. "Croften, you already know everything."

Ainsley turned to him, betrayed. He slapped him on the arm. "You know?"

"Of course." Croften smirked. "Graham's very talkative."

"More like you're annoyingly persistent," Graham mumbled.

"I am too!" Ainsley said. "So, save us all the trouble and tell me now!"

Graham groaned, running a hand down his face. "Very well." He adjusted his seat to be more comfortable. "It's taken some time, but Alexander is going to jail."

Ainsley sat up. "Jail? I thought for sure your parents would have gotten him out somehow."

Graham smiled, all proud of himself. "They might have been able to buy his way out of one account of kidnapping. But that's one of the perks of having once been close to my brother. I know all his secrets." He tilted his head forward, smile turning devious. "And let's just say he hasn't exactly been an angel all his life."

Ainsley shivered, that look on Graham's face sending a jolt of joy through his nerves. Croften's knee bounced, and he said, "I know right? He's hot."

Ainsley chuckled. Croften was right. "That's wonderful news, Graham. You must be working so hard."

Graham shrugged, but his face did look weary. "It's nothing."

"And what about Henri?" Ainsley asked. Croften growled. "He was working with him, wasn't he?" He looked at Croften. "What happened?"

"He lied his fucking ass off," Croften grumbled. "And those idiots believed him. I'd send him to jail right alongside that piece of shit but whatever. I'm not the lawyer so *whatever.*"

Ainsley looked to Graham for answers since Croften was simply going to mope.

"Henri was given a plea bargain for his testimony," Graham said.

"A testimony? Surely my own would have been enough."

"A testimony of extortion," Graham elaborated. "He was working with Alexander because he had threatened harm to Léon. Who then found out about everything and thankfully came and told us."

"Allegedly," Croften mumbled.

Ainsley's head was spinning. He had never really met this Léon, but the fact that he was married to that horrible man didn't exactly prove this whole story true. He was inclined to agree with Croften, that perhaps it had all been a story. But Léon *had* told Croften where to find him. And the story did help put Alexander away. So, Ainsley figured it was best to let it go.

"Thank you for all you've done for me, dear," Ainsley said, placing his hand on Graham's.

Graham smiled and squeezed his thigh. "I'm just sorry all this had to happen in the first place."

Croften could practically feel the frustration radiating off of Ainsley. But it didn't matter. Croften was seriously never going to let go. Not even as Ainsley opened the door, welcoming Mara and Ursula in. Croften had himself draped over Ainsley's back, arms over his shoulders, hands on his chest.

"You weren't lying," Mara said, chuckling as they made their way into the drawing room. It was the last of Alexander's trials and he didn't stand a chance. They were all going to go and watch. Croften at least planned to point and laugh.

Ainsley huffed, not sitting down. "No. I wasn't."

"I can help." Ursula stood up and Croften squinted at her, holding Ainsley closer. She had that 'I'm going to hit you now' look, and Croften positioned himself so that Ainsley was between them, blocking any blows she might have. Let her try and attack him now.

"Really, dear," Ainsley said, shrugging and wiggling. "I'm perfectly fine. Look. I'm here with Mara and Ursula so why don't you go help Graham, hm?"

"Can't get rid of me that easily," Croften muttered in Ainsley's ear. Not even the tantalizing prospect of an undressed Graham was going to get him to leave Ainsley's side.

"Can't get rid of you at all," Ainsley mumbled.

"Glad you're coming to terms with it." Croften smiled and leaned over, kissing all over Ainsley's cheek. He was so busy kissing Ainsley that he didn't notice Mara getting up until he felt a tight pressure on his ear.

Mara managed to successfully drag him away, nearly ripping his ear off in the process, while Ursula untangled Ainsley and freed him. Croften shivered, the lack of Ainsley in his arms unnerving.

Ainsley let out a sigh of relief, fixing his clothes. "Thank you," he said.

"He's in good hands," Mara said, dragging Croften to the hall. "Now go help

Graham get ready. We'll be late."

Croften rubbed his ear and scowled at them. He stepped out of view, but then peaked around the corner. He couldn't just not watch Ainsley at every moment of every day. What if something happened again?

"Thank you," Ainsley said again, sitting on the couches with them. "I love him, but he's really overreacting."

"He's just worried about you," Mara said. "You did go through quite an ordeal."

Ainsley bit his lip and nodded.

"What's wrong?" Ursula asked.

"I just…" Ainsley sighed and looked at them with down-turned eyes. "I feel a bit guilty."

"Whatever for?" Mara asked before Croften could burst in and grab Ainsley by the coat and shake him.

"I feel guilty because I don't feel like I went through all that much. I mean, yes. It was...terrifying in the moment. But...well…" Ainsley took a deep breath and picked at his fingernails. "I know I should be scared about something happening again. But I'm not. Because I know that if it does, they'll fix it. Does that make sense?"

Croften could hear the smile in Mara's voice. "It makes perfect sense, Ainsley. And it's really sweet."

"But why does that make you guilty?" Ursula asked. And Croften leaned closer because he was curious too.

"They're so worried about me," Ainsley said. "As you could tell. And I don't know how to tell them that I'm really okay. They have every right to worry, and I don't want to put that sort of pressure on them."

Croften smiled and finally turned to leave. Ainsley would be fine. Because he was right. If anything did happen, they would fix it. Croften had been so attached because he never wanted to feel that way again, that hopelessness of not knowing what was happening, or what he could do to fix it. But he would never have to go through that alone because Graham would be there.

And there Graham was, standing before his vanity, shirt open, staring off into space as his fingers fidgeted with his cufflinks. Croften smirked and walked up, taking his sleeve and finishing the job. "Honestly, can't even get yourself dressed." He tsked.

"Sorry," Graham said. "Just got lost in thought."

"Yeah." Croften turned Graham around and started buttoning up his shirt for him, a little sad to have to cover up that chest. "Been doing a lot of that myself."

"I'm surprised you willingly let Ainsley out of your hold," Graham mused. He reached over and tried to smooth Croften's hair down. A feat easier said than done.

"Oh, it wasn't willing, trust me." Croften finished the shirt and snagged the tie off the back of the chair before Graham could grab it. There was something warm and soft about dressing someone else. And without being so close to Ainsley, he kind of needed that.

"I keep thinking about what would have happened if we didn't find him," Graham said, staring at Croften's face as he worked the tie.

"I try not to," Croften admitted. But the truth was he thought about it a lot. It plagued him, the idea of Ainsley alone, in that room, locked and hidden away.

His hands started to shake at the idea and Graham grabbed them in his own, warmth spreading over Croften's skin. Croften looked into Graham's eyes and he knew, somehow, that things would be okay. Maybe in the same way that Ainsley knew it would be okay. There was a comforting feeling from knowing that all of them together would never have to face anything alone. That something bad had happened, but it was rectified nearly immediately, because they worked together.

Croften cleared his throat and then shook his head, pushing Graham's hands off so he could finish his tie. "There," he said, patting his chest. "Finally presentable for the court of law."

Graham smiled. "Thank you. You could use some work." He picked at Croften's shirt and Croften just laughed.

"Hey. Think you could distract everyone so I could get one last punch in?"

Graham shook his head. "As your lawyer, I didn't hear that." He smiled. "As your boyfriend, we'll see what can be arranged."

"Are you two quite ready yet?" Ainsley asked, sticking his head through the door. "You know they can't start without you."

"Ready," Graham said. He grabbed his jacket and slipped it on, joining Ainsley in the doorway.

"Croften?" Ainsley asked, holding his hand out to him.

Croften looked at that hand and smiled. He had a lot to worry about still. But none of those worries seemed to mean much when he was facing them with Ainsley and Graham. Everything seemed to just be easier, more manageable.

Croften took Ainsley's hand and placed his other hand on Graham's shoulder. "Ready."

Anna Denisch was born and raised just outside of Baltimore City, but she has never called it home. When not traveling around the world or daydreaming about dragons, she spends her time looking at books she wants to read without actually touching them. She received her M.F.A in Creative and Professional Writing from Western Connecticut State University and considers daily if she is just insane enough to take her family's sometime suggestion of getting a PhD.